We hope you enjoy this boo renew it by the due date.

You can renew it at www.norfolk.gov.uk/libraries or by using our free library app.

Otherwise you can phone 0344 800 8020 - please have your library card and PIN ready.

You can sign up for email reminders too.

11/22

23. FEB 23

ZERTEX
CRIME

NORTHWIND

A ROBERT HOON THRILLER

JD KIRK

For Daphne Broon

NORTHWIND
ISBN: 978-1-912767-48-9

Published worldwide by Zertex Media Ltd.
This edition published in 2021.

I

www.jdkirk.com
www.zertexmedia.com

BOOKS BY J.D. KIRK

A Litter of Bones

Thicker Than Water

The Killing Code

Blood & Treachery

The Last Bloody Straw

A Whisper of Sorrows

The Big Man Upstairs

A Death Most Monumental

A Snowball's Chance in Hell

Ahead of the Game

An Isolated Incident

Colder Than the Grave

CHAPTER ONE

IT WAS, without question, the most frightening moment of her life so far.

There were four of them. Maybe five. She hadn't made eye contact—she knew better than that—but she could hear them. Talking. Laughing. Leering at her from thirty feet behind, their trainers scuffing the pavement as they moved to follow.

She should never have walked. Not here. Not this late. Not alone.

But there had been no taxis to be had, and her phone battery was too low for the GPS to run, so she couldn't summon an Uber. Worst of all, one drink too many had bolstered her courage to dangerously high levels.

It had seeped away again, quick smart, at the first cry of, "Show us your tits."

She'd walked on, head down, hand clutching the strap of her bag. Eyes on the pavement. One foot in front of the other. *Don't engage, don't engage.*

They were young. Teenagers. Three or four years her

junior. A mix of races, and sizes, and facial hairs. London was a real melting pot of colours and cultures. But, bring a group of young men from almost any background together, and the results in her experience were always the same.

"Oi, you stuck up slag! We're talking to you."

She picked up the pace, and heard their laughter over the clacking of her heels. Taking a shortcut across the estate had been a bad move. She should've waited on a cab. Taken the long way. Anything but this.

'Her skirt was too short.'

That's what they'd say. Afterwards. The police. The papers. The courts, if it ever got that far.

'Dressed like that? Out on her own? She was asking for it. What did she *think* was going to happen?'

There was a corner up ahead, where the path turned down the side of a block of flats. She'd reach it in a few seconds.

Then what?

She tried to picture the next street, but she hadn't lived here long enough to know them all. It was a road, she thought. There might be cars.

Even if there wasn't, the moment she was out of sight, she could run for it. Try to put some distance between herself and the pack of lads behind her.

Or... was that the wrong move? They were just following her for now. They might get bored. But if she ran, would that trigger some primal urge to give chase? Would her running provoke the hunt?

She was three or four minutes of flat-out sprinting from her flat. Thanks to an overpriced gym membership, she had the lungs and the legs to do it, but not the shoes. They'd be on her in seconds, pulling her down, tearing at her clothes, and at her hair, and at her skin. Forcing her down. Forcing her legs apart.

Her breath became short. A bubble formed at the back of her throat. Oh, God. What had she done?

Behind her—several steps behind, but keeping pace—the hyenas sniggered and sneered.

She made it to the corner and risked a glance back. They must've seen something then—read it on her face, or in her movements—because they sprang forwards as one, breaking into a run, lust and glee twisting their faces into something monstrous. Something inhuman.

Hurrying around the bend, she saw a road. A car. A man walking towards it, whistling, twirling a set of keys around a finger.

She ejected a sound. A sob of relief. A cry for help. Some combination of the two.

He turned towards her, eyebrows rising in surprise, the tune dying on his lips.

She ran to him, tears streaming, the clatter of footsteps closing fast behind.

It was, without question, the most frightening moment of her life so far.

But the night was still so very, *very* young.

CHAPTER TWO

ROBERT HOON, former Detective Superintendent of Police Scotland, eyeballed the man on the other side of the glass, scrutinising him, judging him, staring him down.

He enjoyed a good eyeballing. Always had. There were few better ways to show utter disdain for a person, he thought, than with some intense squinting and a lengthy spell of not blinking.

The man on the other side of the glass, to his credit, had not blinked either, and showed no signs of turning away.

"Look at the state of that poor bastard," Bob remarked. He took in the dark hollows of the man's eyes, and the white outline of dried sleep drool that had gone wandering through a salt and pepper forest of stubble.

He ran a hand over his chin, and his reflection in the bathroom mirror followed suit. He should probably shave, he thought. First day of his new career, and all that. Good to make the effort.

He upped the quality and intensity of his eyeballing, as if

the man on the other side of the glass had betrayed him by even thinking such a thing.

"Shave? For a fucking Tesco security man job?" he spat. "I don't think so."

Besides, he wasn't looking *that* bad, was he? Not for a man in his fifties.

Aye, his eyes were so sunken they looked like they'd been put in with a riveting gun, and he couldn't quite pinpoint when he'd last brushed his teeth, but he was looking better than he'd looked this time last month, and better still than the month before.

He was getting there. Even if 'there' was just a security guard in Tesco, it was still somewhere.

And anywhere was better than where he'd been over this last year or so.

He reached for the razor. It was not the first time he'd reached for a razor in the last few months. Unlike on those occasions, though, this time he intended to use it for the purpose for which it had been designed.

"Onwards and upwards, you crusty old cocksplash," he muttered at the man in the mirror. "Onwards and fucking upwards."

———

Hoon stepped off the bus, glowered furiously at the big 'Tesco' sign above the entrance to the Eastfield Way superstore, then strode on inside like he owned the place.

The security guard stationed just inside the front door was gazing blankly at one of two black and white screens mounted on the terminal before him. He blinked in surprise when Hoon prodded him on the shoulder.

"Haw. Pal. Where do I go?"

The security guard was somewhere in his mid-thirties, Hoon guessed. He was heavily built and had the look of a pub bouncer about him.

"What?" the guard asked, giving the newcomer a slow look up and down. Hoon could practically hear the cogs creaking into life.

If this was the best the supermarket had, shoplifters must be having a field day.

"Jesus. Wakey-wakey, son. I'm the new guy. It's my first day." He shrugged. "Well, technically my first day was last week, but I've been busy. Where do I go?"

The security guard shot an indifferent look in the direction of the Customer Services desk. "Dunno. Manager?"

Hoon muttered something below his breath. "Cheers, you've been a big help," he said, then he pointed to the screens. "I'll let you get back to your glassy-eyed waking death, or whatever the fuck it was you were doing."

Turning away from the guard, Hoon was halfway to the Customer Services desk when he heard his name called and saw a man with a face like a sexually frustrated wasp come scurrying towards him.

"Robert Hoon?" he said again. "Are you Robert Hoon?"

"Depends who's asking," Hoon replied, sizing the other guy up and quickly getting the measure of him.

Thirties, but older looking. Single. Cuts his own hair. Big glasses, skinny suit, and probably not an inch of spine to be had anywhere on him.

"Wayne Gilhooley." A hand was thrust in Hoon's direction. "Deputy Under Manager."

Hoon briefly gave the hand the contempt it deserved, then relented and shook it.

"I thought that was the younger fella who did my interview? Fat Harry Potter."

Wayne smiled. It was the sort of smile that suggested he was aware there was a joke somewhere in the vicinity, but he was damned if he knew where it was.

"Ahahaha," he said. Not laughed. *Said.* "That's Gavin. He's the Junior Manager."

"Right. And you are...?"

"Deputy Under Manager."

Hoon contemplated this for a second or two. "And both those jobs need to exist, do they?"

If the 'Fat Harry Potter' comment had confused him, Wayne was completely lost now. He spoke the words, "Hahaha," again, added a, "Quite," then hastily changed the subject. "So, I hear you were in the police."

"Among other things."

"Detective Superintendent, wasn't it?"

Hoon grunted. "Among other things."

Wayne rocked back on his heels and gestured to the store around them. Customers plodded along the aisles like cattle waiting their turn for the slaughterman's bolt gun. Staff buzzed between them, decked out in matching blue uniforms and auras of despair.

"This must feel like a bit of a step down!" Wayne said.

"Too fucking right it does," Hoon confirmed. Which, judging by the Deputy Under Manager's face, was not the response he'd been hoping for.

"Right." Wayne's arms flopped back down to his sides. "Well. We should get you your uniform."

"Uniform?" Hoon shook his head. "I don't do uniforms, pal. No' in a long time."

That vague, not-quite-getting-the-joke smile returned. "Well, company policy is that—"

"Fuck company policy. What do wankers in suits know about anything?" Hoon asked. He waved a hand in Wayne's direction. "No offence."

The Deputy Under Manager looked down at his blue nylon suit. It had gone shiny at the knees from all those hours spent filling bottom shelves when staff failed to turn up for their shift. "It's... The uniform is a deterrent. It stops people nicking stuff."

Hoon put a hand on the younger man's shoulder. "But we don't want to just deter the bastards, do we? We want to catch them in the act, so we can teach them a lesson they'll no' forget. Believe me, I've seen enough rookie constables dressed as fucking squirrels to know that crime prevention doesn't work. We need to nab the thieving wee pricks and cut their hands off."

Wayne swallowed. Blinked. "Yeah, but... Not... not literally?"

"Jesus Christ, son. No. Not literally." Hoon pointed to the door. "But see all these bastards coming in and swiping stuff? They're laughing at you. Right now. Wherever the fuck they are. They're laughing. At *you*. And they'll keep coming in and nicking stuff, and they'll keep laughing, because they keep getting away with it. Is that what you want, Wayne?"

"Well..."

"Sticky fingered wee neds laughing their arses off at you. Is that what you want?"

The Deputy Under Manager shook his head. "No. No, I don't want that." He puffed out his chest, his fingers practically balling up into tight, sweaty fists. "I don't want them laughing at me at all."

"No. Thought not." Hoon gave the other man a clap on the shoulder. "So, best if I blend in, eh. Go incognito, and keep my eyes peeled. See if we can catch some of them in the act."

"Yes. *Yes!* I like that. Catch them in the act. Throw the bloody book at them. Bastards!"

Hoon had expected a bit more resistance, and was surprised by Wayne's enthusiasm. Clearly, the thought of being secretly mocked by shoplifters had touched a nerve.

"Good lad," Hoon said. "Now, quick question." He pointed up to the far end of the first aisle, to where the technology department lay. "See them big tellies on the far wall that show all the demo stuff? Can you turn those over to other channels, do you know? Because it's just about time for *Bargain Hunt*."

CHAPTER THREE

THERE WAS a right neddy wee bastard over by the DVDs. Zipped-up hoodie and baseball cap combo, fat gold chain, and tracky bottoms tucked into his socks. No' just a ned—maybe *the* ned. The definitive, original specimen. The ned on which all other neds were subsequently based, standing right there, in the flesh. Hoon almost felt honoured to be in his presence.

The ned had been acting shady since he'd come sauntering in. Hoon had clocked him almost at once, some rusty old sonar from back in the day crackling into life as soon as he came within sensor range.

He'd spent a full five minutes in the stationery aisle, picking up packs of pens, studying them for anything up to sixty seconds, then hanging them back onto their hooks like he had some serious writing to do, and these wouldn't *quite* cut the mustard.

Next, he'd lifted a pack of printer paper, weighed it in one hand, then returned it to the shelf, all the while glancing around like he was about to make a grab for the coloured pencils and *Pritt Stick,* and have it away on his toes out the door.

"Aye, just you try it, ya treacle-fingered bawbag," Hoon had muttered below his breath, as he watched the ned from the other end of the aisle.

This was why you didn't wear uniforms in a job like this —for the element of surprise.

Well, that and the dignity.

The lad had appeared similarly interested in the kitchen-wares, then had spent a few minutes admiring the selection of towels on offer. Each aisle he moved through brought him closer to the media and technology departments, and his anxiety levels were creeping higher and higher now that he was there.

It was embarrassing, really. Back in Hoon's day, down in Glasgow, a wee bit of shoplifting in Tesco would be neither here nor there to a ned. There'd be no panicky glances, or pissing about looking at ironing board covers. They'd come in, head straight for what they'd come for, and walk off with it, practically daring security to try and stop them.

The way he was acting, you'd think this clueless bumble-fuck had never half-inched anything in his life.

Hoon almost felt sorry for him. What a day to pick to start a life of crime.

He had a DVD in his hand now, and was studying it with the sort of intensity Hoon had last seen on the faces of the boys in the bomb disposal unit.

The unsubtle wee scrote looked up and around him, making sure nobody was watching. From where he was standing, the coast would've looked clear. Hoon lurked at the end of the next aisle over, watching the ned's reflection in the darkened screen of a big telly. He was coiled. Eager. Ready to pounce just as soon as—

"Settling in alright, Bob?"

Wayne Gilhooley was all smiles and enthusiasm when he appeared out of nowhere with a big box of nappies in his hands. He had removed his suit jacket and had his sleeves rolled up. A slick of sweat on his forehead gave the impression he was working harder than usual.

"Eh?" Hoon asked, trying to look past him to the reflection on the screen.

"I was just asking how you're settling—"

"Out of the fucking road, I'm trying to see the telly."

"I beg your pardon?" Wayne said. "You can't talk to me like that. I'm the Deputy Under—"

"Fuck's sake!" Hoon hissed, eyes widening and nostrils flaring like a bull who'd just had his pint spilled.

Wayne almost dropped his nappies in fright. "Look, I'm sure whatever's upset you, we can—"

"You let him get away, ya daft bastard!" Hoon retorted, and then he was off and running, much to Wayne's confusion. And, if he were honest, relief.

Hoon skidded around the end of a shelving rack, scanned the throngs of shoppers who congregated in the middle aisle to marvel and coo at this week's specials, then caught a glimpse of the distinctive hoodie-and-cap combo that marked his prey.

The ned was speed-walking for the exit now, already well ahead. In a few seconds, he'd be out the door, and with the best will in the world, there was no chance that Hoon was keeping up if he decided to go full pelt.

Fuck it, then. It was now or never.

"Stop that wee bastard!" he bellowed, drawing the attention of the security guard at the door.

The guard looked up from where he was peering disinterestedly into the bags of some old woman who had triggered the alarm by the door.

The ned's reactions were quicker than the security man's. It wasn't even a close-run thing, either. Hoon's voice was like the crack of a starting pistol that launched him into a sprint. He powered past the granny and the guard, who were each holding a handle of her hessian shopping bag as he shone his torch inside.

"Hey, stop!" the guard instructed, but there was no urgency to it, and he made no move to physically intervene.

"Lot of bastarding use you are," Hoon spat when he raced by them a few seconds later. And then, he was out through the sliding doors, urging pedestrians to get out of his way with a few well-aimed expletives and insults.

The ned, as expected, had already hit top gear. He had hung a left out of the doors and was racing along the path in front of the store, headed for the wider retail park. He may not have been an expert thief, but he was an accomplished bloody sprinter. There was no way that Hoon was catching him.

Not on foot, anyway.

"You. I need your car," he said, striding over to where an elderly man sat idling in his Vauxhall Corsa at the pick-up and drop-off point.

"S-sorry?" the old fella said, squinting out through his open window.

"I'm commandeering this vehicle," Hoon barked.

"What? Why?"

Hoon pointed after the fleeing ned. "So I can catch that thieving wee bastard!"

"And... who are you?"

"I'm the fucking poli—" Hoon began, then he corrected himself. "I'm store security, and that little shite's getting away!"

The old man looked him up and down, then began to wind his window up. The car was an ancient model with a manual window winder, and it took him forever to crank it closed.

By the time he had, Hoon was already sitting behind him, gripping the headrest of the driver's seat. "Fine. You drive, then," he ordered. "But if you let him get away, you and I are going to have some serious—"

The car lurched forwards, throwing Hoon back in his seat.

"Jesus fuck!" he ejected. A horn blared behind them. An angry shout followed hot on its heels. Hoon responded with a raised middle finger, then jabbed the one next to it ahead, indicating the target. "That one. That's the one we're after."

"I see him!" the old fella up front said. He swung sharply, pulling past a stationary taxi and forcing a delivery van coming in the opposite direction to slam on the anchors.

Hoon gave him a hearty pat on the shoulder as they swung back in. "That's ma boy!" he cheered.

The fleeing ned was right ahead now. He risked a glance back over his shoulder, but he was looking for security to be chasing him on foot, not in the back of a rusted old Corsa with the ghost of Ayrton Senna behind the wheel.

"Right, he's no' seen us," Hoon said. "Pull up just ahead and I'll—"

The car swerved to the left. There was a solid and somewhat stomach-churning *clunk* as wing mirror met hip. Through the side window, Hoon watched the ned perform a near-perfect pirouette, arms flung up towards the sky as if seeking salvation.

Then, the brake pedal was kicked all the way to the floor, and Hoon was slammed violently against the back of the seat in front.

"Christ Almighty, calm down you mad old bastard!" he spat, throwing open the door. "We're chasing a shoplifter, no' the fucking Zodiac Killer."

"Can I let you off here?" the old man asked, ancient bones creaking as he craned to look back over his shoulder. "My wife will be wondering where I am."

"Aye. On you go," Hoon said, then he gave a yelp when the car began to pull away. "Wait until I'm out of the car! You nearly had my bastarding leg off there!"

"Sorry. I didn't see you had your door open."

"You knew I was getting out of the... forget it," Hoon retorted, then he jumped out of the car and had barely got the door closed when the Corsa pulled a U-turn into moving traffic, and drove off to a chorus of honks and abuse.

The ned, meanwhile, was rolling around on the ground, winded and grimacing in pain. The DVD that he'd nicked was on the path beside him. Hoon bent to retrieve it while he waited for the lad to get his breath back.

"*Moana*," he said, contemplating the DVD's title, and the stoic face of the animated Polynesian princess emblazoned across the cover. "I'll be honest, no' what I was expecting. I had you down as more of a *Fast and the Furious* man myself. That's the sort of thing you predictable wee fucks are usually into."

Down on the ground, the ned pulled himself together

enough to start looking for an escape route. Hoon pressed a foot down on one of the lad's arms, pinning him in place.

"Aye, I wouldn't think about it," he warned, then he waggled the DVD at him. "What's with this?"

"Fuck off! Get off my arm!" the ned protested.

He was younger than Hoon had been expecting, which went some way to explaining the nerves. He had the frame of a ten-year-old, but the acne and bum fluff of someone who had very recently entered their teenage years.

"What are you going to do, son? Call the polis? Just you go ahead. I'd give you my phone myself, but I'd worry you'd try to run off with it, and then you'd *really* be on my bad side," Hoon said. He applied fractionally more pressure to the arm, drawing a hiss from the lad. "And believe me, you don't want that."

"Ow, alright, alright!"

Hoon caught a look of concern from a passing couple and gave them a reassuring wave. "Store security. It's fine. On your way," he said, then he turned his attention back to the boy on the ground and waved the DVD at him again. "Why this?" he asked again. "I mean, I'm no' saying it's no' a good film. It's fucking top tier *Disney*, if you ask me. Granted, it's no *Up*, but then what is? My point is, what the fuck's a lad like you doing nicking *any* tier *Disney* in the first place? Did they no' have anything with guns and tits?"

"It's for my wee sister," the ned spat back.

Hoon snorted. "What, she the brains of the outfit, is she? She the one selecting the targets?"

"It's her birthday. I just... I wanted to get her something, alright?" He squirmed, tears springing to his eyes. "You're breaking my arm."

"You'll know I'm breaking your arm when you start spitting jaggy wee fragments of it out of your arse, son," Hoon told him, but he eased his foot up a milimetre or two and the boy gave a strangled sob of relief. "How old is she?"

The ned frowned. "Moana?"

"What? No! Not fucking... No' Moana. Why would I be asking how hold Moana is? Your sister."

"I'm not telling you that!" An increase of pressure on his arm changed the boy's mind. "Ow, shit, OK, OK, she's eight."

Hoon regarded the DVD cover again, then looked up at the enormous *Tesco* sign emblazoned across the front of the store.

"Did you get her a card?" he asked.

Down on the ground, the boy blinked. "Eh?"

"Fuck me, are you sure it was your hip that got winged and no' your head?" Hoon asked. "A card. Did you get her one?"

"No. No, I didn't. Honest. It was just the DVD. That was it. I swear."

"That's the problem wi' criminals these days. They don't think things through. You need a bloody card for a birthday, son. That's just common sense."

There was a buzzing from Hoon's pocket. He took out his phone and saw an unrecognised Inverness number emblazoned across the screen. Probably the store. They'd given him the number, but he hadn't bothered sticking it into his contacts.

Hoon dropped the DVD so it landed on the ned's chest. "You'll have to excuse me a minute. I have to take this call," he said, removing his foot from the boy's arm. "I'll have my back turned for a while, so don't you go running off, eh?"

The ned nodded, then realised this could be miscon-strued and shook his head instead. "I won't."

Hoon hesitated. His phone continued to buzz at him. "Aye. Because I'll have my back turned and my attention will be elsewhere for the next sixty seconds at a minimum."

"I won't go anywhere," the lad replied. "I promise."

"Jesus Christ, son, are you thick?" Hoon snapped. He pointed away to the far end of the retail park. "Go. Take your film, and fuck off before I have a change of heart."

There was some stunned staring from the lad sprawled out on the pavement, then he grabbed the DVD, rolled over, and kicked off into a sprint.

"There's a *Birthdays* shop down that way," Hoon bellowed after him. "Get her a card, you bloody savage."

"Fuck you, you mad old bastard!" came the reply.

Hoon tutted. "Well, that's charming," he muttered, then he spun around, stabbed a finger at the insistently buzzing mobile and demanded, *"What?"*

———

When Hoon jogged back into the store, he found the Deputy Under Manager taking security matters into his own hands.

"There you are!" Wayne chirped. He was gripping the arm of a struggling young woman with both hands, and hauling her over to the security desk, his face red and shiny with glee. "I got one! I bloody got one!"

"Ow! Quit it. Let me go!" the woman protested. "I didn't do nothing!"

She was in her twenties, with shoulder-length hair and a tartan coat that was far too big for her. A hand-me-down, or a charity shop bargain, Hoon reckoned. Not a good fit, but perfect for stashing a haul.

"You hear that? 'Didn't do nothing,' she says!" Wayne

tugged harder on her arm, practically giggling with nervous excitement. "You've got two big tubs of powdered baby milk up that coat. I saw you put them there."

"I don't!" she insisted, then logic prevailed. "I mean, yeah, I do, but I was going to pay for them. I was, I swear!"

Hoon glanced over to the security stand, but found it unmanned. "Where's that dead-eyed bastard gone?"

"Tea break," Wayne said. "This one thought she could take advantage of that, but she didn't count on me clocking her!"

"Aye, well, you're going to pull her arm off," Hoon said. "Let her go."

"*Let her go?*" Wayne cried. "Not bloody likely! She'll only make a run for it." He inhaled deeply through his nose. "You were right, Bob. She's one of them you told me about. She's one of them ones who'll have been laughing at me." He gave the hardest yank yet on her arm, drawing a yelp of pain. "Not laughing now, is she?"

After the flash of pain, Hoon saw the woman's face change. She smiled, just for a moment. It was a desperate and unconvincing thing that fooled nobody.

Not even the wee lad Hoon now spotted hovering just inside the door. Two years old, and terrified. Eyes red and puffy, a couple of lines of snot forming the number eleven on his top lip. His hands were clasped together, chubby wee fingers intertwining anxiously.

Hoon was so transfixed by the child that he didn't hear his name until the third or fourth time it was said. "Bob? Bob! The police, Bob. Call the police!"

"Why don't you just leave this to me?" Hoon suggested. He turned back to the tussle, and saw another tug, and another grimace of panic and pain. "And stop pulling on her arm, for fuck's sake! That's not how you restrain someone. You're hurting her."

"She's a thief! She's a dirty bloody thief!" Wayne announced to everyone within earshot. Given that this little tableau had started to draw a crowd, that was quite a lot of people.

"It was just... Please. I just needed baby milk!" the woman pleaded.

Hoon looked at the boy in the doorway. *Thomas the Tank Engine* jumper. Swollen arse from the nappy he wore below his trousers. Tears tripping down cheeks that weren't as pudgy as they should've been.

"What's the problem? You've got tits, haven't you?" Wayne retorted, all flared nostrils and toothy leer.

Later, Hoon would only dimly recall his fingers forming fists. He'd vaguely remember his arm drawing back, and the moment that the punch connected.

What he would always remember—what he would take great pleasure in recalling--was the look on Wayne's face as he staggered back, blood fountaining from his ruptured nose.

It was the rage that did it. Activated some auto-pilot. Made him act without thinking, even after all these years.

Sure, he could bury it. Package it up and stash it somewhere. Lock the beast away.

But it would always find a way out. It was only ever a matter of time.

It was a fog that clouded his judgement, and made it hard to think clearly.

That was why, when questioned later, he would struggle to remember picking up the wee lad and handing him over to his mum, then silencing the Deputy Under Manager's protests with a slap, and a shove, and an outburst of swearing.

Later still, he would find out that this was, by quite some margin, the most impressive resignation in the history of the Tesco Eastfield Way superstore, albeit only the fourth quickest.

Before then, however, there was the small matter of his arrest.

CHAPTER FOUR

HOON WAS no stranger to the police station on Inverness'
Burnett Road. God knew, he'd worked there long enough.

He was less familiar with this part, though. The cell he
was in was a little longer than six feet, and a little narrower
than four. Something that could generously be described as a
bed, but which more closely resembled a lightly padded
shelf, took up almost half of the available space.

Hoon lay on it, one hand tucked behind his head, point-
edly ignoring the room's only other notable feature—a
towering big bastard of a detective who had no doubt come
here to gloat.

"New job going well then, Bob?" the detective asked.

DCI Jack Logan was one of the many officers that Hoon
had previously been entitled to boss around and throw things
at, back before all the... *unpleasantness* that had seen his
career go up in flames.

"That's got to be some sort of record, surely?" Logan
continued. "I mean, how long did you last?"

"Four hours," Hoon retorted. He had his eyes closed, like

he was trying to catch up on lost sleep. "And they'd better fucking pay me for it, or I'll be ripping it out of their arses with my bare hands."

"He says he wants to press charges," Logan said.

This was enough to warrant the opening of one eye, but not two. "Who?"

Logan scowled. "What do you mean 'who?' The manager. The guy you lamped in the face and then called a... Hold on..." He took a notebook from his pocket, flipped to a page, then read part of Wayne's statement out loud. "...'a back alley finger bang that got out of hand.'"

Hoon grunted. "Aye, well, he was out of line. Also, what even is an *Under Junior Deputy Departmental*... whatever the fuck he is? How's that a job?"

"Why did you do it?"

"Why do you think?"

Logan shrugged. "I honestly have no idea. Boredom?"

"Fuck's sake, Jack," Hoon scowled. "What do you take me for?"

"A hate-filled, self-destructive, bitter old bastard."

"Fuck off!" Hoon spat. "*Old*? I'm no' old. I'm fifty-fuck-ing..." His lips moved as he did some silent calculations, but failed to settle on a definitive answer. "I'm mid-fifties."

"Interesting that's the only bit you took issue with," Logan said. He sighed, and returned the notepad to his pocket. "Jesus Christ, Bob. I thought you wanted this job? You shouted at me to write you a reference enough times."

That was enough to open Hoon's second eye, and make him swing his legs down off the bed. "Which you didn't fucking do!"

"Aye, well... Whatever. The point is, I thought you wanted the job. *A* job. Of some kind." He gestured around the room. "How is this going to look on your next application form?"

"Don't patronise me, Jack," Hoon spat. "I'm not one of your wee fan club. I don't need your advice, and I certainly don't need your fucking help."

Logan thrust his hands deep down into his coat pockets and shrugged. "Right. Fine. That works for me," he said. "I mean, I was going to talk to the victim and see if he might consider dropping the charges. You know, given that a dozen witnesses saw him physically manhandling a young single mother. But, if you'd rather I didn't..."

Hoon stood up. "Well now, I might've been a bit hasty," he said, then he gave the DCI a couple of light slaps on the cheek. "Maybe you're no' such a useless big arsehole, after all."

———

Two hours, some light persuasion, and a significant amount of paperwork later, Hoon sat in the passenger seat of DCI Logan's BMW SUV, watching the streets of Inverness roll by. It was early evening, and the Highland capital was in that transition period between the day and night economies. Shops were shutting, takeaways were opening, and pubs were just starting to get interesting.

Hoon had suggested they stop somewhere for a drink, but Logan was having none of it.

"You know the only thing more tedious and infuriating than a reformed alcoholic?" he asked, watching the lights of another perfectly good pub go sliding past the rain mottled window.

"No, what?" Logan asked.

Hoon met his eye. "Absolutely nothing."

They continued on. Roadworks on the A82 had forced them to detour through the town centre, and rejoin the main road on the other side of the Ness Bridge. They were not the only ones. Half the cars in the city appeared to be crawling through the same overloaded network of narrow roads and side streets.

They both blamed the tourists.

But then, they always did.

"You get your man for that case down in Glencoe, then?" Hoon asked, his eyes fixed on the city out beyond the glass. *Johnny Foxes* was starting to get busy. Not really his scene, though. Too many young people making tits of themselves for his liking.

"We did, aye," Logan confirmed. He shifted in his seat and shot his old boss a sideways look. "And... thanks again for your help down in Glasgow. I shouldn't have got you involved."

Hoon didn't acknowledge the thanks, nor the attempt at an apology. "How's what's his name doing? With the hair?"

"He's fine. Recovering. Oncologist is pretty happy."

Hoon pointed to his crotch. "Did he get it...?"

"One of them, aye," Logan confirmed, and Hoon wriggled around in his seat.

"Aye. Well, I told him he'd fuck all to worry about," he grunted, going back to watching the passing streets. "He's a drama queen, that one."

Logan nodded. "Aye. He can be, right enough."

They sat in silence at a set of traffic lights, Logan lightly tapping his fingers on the wheel, Hoon gazing glumly out at the rain. The junction was a complicated crossroads, and it always took forever for the lights to work their way around.

"So... what now?" the DCI asked, tearing his eyes from the traffic signals just long enough to shoot the other man a sideways glance.

"Now?" Hoon puffed out his cheeks. "Home for a shite and a bite to eat. Not necessarily in that order."

"I meant beyond that," Logan said. "Job-wise."

"Oh. That." Hoon shrugged. "Fuck knows. No rush."

"I thought you were skint?"

Hoon shook his head. "Skint? No. Why would I be skint? I was in a well-paid job for twenty-odd years, and I buy nothing. Don't you worry about me, Jack. I'm A-O-fucking-Kay on that front."

"Then... why did you go for a job in Tesco?" Logan asked.

The lights changed. The car in front stalled. Hoon leaned over and gave a blast on the horn until the other vehicle chugged back into life and scurried off in shame.

"Just you help yourself," Logan said, shooting deliberate looks to Hoon and the horn in turn.

"Well! Useless bastard," Hoon said, firing off a single-finger salute to the car ahead. "If you can't drive, you shouldn't be on the bloody road." He sat back in his chair, sniffed loudly, then shrugged. "And I was bored."

Logan frowned and stole another look at the button for the car horn. "Bored?"

"No' then. When I applied for the job," Hoon told him. "I thought... I've spent long enough sitting on my arse in the house. Time to get out and do something."

"Well, you did something, alright," Logan said, fighting back a smirk. "I mean, breaking your boss's nose on the first day... That's definitely something."

Hoon gave a snort. "Aye. Well, the goblin-faced wee prick

was asking for it. To be honest, it was probably my favourite day at any job I've ever done. Did you see his face?"

Logan nodded. "What was left of it, aye."

"Would you no' just love to punch that thing over and over again forever?"

"I can't say the thought had occurred to me, no."

"What, not even once?" Hoon turned in his seat and gave the DCI a long, hard look. "Fuck me," he muttered, after several seconds of staring. "You've changed, Jack."

"Maybe," Logan conceded. The car gave a *thu-thunk* as it crossed the bridge over the Caledonian Canal, and they left the bulk of the city behind them. "Now, let's get you home. Because one of us in this car has got a date tonight."

"A date? Jesus." He gave the DCI an appraising look. "Who with? Stevie Wonder?"

Logan said nothing, just indicated right and slowed while he waited for the traffic coming in the opposite direction to pass.

Hoon raised his head and sniffed a couple of times, like he was picking up the scent of his house now that they were closer.

"Aye, well," he muttered, looking out across the dreich and dreary fields that passed for the Inverness suburbs. "Maybe you're no' the only one with a hot date lined up."

CHAPTER FIVE

HOON'S 'DATE' was with a fiery young gentleman by the name of *Johnnie Walker*. He'd kept the bottle—or a good three-fifths of it, anyway—tucked away at the back of the cupboard in the hall.

It was Black Label, and about as close to 'the good stuff' as he got these days. He'd told himself he was keeping it for special occasions, but that had turned out to be any occasion where there was no other alcohol left elsewhere in the house.

Today, though, did feel special. Today, he'd taken fuck-uppery to a whole new level.

He grasped for the bottle and brought it in closer to an old metal cup that he nursed against his stomach. There was a moment of intense concentration as he attempted to pour approximately two inches of the amber liquid from one container to the other. This process involved some squinting, some tongue biting, and an urgent *shh* aimed at the empty room around him.

Finally, and with only some light spillage, he poured himself another drink and returned the bottle to the coffee table with all the care of Indiana Jones trying to outfox some ancient booby trap.

Craning his neck forward, he managed to inhale a few sips of the drink, then he let his head fall back onto the arm of the couch and enjoyed the burning sensation in his throat.

It was smoother than his usual whisky of choice. Given that his usual whisky of choice was whatever represented the best ratio of alcohol content to price, this was no real surprise.

He found himself resenting its subtlety, though. A good dram was a double-edged sword of both pleasure and pain. Afterwards, you should feel like you'd achieved something. Like you'd conquered it. Like you'd crawled through Hell and somehow made it out the other side.

That was the experience his usual tipples provided, at least. This one, though, was actually palatable, which largely defeated the point.

Not that he was about to let it go to waste.

He brought his mouth up to meet the rim of the glass, took another sip, and lay back.

There had been a more optimistic guy hanging around here this morning, he seemed to recall. He'd spoken to him in the mirror. That daft bastard had gotten his hopes up. Allowed him to start believing that things were about to get better. That he somehow deserved another chance.

Lying on his couch, Hoon raised his glass to the ceiling, toasting the man who was no longer there.

"Onwards and fucking upwards, eh?" he sneered, then he brought the glass down, missed his mouth completely, and emptied half a glass of Scotch into his eyes.

Blinded by whisky and pain, he flung himself off the couch, tripped over the coffee table, and went tumbling towards the floor.

Even as he fell, some protective instinct screamed at him to save the open bottle, and he grabbed for it, fingers splayed in what he prayed was the right direction.

His fingertips brushed against glass. There was a *clack*, then a *thud*. By the time Hoon connected face-first with the carpet, he could hear the liquid gushing out onto the floor somewhere just beyond his reach.

It was at this point that the doorbell rang. Hoon reared up, the heels of his hands jammed into his burning eye sockets. If the pleasure-pain pendulum had previously been swinging too far in one direction for his liking, it was sure as fuck making up for it now.

The doorbell rang again. It was a bright, cheerful sounding *ding-dong*—far too perky for its own good. He disliked the bloody thing at the best of times. Now, with his eyeballs practically melting down his face, his opinion of it had not improved.

"Alright! Argh! Jesus!"

Ding-Dong! Ding-Dong!

"I'm fucking coming! Hold your horses!"

He found the couch and fumbled himself up onto his feet, using it for support. He tried to open his eyes, but the lids were having none of it until he physically forced them apart using his fingers and thumbs.

Agony swept in, drawing a bellowed, "*Fuuuuuuuuuck!*" that shook the dust from the light shade above his head.

The cheerful bastard of a doorbell chimed again, and he threw himself in what he hoped was the direction of the hall, his vision still too blurred to be sure. Blinking through the haze of whisky and tears, he felt his way along the hall.

After knocking a couple of pictures off the wall, and almost breaking his neck when he tripped on the phone cable, he finally reached the front door and pulled it open in the nanosecond of silence between another *ding* and its accompanying *dong*.

He bellowed a *"What?"* into the darkening night, then physically peeled both eyes open again when he realised there was nobody standing on the step.

Something thin and pointy prodded him in the stomach. He grabbed for it, but it was whipped away before he could close a hand around it.

The evening air cooled the burning sensation a degree or two. It was just enough that he could peer through the tears and find the outline of the figure sitting on a chair on the path.

"Good God, man. What happened to you?"

Hoon recognised the voice at once, and suddenly the shape made sense. The metal pointer, too - an old extendable car aerial, which would've been used to reach up and press the bell with. It could also, in his experience, give you a right nasty whipping across the back of the legs.

He gave his eyes another rub and peered down at the man in the wheelchair. "Bamber? That you?"

"It is," the visitor confirmed. The voice was recognisable but different. Its usual levity—forced as that sometimes was— was gone. "And I really need your help."

———

Hoon had retreated into the house, knowing better than to offer Bamber a hand up the steps. He'd lost the majority of both legs to a roadside IED way back in the day, but had done his damnedest to hold onto as much of his independence as possible.

He had been a big, brash, bombastic bastard prior to the explosion. Always on the wind-up, even when things were at their worst.

His laugh was legendary. It was the sort of laugh that should by rights always be accompanied by the clanking of metal tankards and the sound of roast chicken being torn from the bone. You could imagine it echoing around the great hall of Valhalla on a particularly rowdy Saturday night.

He had laughed less often and less heartily after the bomb had as good as ripped him in two. Of course, it was a miracle that he'd laughed at all. But he had. Not right away, granted, but eventually, once the anger had burned out of him and the tears of self-pity had for the most part dried up.

It had been a turning point, that first post-explosion laugh. That was the day he'd stopped feeling sorry for himself, and insisted that no other bastard should feel sorry for him, either. The extent of his injuries meant prosthetics were out of the question, but he let his wheelchair take him wherever it could, and crawled through the places it couldn't.

He wasn't an invalid, he insisted. Offer to wheel his chair for him, reach anything, or—God forbid—carry him, and you were opening yourself up to levels of vitriol and abuse that even Hoon could only aspire to.

And so, to even hear him say the word "Help," had almost knocked Hoon off his feet. Something was wrong. Something major.

Now that Hoon's vision was starting to clear, he retrieved the fallen bottle of *Johnnie Walker* and gave it a shake. A couple of mouthfuls swished about in the bottom. He poured half into his metal mug, then found a glass in the kitchen and tipped the rest into that.

By the time he'd returned to the living room, a slightly out of breath Bamber was wheeling himself in through the other door, his waterproof jacket rustling in time with his arm movements. He took the offered glass without a word, clinked it against Hoon's raised mug, and then knocked it back in one.

"You know your eyes are all bloodshot?" he asked, after the customary post-whisky grimace.

"Eh, aye. I've no' been sleeping well," Hoon said.

Best not to tell him how he'd almost blinded himself a few minutes before. He'd never hear the end of it.

Bamber gave a grunt. "You and me both, then."

He didn't add anything else. Not yet. Instead, he looked around at the living room, with its stacks of dirty dishes and ramshackle piles of old newspapers that Hoon fully intended to chuck in the recycling bin just as soon as he could remember where it was.

"Been a while," Hoon said. "How's things?"

"Shite," Bamber replied. "You?"

"Just hunky-dory, as you can see," Hoon said, gesturing at the squalor around them.

"I hear you lost your job," Bamber said.

Hoon's bloodshot eyes widened. "Fuck me. That travelled fast." He took a sip of his drink, then burped. "Aye, well, it was just a shitty security guard gig."

"What?" Bamber looked him up and down, like he was seeing him for the very first time. "I thought you were in the police? I thought you were a Superintendent or something."

"Oh, that? Christ. No. I lost that ages ago," Hoon said. "Through no fucking fault of my own, I should add."

Bamber noted the empty whisky bottle, and ran a finger around the inside of his glass, mopping up the dregs. "That's not the way I heard it," he said.

"Aye, well, never mind the way you heard it," Hoon retorted. "What do you want?"

Under other circumstances, Bamber would have laughed at the directness of the question, and the sound of his merriment would have shaken the walls.

Today, though, he just nodded, like he was grateful to be skipping the small talk. He wasn't here for a catch-up, or to talk about old times. He was here for a reason, and Hoon wanted to know what it was.

"You, eh, you remember Caroline, don't you?" he asked. Met by Hoon's blank expression, he added, "My daughter."

"Oh. The baby! Fuck. Aye," Hoon said.

"Yes, well, she got bigger over the subsequent twenty-two years, but yes."

Hoon whistled through his teeth and flopped down onto his couch. "Twenty-two years. Jesus. Has it been that long since I saw you?"

Bamber shook his head. "Reece's funeral. Two-thousand-and... what? Twelve? Thirteen? Something like that."

Hoon slapped a hand against his forehead and grinned. "Christ, yes! Reece's funeral. That was some fucking night out. No wonder I couldn't remember. Did you no' end up getting a hand-job off that lady vicar?"

Bamber shot a worried look at the window. "Lizzie's outside," he warned.

Hoon followed the other man's gaze. "And what, has she got fucking bat ears these days?" he asked. "Why did you no' bring her in?"

"Because she still hates you and wants you dead," Bamber replied.

Hoon ran his tongue across the back of his teeth, then nodded. "Aye, that's fair enough," he conceded. He raised his mug in a toast to the window, then knocked back the contents. "So... your daughter?"

Bamber exhaled slowly like he was in the early stages of labour. After the explosion, he'd physically been half the man he used to be. Mentally, though—once he'd worked through it all—he'd still been more or less the same guy. Larger than life. Legs or no legs.

Now, though, he looked shrunken. Small. A shadow of that other man.

"She's in uni. Studying Chemistry."

"Aye? Where'd she get the brains from?"

Bamber smiled at that, but it was a distant, wistful thing. "Lizzie says it's from her side. But she's smart, right enough. Caroline, I mean. She's always been that way. I mean, you wouldn't believe some of the things she used to come out with when she was—"

His voice cracked. His head bowed. Hoon sat quietly, as Bamber's broad shoulders shook their way through a series of silent sobs.

"Sorry, Bob. Sorry, I just..." Bamber inhaled sharply like he was sucking his grief in, then swallowing it back down. "We wanted her to go to Edinburgh. They don't pay for it up here. Uni, I mean. Free education. But, she wanted London. She had her heart set on it. She'd always loved the place. Saw something magical in it, where I just saw dirt and noise and shady bastards up to no good."

He sat up straighter and looked to the window again. Hoon could just make out the outline of an estate car parked out there, beyond the lights of the house. The silhouette of a woman watched from the driver's seat.

"We gave in. We let her go. Didn't want to hold her back. Or didn't want her to be able to say later that we'd held her back, if we'd talked her out of it," Bamber continued. "I thought if we told her she could go, she'd change her mind. Like... I don't know. She was testing us, or something. We thought, if we called her bluff, she'd go to Edinburgh."

"Did it work?"

"Did it fuck. She was off like a shot," Bamber said. "Been there nearly three years. Due to graduate this year."

Hoon stole a glance into his mug and was disappointed to find it empty. He set it down on the table and remained sitting forward. "But?"

Bamber raised his gaze to the ceiling. His fingers flexed a couple of times, then tightened around the arms of his wheelchair. When he spoke, his voice had to fight to escape his narrowing throat.

"But something happened, Bob. Something happened to my wee girl."

CHAPTER SIX

"ARE YOU OK, miss? Who were those lads? Did you know them?"

She turned in the passenger seat and saw them through the rear windscreen, picked out in the red of the rear lights. Five of them, shouting and gesturing after her, growing smaller and smaller as the car sped away.

"Did they hurt you? Are you alright?"

She faced forwards, and the glass in front of her fogged as she breathed out several minutes' worth of tightly packed fear. "No. No, they didn't. I'm... I'm fine. They were just following me. That's all."

"They didn't... do anything? They didn't hurt you?"

"No. Nothing like that."

They would have, though, she thought. Given the chance. She had sensed their hunger as they'd closed in on her. Their lust. Their urge to dominate.

She tried not to think about what they might have done to her. Tried, but failed, and a thousand violent indignities filled her head.

Beside her, the driver gave a little sigh of relief. "That's good. Thank God." He double-checked the rearview mirror to make sure they weren't being followed, then spat a, "Pricks!" when he was sure they were safely out of earshot.

"You can say that again." She tapped out a message on her phone, then hit 'send' just as the battery flashed and the screen went dark. "Shit."

"Everything OK?"

"Hmm? Oh. Yeah. Sorry. Phone's died."

He indicated the glove box. "I think there might be a charger. iPhone?"

"Android."

"Ah. Then no. Sorry."

He checked the mirror again, squinting into the red-tinted darkness of the road behind them.

"A lot of these lads have scooters these days," he remarked. "But doesn't look like anyone's coming. I think we're in the clear. You should be safe now."

She chewed on a thumbnail, her hand shaking as her mind continued to conjure up images of what could have been. "I don't know what would've happened if you hadn't been there," she said, the words coming out as a whisper. "I don't know what they'd have done."

"Don't think about that. You're fine. I'm just glad I was there," the driver said. "What were you doing wandering around at this time of night, anyway?"

"Couldn't get a taxi," she explained.

"Wasn't there someone you could've walked with? Strength in numbers, and all that?"

She shifted in her chair, but said nothing. The driver smiled, then shook his head.

"Sorry, none of my business," he said. "Where to?"

"What?"

"Where am I dropping you?"

"Oh. Yeah. Sorry. Just... um. Could you just take me home?" she asked.

The driver waited, then gave a little chuckle. "I'm going to need a little more than that, I'm afraid."

She frowned, then realised what she had done. "Oh! Shit. Sorry! Yeah. I'm still not really thinking straight." She pointed ahead. "Just keep going down here and I'll tell you where to turn."

"Righty-o." The driver tapped his fingers on the steering wheel for a few seconds, then checked his mirrors again. "Still nothing. I think we're clear."

She looked over her shoulder at the rear window. "Yeah, I doubt they'd follow us now," she said.

The noise the driver made was a noncommittal one that made her heart beat a little faster.

"You don't think they would actually chase us, do you?"

"No. Probably not. I seriously doubt it. But they did seem quite determined," he said. His eyes flitted to her. "And you are a very pretty girl."

She picked at her thumb. "Thanks."

"I mean it. You're really... you're gorgeous. I hope you don't mind me saying."

She shook her head. "No. Um, thanks. It's just up here in a minute."

"What is?"

"My flat."

"Oh. Right. Yes. That. Just you tell me when to turn." He turned to her. Smiled. Showed too many teeth. "I'll make sure you get home safe and sound."

CHAPTER SEVEN

"THREE MONTHS," Bamber said. "Ninety-two days, actually." He shrugged. "I won't bore you with the hours and minutes. Though, I could."

Hoon sat back and surrendered to the cushions of the couch. "Jesus Christ, Bam. That's... Jesus Christ. What are the polis saying?"

"Not a lot. They're still looking, of course. Officially. But they don't check in with us now. We have to phone them. Half the time, the bastards don't even call us back." His lips drew back over his teeth like he'd just taken another shot of the *Johnnie Walker*. "People go missing all the time in London, they say. We can't say for sure that she didn't just take herself off somewhere."

"And would she?" Hoon asked.

Bamber bristled in his wheelchair, his head snapping up until he met the bloodshot, red-ringed eyes of the other man. "No!"

Hoon held up his hands like he was surrendering. "Sorry, Bam. Had to ask."

"Why?"

The question caught Hoon off guard. "Eh... force of habit, I suppose."

"You can take the man out of the police..."

"Something like that, aye," Hoon said. "So, they've got nothing?"

Bamber shook his head. "Nothing concrete. Or not that they're telling us, anyway. But her phone's been off, and she hasn't touched her bank account. Flatmate's not seen or heard from her."

"Flatmate? Male or female?"

"Female."

"You know her?"

"Vaguely. She's not... She's not involved. She's just a kid. They're both just kids."

"She still could know something," Hoon said. "I take it the Met's spoken to her?"

Bamber sighed. "The Met. Us. Chuck. You remember Chuck, aye? From the unit?"

"What, Bookish?" Hoon asked.

The name stirred a memory that almost brought a smile to Bamber's lips. "Bookish. Aye. He lives down in London. Got some police contacts. He's been digging around for us."

"Good. That's good. He's a good guy. Right fucking smart arse," Hoon said. "He find anything?"

"Bits and bobs. A few leads here and there," Bamber confirmed. "I think he's pretty much done all that he can, though."

Hoon reached for his mug, and only remembered he was out of alcohol when he found it empty. Shame. He could really do with a drink.

Although, judging by the other man's face, not nearly as much as Bamber could do with one.

"That is fucking..." He blew out his cheeks. "I don't know what to say, Bam."

Bamber's wheelchair creaked as he shifted his weight around in it. "You can say yes."

Hoon's brow creased. "To what?"

"To the question I'm about to ask you," Bamber said. He was perfectly still now. Had it not been for his lips moving, he might've been a statue. "Will you find her for us, Bob?"

There was a cough. A snort. An incredulous, *"Find her?"*

"Yes."

"What, me?" Hoon prodded a finger against his chest, as if to demonstrate just how ludicrous a candidate he was for this particular job. "How the fuck am I meant to find her? Have you seen the state of me? I can barely find my arse with both hands. Keep Bookish on it. If anyone can find her, it's him."

Bamber shook his head. "He's a good guy, but he's a thinker, Bob. That's his strength. We don't need a thinker. Not now. We need someone who can..." He looked down, took a moment to compose himself, then tried again. "We need someone who can get answers. Who can throw their weight around a bit. A blunt instrument."

"Well, that is fucking charming, that is," Hoon retorted. "You could have said, 'We need a man of action,' or a 'rakishly handsome hero type,' but you settle on 'blunt instrument.' What, was 'We need a big fucking mental bastard' too on the nose?"

"I can pay you. Lizzie and me. We've got some money put away for—"

Hoon extended a finger and a warning. "You better watch what you fucking say here, Bam."

There'd be no talk of money. Whatever happened, payment was off the table.

Bamber winced, having clearly been bracing himself for just such a reaction. "Sorry, Liz told me to say it. I told her it wasn't..."

Hoon waved the apology away, then looked out of the window at the outline of the car in the darkness. "She knows what you're asking me, then? She knows why you're here?"

"She does."

"And she's OK with that?"

"She's not delighted. But right now, she doesn't care. We just want Caroline home, Bob. We just want our wee girl back home."

"I get that, Bam. I do. I really fucking sympathise. And I can make a few calls—"

A fist slammed down on one of the wheelchair's arms. Bamber's voice was harsh. Raw. "We don't need someone to make calls! We've done that bit! We've got all we can from doing that, and we're no closer to finding her!"

He inserted the first knuckle of his fist into his mouth, stopping the flow of words rushing out, and sat like that for several seconds, bringing his emotions back under control.

Once he had, he forcibly cleared some blockage from his throat, then spoke in a voice that was almost supernaturally measured, given the circumstances. "We don't need someone to look for her. We need someone to *hunt* for her. And you're our best chance. You're *her* best chance."

"Jesus, Bam. Look at me. If I'm her best chance, she's got *no* fucking hope."

Bamber closed his eyes. Ran a hand down his face. Steeled himself.

He was going to say it. After all this time, he was actually going to say it.

Hoon had been waiting years for these words. Decades. So long, in fact, that he'd almost started to believe he'd never hear them.

Almost.

"You owe me, Bob."

And there they were. Hanging there in the present, loaded with the weight of the past.

Hoon sat forward slowly, carefully choosing his words.

"Aye. I do. I owe you big time," he agreed. He met Bamber's eye, saw hope spluttering there, and moved swiftly to stamp it out. "That's why I'm telling you to get someone else. I'm not the man for this job. I'll only let you down. And I can't do that." He struggled to stop his gaze flitting to the stumps of the other man's legs. "Not again."

"Bob—"

"It was good to see you again, Bam. I hope you find her, mate, I really fucking do." Hoon stood. Nodded to the door. "But, I think it's time you were on your way."

For a moment, it looked like Bamber was going to argue. But only for a moment.

He nodded, just once, muttered a quiet, "Right, then," and unzipped a pocket on the front of his jacket.

A photograph was placed face down on the coffee table, between Hoon's mug and Bamber's glass.

"I'll be on my way, then," Bamber announced. He turned his chair to face the door. "Thanks for the drink."

"Any time, Bam," Hoon said. "And... you know. I hope it all works out. I really hope you find her."

"Yes." Bamber's wheels creaked as he rolled out of the room. "You and me both."

———

He had clicked the lights off the moment the front door was closed. Sat there in silence, listening to the sound of the wheelchair on gravel, and the thunk of a sliding car door rolling closed.

There were voices then. Muffled so he couldn't make out the words. He got the gist of it, though. If Lizzie had disliked him before, she positively loathed him now.

There was shouting. Sobbing. A noise like a wounded animal, then words of comfort spoken so softly he could barely hear them at all.

And then, the engine started, headlights ignited, and two glowing red dots went trundling away across the uneven surface of his drive.

Then, and only then, did Hoon let out the breath he'd been holding.

He swore a few times at nobody and nothing in particular, checked to make sure the car hadn't turned around, then pulled the curtains shut like they were a shield keeping the outside world at bay.

The photograph taunted him from the table.

"No," he told it. "Fuck off!"

He stormed through to the kitchen, searched the cupboards there for the emergency half bottle of *Co-op* brand Vodka that he was sure he hadn't completely polished off.

"Come on, come on," he muttered, hands shaking as he rifled behind jars and cans, and emptied the contents of a couple of drawers.

A memory—dim and distant—of a cereal box came creeping back to him. Abandoning the cutlery drawer, he pulled open one of the lower cupboards, hauled out a box of *Frosties*, and thrust a hand inside, spilling sugar-coated flakes of corn all over the floor.

Nope. Not there.

He hunted in another two boxes—*Coco Pops* and *Shreddies*—and was coming to the conclusion that he bought far more cereal than any single adult man probably should, when he found a hunk of glass buried in a bag of *Rice Krispies*.

With a cry of triumph, he pulled it free, fingers trembling as he twisted off the bottle's metal lid. It clacked on the floor and got lost somewhere under the fridge.

Fuck it. Didn't matter. Not like he planned using it again now that...

His heart was sucked down into his lower intestines when he saw the bottle was empty. He gave it a shake, then raised the bottle's neck to his mouth, refusing to believe the evidence of his own eyes.

Not a drop emerged. Not a snifter.

"No, no, no. Fuck off!" he ejected.

Snatching up the box of *Rice Krispies* again, he pulled out the inner bag and tipped the contents onto the kitchen worktop, letting it cascade over the edges and onto the floor. The cereal snapped, crackled, and popped beneath his feet as he grabbed for various other boxes and emptied them all, one by one.

On the table in the living room, the photograph waited.

"Fuuuuuck!"

The empty bottle exploded against the wall, denting the plasterboard, and spraying slivers of glass in every direction. Spinning, he punched the front of a cabinet. Once. Twice.

Pain burned through his knuckles and bloodied the cabinet door.

Teeth gritted, he clutched the overhanging edge of the worktop and heaved, like he could topple the whole kitchen over, send it crashing through the house and into the garden.

Something in his back gave an audible *twang*, and an entirely new, never-before-heard swear word was born and died on his lips.

He folded forward until his forearms were on the worktop, nestled among a rolling landscape of *Crunchy Nut Cornflakes* and *Cookie Crisps*.

He really did have an awful lot of cereal.

Were there other hiding places? Other secret stashes dotted around the house?

Maybe. Almost certainly, in fact.

Could he remember where any of them were?

Could he fuck.

"Well, that's that, then!" he announced to the Universe in general. It came out like an accusation, like this thing he was feeling—whatever the name for it was—was someone else's doing. Someone else's fault.

The Universe, for its part, did not offer a response.

"Fine. Right. Fine. I'll fucking look. Happy?"

The crunching of the cereal was joined by the cracking of glass as he plodded out of the kitchen and into the adjoining living room.

The photograph hadn't gone anywhere. Of course it hadn't.

The bastard.

His legs felt heavy. His head, quite the opposite. He perched himself on the arm of the couch, about as far from the photograph as it was possible to be while still being within reaching distance.

It was a little bigger than standard photo size. Five inches by seven, rather than the usual six by four. The back of it was giving nothing away, of course. It was plain white, aside from a string of numbers written neatly in one corner that dated it to eight months ago.

"Jesus Christ," Hoon whispered.

He stood up.

Sat down again.

Rubbed the palms of his hands on his knees like they'd suddenly become infuriatingly itchy. The blood from his damaged knuckles trickled between his fingers, smearing his trousers with streaks of crimson.

He edged closer along the couch, flexing the fingers of his uninjured hand. Warming them up.

A deep breath. A silent curse. The fingers hovered above the back of the photograph, dancing slowly in the air as if carried on some invisible current.

He touched the back. A tap. Just one, like he was checking the picture was really there.

"Right, get a grip," he told himself. "Just look at the fucking thing."

And he did. Less than fifteen minutes later, he picked it up, turned it over, and looked into the eyes of a smiling young woman who had no idea what her future held.

He hadn't seen her since she was a baby, but he'd have recognised her a mile away. She had her mother's eyes, and her father's smile. That big daft grin that Bamber had, all teeth, and spit, and gums. She was a bit more self-conscious about it than her old man, maybe, but it was there. No mistaking it.

Almost immediately, Hoon turned the photo over, dropped it, and threw himself to his feet.

He turned his back. Walked away. Stood by the window and stared out, like the closed curtains weren't even there.

He gave his mind something to do, and tried to remember where he'd stashed the drink.

When that didn't work, he grasped fitfully back at the day's events, searching for something to hold onto. Something to distract him.

The early optimism over his first day in a new job. The chase with the ned. The scared wee boy watching his mum being manhandled.

The immensely satisfying *crunch* of the manager's nose giving way.

The cell. The car ride.

The man in the wheelchair. The desperation in his voice.

You owe me, Bob.

And he did, of course. Hoon owed a lot of things to a lot of people, but Bamber more than most.

Bamber, more than anyone.

On the table behind him, tucked out of sight, a lost girl smiled self-consciously, all teeth, and spit, and gums.

CHAPTER EIGHT

HOON STARED at the woman on the other side of the glass in a mute disbelief that lasted all of three seconds.

"Sorry, maybe you misheard me, sweetheart," he said. "I said I wanted a one-way ticket to London, no' to the fucking moon."

On the other side of the dividing window, the woman in the ticket booth gave an almost imperceptible sigh. "Aye. And that's the price. Two hundred and twenty pounds."

"Can I assume that comes with a veritable fucking smorgasbord of sexual favours?" Hoon spat back.

"No. It comes with a bed and a bacon roll, and I'll be honest, neither one's up to very much," the teller replied, unfazed. She'd dealt with her fair share of arseholes over the years, of which Hoon was just the latest. "But, it's the only berth we've got left on the Sleeper tonight."

"What about without a bed?" Hoon asked.

The woman's nostrils flared. "What, seated? You don't want seated."

"Why not?"

"Because it's eleven hours."

"I think I can manage eleven hours of having a seat, sweetheart. It's hardly one of the twelve fucking labours of Hercules, is it? *Having a sit down.*"

She shook her head. "You'll regret it. Trust me. You don't want seated."

"I'll be the fucking judge of that. How much is it?"

The teller tapped at her keyboard. "Seventy-three pounds."

Hoon slapped the counter in triumph. "Aha! That's why you don't want me taking the fucking seated, you upselling bastard. No bloody wonder. I'll take one of them."

She peered at him through the glass, shrugged, then went back to tapping on her keyboard. "Aye, well, it's your arse."

"Does that come with the bacon roll, by the way?"

She answered him with a disparaging look that said he should be so lucky, then indicated the card payment terminal on the counter. "Seventy-three pounds. Ready when you are."

Hoon inserted his card, shielded the keypad from the woman's prying eyes, then poked in his PIN.

He took the offered tickets and waved them at her like they symbolised some great victory.

"You're going to regret it," she told him.

He sneered. "Dry your eyes, you robbing bastard," he retorted. "This is going to be a fucking breeze!"

———

It was thirteen hours later, and Hoon wished he was dead.

The journey had been thoroughly enjoyable for the first forty minutes, gone downhill somewhat over the next three or four hours, then become an unrelentingly grim test of endurance as the night had worn on.

He'd started out confident that the right decision had been made. The seats were big. Plenty of room to get comfortable in. When he'd discovered they reclined, too, he actually laughed out loud at the bare-faced cheek of the ticket seller who'd tried to talk him into wasting a hundred and fifty quid on a bed he didn't need.

By the time the train had reached Edinburgh, the seat had lost almost all of its appeal.

Before they were even over the border into England, he was fantasising about amputating his whole arse.

Sleep rarely came easy these days, even when tucked up in bed at home. Here, wedged on an awkward incline, surrounded by coughing, wheezing, farting strangers, it evaded him completely, and by the time he saw the sun rising above Watford Junction, he didn't know whether to laugh or cry.

It may have been the lack of sleep, the pain in his back, or the near-total loss of feeling below his waist talking, but he fucking hated London. Even the fleeting glimpses of the outskirts that he was able to make out between the heads of the other zombified passengers was enough to set his teeth on edge.

The bottlenecked roads. The graffitied bridges. The shuttered shops. The blocks of mocket-looking flats that were the size of postage stamps yet for some reason cost a million quid each. He despised it all.

Quite why anyone would want to visit the place was beyond him. And as for living there...

Somewhere about his person, his phone rang. He felt

around for it, patting pockets and rummaging in the rucksack that was jammed in next to his legs.

Two seats away, a man who had snored and fidgeted his way through ten of the longest hours of Hoon's life shot a look of irritation in the direction of the ringing phone, earning himself a, "Don't you even open your fucking mouth, pal. I'm warning you!"

The phone rang off just as he found it wedged under the marginally more paralysed of his two buttocks. He checked the number and called back, and was surprised when a woman's voice answered.

"Who's this?" he demanded. "You're not Gwynn."

"I'm aware of that. Who's this?" the woman asked, and over the clacking of the train on the tracks, Hoon picked up the hint of an accent that the years had chipped away at.

Shite. What was her name again? He closed his eyes and pictured her as she'd been two decades before. Long legs and deep tan. Wee floral skirt. They'd all be green with envy, and Welshy had loved every bloody minute.

"Gabriella? That you?"

There was a moment of silence, then, "Depends. Who's this?"

"It's, eh, it's Bob. Hoon. From... Me and Gwynn served together in the Gulf."

There was another pause while the woman on the other end of the line considered this. "The angry one? Face like a hamster?"

Hoon frowned. "What? How's it like a fucking hamster?" He ran a hand down his face, presumably checking for any hamster-like qualities. "But... aye. Maybe, I suppose."

"You called here. Twice. Both times after three in the morning," Gabriella told him.

"Was it as late as that?" Hoon asked. "Sorry, I was half-shot, and trapped in a never-ending fucking hellscape of misery. I must've lost track of time. Is Welshy there? Gwynn, I mean. I wanted to ask him a favour."

Another pause. Longer this time. A garbled announcement resonated through the carriage, alerting any blind or particularly dim-witted passengers to the fact that they were now in London.

"Hello? Still there?" Hoon asked, jamming a finger in his ear to drown out the din.

"You don't know?" Gabriella asked.

"Don't know what?"

"About Gwynn."

The rest of the world dulled into shades of grey. Hoon let his head fall back against the top of the chair. "Shite. No. Is he... He's not dead, is he?"

"No," Gabriella replied, but there was something in her voice that told Hoon this wasn't the good news it might appear to be. "He's not dead. Or... not exactly."

CHAPTER NINE

GWYNN EVANS WAS NOT WELSH. He had never, to the best of his or anyone else's knowledge, so much as set foot in Wales in all the twenty-seven years up to the day he had started serving alongside Bob Hoon. Despite this, he had carried the monicker 'Welshy' for almost a decade by that point, and it had stuck with him through the rest of his military career and beyond.

His name had a lot to do with it, of course—Gwynn Evans was arguably the most Welsh name in the whole of human history—but the rest of him contributed its fair share, too. He was a big fan of the rugby, enjoyed a drink, and could belt out *The Green, Green Grass of Home* until there wasn't a dry eye in the house.

For a man who'd never visited the country, he was as Welsh as rarebit and sheep shagging. Hoon had liked him immediately. They'd become friends, and had pulled each other's arse out of the firing line more than once.

And now, here he was lying on a rubber sheet, one good

eye swivelling around the room, the other tucked away beneath a drooping lid.

He hadn't noticed Hoon. At least, it didn't seem like he had. Gabriella had warned that her husband might not recognise him, but that he shouldn't take it personally.

"He doesn't recognise many people. Sometimes, not even me," she'd said, before adding that all this was just a feeling she had, and that there was no real way to tell for sure.

It had been a stroke. A massive one. There had been complications. Delays. Bad medical decisions. Recovery wasn't impossible, just statistically improbable.

The bed was tucked away against the wall of what had once been a small dining room. There was something surreal about it—a fully-equipped hospital bed, surrounded by bleeping and pumping machines, standing next to a folding table and a rack of painted crockery.

"I eat in here most days," Gabriella said, slipping in through the door at Hoon's back. "We talk. Or... I talk. I think he likes the company."

"Aye. I'm sure he does," Hoon said. He set his rucksack down against the wall by the door and approached the bed, voice raising like a foghorn to announce his presence. "Alright, Welshy, you malingering bastard?"

The eye shifted, finding focus on the new arrival. There was no reaction. Not at first. No change in his breathing, or flicker of recognition.

But then, a sound emerged. It came from deep within him, and somehow found its way out without his lips moving. There were no words, yet it was a question, Hoon knew.

"Aye, Welshy. Aye, it's me." He took one of Gwynn's hands in both of his. It was a dead fish of a thing, limp and cold. "The fuck's all this, then?" Hoon demanded, indicating the banks of medical equipment. "Still a bloody drama queen, I see."

The eye remained fixed on him. Staring. Scrutinising.

Pleading?

It was painful to look at. Or maybe painful to *be looked at* like that. Either way, Hoon didn't flinch or turn away. Instead, he watched a tear roll down a sunken cheek. He interlocked his fingers with Welshy's and tightened his grip.

"You're alright, big man. You're alright," he soothed. "I suppose this explains why you stopped sending me all those shite jokes by email, eh? Thought maybe you'd just developed a decent fucking sense of humour, at last."

"Wait, he sent those to you?" asked Gabriella. She joined Hoon at the bed and put a hand on her husband's arm. Welshy's attention didn't shift from Hoon.

"Unfortunately, so. Fucking honking, they were."

Gabriella laughed. It was the first time the room had heard laughter in months, and Welshy's eye shimmered at the sound of it.

"He did that on purpose. He knew they wound you up. He used to hunt out the longest, most unfunny jokes he could find, just to annoy you." She laughed again and stroked Gwynn's arm. "He'd said he was sending them to... It was you. Of course. I should have realised. You're Boggle."

At least two different parts of Hoon's face twitched at the mention of his old nickname. It had been an abbreviated form of 'Boggle-Eyed-Bastard,' a title given to him on account of the way his eyes could sometimes get a little bulbous when he lost his temper.

Which, back in those days, was often. He had been foul-tempered and fouler mouthed as a younger man. Compared to back then, the Hoon of today was practically a Buddhist monk.

Hoon looked down at the man on the bed. "You know, I actually wondered if that might be it," he said. "'Not even that unfunny fuck can actually laugh at these, surely?' I used to say. Thought it had to be a wind-up."

"It was," Gabriella confirmed. "He always got a real kick out of your reactions."

"Just as well he wasn't closer, or he'd have got an actual fucking kick, right up the jeb end."

Gabriella gave her husband's arm one final pat, then stepped away. "Come on, you must be hungry."

Hoon's stomach gurgled its confirmation. "I wouldn't say no to a bacon roll, right enough," he said. He tried to detach himself from Welshy, but the man in the bed tightened his grip, hanging on, refusing to let him go.

Hoon didn't struggle. Instead, he just rubbed a thumb across Welshy's wrist, nodded, then turned to the woman in the doorway. "But I'll maybe take it in here, if it's all the same with you?"

———

It was mid-morning when Hoon finally managed to get away. Gwynn's grip had slackened over the course of their decidedly one-sided conversation, and Hoon had sat and watched his old mate's good eye turn glassy, then close over as he was pulled down into sleep.

He'd untangled his fingers, picked up his plate and cup, then found Gabriella asleep in an armchair in the living room.

It had been the first chance he'd had to see her properly,

having been steered straight through to see Welshy the moment he'd arrived.

She'd aged well. Far better than her husband, certainly, though that wasn't saying much. But better than most other people, too.

She must've been in the latter half of the forties now, but could've passed for ten years younger. She was a little plumper than she'd been back in the day, but then weren't they all? The thigh-length floral skirts had been replaced by much more practical jeans and a V-neck jumper with a t-shirt underneath.

Hoon realised he had been staring for several seconds now, gave himself a shake, and turned his attention to his surroundings, instead.

The house was a compact two-bedroom end terrace on Lampard Grove in North London, with a big bay window looking out onto a relatively quiet residential street. It was decorated sparsely, with a couch, an armchair, and some largely featureless laminate flooring.

The only two interesting additions were a battered old piano in the corner, and a coffee table that had looked as if it had been produced by either *Ikea*, or one of the lower circles of Hell. The thing was the epitome of style over function, with an angular wooden knot as a base, and a top made up of three distinct circles of glass, none of which met the others at any point. It looked like a puzzle, and not one that was worth the effort of solving.

It was a decent enough house, though, as houses went. Up in Inverness, it would've cost less than two-hundred grand. Here, you'd be lucky to get change back from a million.

Welshy had inherited the house fifteen years ago, back

when prices were merely eye-wateringly expensive, and not bowel-shatteringly so. There was little chance he could've afforded to buy a place like this back then, and absolutely no way he could do it in today's market.

He'd spoken in his emails—between the awful jokes— about selling up someday and using the money to travel the world. He'd always been more of a nomad than a home-steader, Welshy, and when he'd stopped emailing a year or so back, Hoon had assumed he'd gone wandering.

He should've checked. Should've reached out.

One more *should've* in a long list of the bloody things.

The kitchen looked like it had once been part of an open plan with the living room, but was now partitioned off with some stud wall and a sliding door. Hoon washed his plate and cup, and left them drying on the rack.

When he returned to the living room, Gabriella was unfolding herself and stretching like a cat in a sunbeam.

"Sorry, did I disturb you?" Hoon asked.

"What? No. No. I mean, not then. Last night? Yes." She held up two fingers. "Two phone calls."

"Aye. Sorry about that. Again," Hoon said. "Because, you know, I did apologise already. Maybe you remember...?"

Gabriella looked over at the door to the dining room. Technically, it was the spare bedroom that they'd converted a few years back. Now, it was neither one thing nor the other. "He asleep?"

Hoon nodded. "Aye. Out for the count."

"Thanks. For sitting in with him, I mean. For not freaking out."

Hoon shook his head. "No bother."

"He recognises you."

"You think?" Hoon asked. He thought of the shimmering

eye, and the other man's fingers in his. "Aye. I think he does, right enough. What happened? If you don't mind me asking."

Gabriella exhaled and shook out her arms, like an actor preparing for a big audition. There was no performance when she spoke, though. Every ounce of pain in her recollection was real.

"We were in Turkey," she began. "Anniversary. He surprised me. Nearly left it too bloody late, so we had to sprint the last bit at the airport. Almost didn't make it through security. But we did. We got there—to the hotel, I mean—eventually. He wasn't usually the most romantic guy, but he'd thought of everything."

Her hands were pressed together, fingers dancing and rippling in unison like each hand was a reflection of the other. She wasn't looking at Hoon, but wasn't quite looking anywhere else, either. She had abandoned the here and the now for the there and the then, and was reliving the memory even as she spoke it out loud.

"We went for a walk. Night before our anniversary. Along the beach. At midnight, he played music on his phone, and we danced. Just the two of us and the water swishing around us." She smiled fondly, but it was a struggle to maintain it and it soon crumbled away. "And then... he fell. He just fell. Onto the sand." She shut her eyes, screwed them up tight. "And he was... He made this noise. Like an animal. Just this... groan. This cry of pain, or for help, or... I don't know."

"Jesus. And it was a stroke, you said?"

She nodded. "And then he had some sort of fit, and... I kept shouting for someone to help us, but nobody came. Nobody heard me. So I had to leave him. I had to run and find someone." The lines of her face etched themselves deeper into her skin. "It was an hour and a half before we got him seen to. Before the ambulance arrived. Everyone thought... *I* thought he was dead."

With a blink, she brought herself back to the present, and glanced over at the door. The bleeping and wheezing of the medical equipment echoed from the room beyond.

"But he wasn't," she said, then she stretched again, yawned, and got to her feet. "Anyway. What was the favour?"

"Eh?"

"The favour. On the phone. You said you wanted to ask Gwynn a favour."

"Oh. Right. Aye. No, it was nothing. Nothing important."

"You need a place to stay."

Hoon hesitated. "Eh... I mean..."

"We only have the one bedroom," Gabriella said.

"Aye. Of course. No, I can just get—"

She indicated the couch with a nod. "But I think that unfolds. Don't know how, though. You'd have to work it out."

Hoon regarded the couch like a predator scoping out its prey. "I'm sure I could figure it out," he said. "But, fuck, listen, you've got enough on your plate. If it's putting you out..."

"Gwynn would want you to stay," Gabriella said, in a tone that made it clear the matter was settled. He was staying. And that was that.

"Right. Well, that's grand. Thanks."

"What are you down here for, anyway?" Gabriella asked. "Business?"

Hoon nodded. "Aye," he said. "I suppose you could say that."

CHAPTER TEN

CHARLES 'CHUCK' Mundell sat on a barrel-shaped chair at a *Starbucks* in Canary Wharf, scrolling through a book on his phone's *Kindle* app.

As he reached the end of a page, he sipped some of his ice-cold drink through the straw, then shut one eye and spent the next thirty seconds fending off a bout of brain freeze.

Once recovered, he checked his watch, then looked up in time to see the boggle-eyed face of his past storming across the shopping mall in his direction.

"Fuck me, how many of these places are there?" Hoon demanded in a voice loud enough to make the coffee shop's half-dozen other patrons momentarily look up from their Macbooks. "'Meet me in Starbucks,' you said. You neglected to mention that there's two fucking thousand of the things within a half-mile radius. And Jesus, there's a lot of wankers in suits around here, isn't there? Chatting away into their fucking Bluetooth headsets. Everywhere's hoaching with the bastards."

Chuck smiled, and clicked the button on the side of his

phone that made the screen go dark. "Boggle," he said, and his Essex accent rang out sharply in even just that one word.

Hoon grunted. Nodded. "Bookish," he replied, then he pointed accusingly at the plastic cup on the table between them, crammed almost to the brim with something the colour of candy floss. "What in the name of all that is fucking holy is that?"

Chuck's eyes flitted to the drink. "It's a Flamingo Frappuccino."

"Sorry? It's a what?"

"It's a Flamingo Frappuccino."

"No, I heard the fucking words you said," Hoon replied. "I just didn't understand them, or why you'd be drinking what appears to be the contents of the Pink Panther's ballsack."

Chuck picked up the cup. "Because it's nice." He took a sip. "You want one?"

"Hang on. Wait and I'll check if I'm a pre-pubescent child," Hoon said. He shoved a hand down the front of his creased combat trousers, had a good rummage, then withdrew it again. "No. Seems not. So, how about you bin that Day-Glo liquid shite, and we go and get ourselves a proper fucking drink?" He looked around at the Londoners tapping away on their Macbooks. "Ideally, somewhere where we're no' flanked on all sides by pricks."

"In Canary Wharf? That's a big ask." Chuck sucked one last slurp of his Flamingo Frappuccino up the straw, then got to his feet. "Lucky for you, I've got just the place."

———

"A boat?" Hoon looked down at what was, very clearly, a boat. There was no mistaking its boatiness, in fact, rendering the question completely pointless.

"Well spotted, Boggle," Chuck said. "What gave it away? The pointy bit at the front, or the way it's floating on the water like that?"

"Since when did you become a funny fuck?" Hoon asked. "I meant why are we looking at a boat?"

"Because it's my boat," Chuck said.

Hoon regarded the boat, then the man beside him. Neither one was particularly impressive on its own—the boat was a somewhat dilapidated old motor yacht that was long overdue a coat of paint, and Chuck had put on three or four stone since Hoon had last seen him. He reminded Hoon of a fat Buzz Lightyear. He had told Chuck this, and his remark that, "'To Infinity and Beyond' isn't meant to refer to your fucking waistline," had not gone down particularly well.

Despite the individual failings of the boat and the man, though, Hoon found himself impressed by the sum of their parts.

"You must be doing helluva fucking well for yourself," he remarked.

Chuck wrinkled his nose. "Not really," he said. "I live on it. It's cheaper than rent. A *lot* cheaper than rent. Especially round here. And buying a flat's out of the question, but I picked this up for under a hundred grand."

Hoon gasped in a breath. "*A hundred grand?* For a shitty wee boat? What, does it fly or something? Has it got a wee voice inside it like the car in *Knight Rider?*"

"It's not that small!" Chuck protested.

"A hundred fucking grand." Hoon shook his head and

tutted. "I hope it came with a shitload of Class A drugs in the hold, otherwise some bastard saw you coming."

"It's nice inside."

"Aye, well," Hoon stepped down off the dock and landed with a *thud* on the deck. "I'll be the fucking judge of that."

"No, fair enough. It is nice inside, right enough."

And it was. Much as Hoon hated to admit it. The outside might have been rough, but the interior of the boat was like some quaint Tudor cottage with exposed wooden beams across the ceiling, and a deck of aged wooden floorboards running underfoot. All it was missing was a thatched roof and a big brick fireplace, and the effect would be complete.

There were some modern touches, too—electrical sockets, a TV, some sort of black obelisk that Hoon presumed was something to do with the internet. The telly was a fifty-incher, and fixed to the wall across from either a couch or a padded bench, depending on how generous you wanted to be with your description.

Through a door on his right, Hoon could see a galley kitchen which, while small, looked to be well equipped. Beyond that, another door led to what he guessed would be a bedroom and bathroom, assuming Bookish didn't just piss in a bucket and chuck it over the side.

No, that wasn't his style. Most of Hoon's other old mates, maybe, but not Bookish. His toilet would more likely have an automatic air freshener that pumped out a rose-scented spritz after every use. Hoon couldn't quite decide if that made him less of a man or more of one.

"Yeah, it's not bad, is it?" Bookish said. He looked around

and nodded, like he was seeing it for the first time and was impressed by what he saw. "I'd pay ten times what I paid for this for a flat on the same spot."

"Would a flat no' sink?"

"You know what I meant," Bookish said. He sighed, but it was good-natured enough. "In the same area. Canary Wharf. Not this exact spot."

"Does it not cost to park it here?"

"Moor it, you mean?"

"Whatever it's fucking called. That can't be cheap, can it?"

"Twelve grand."

"For life?"

"A year."

Hoon whistled through his teeth. "Jesus fuck."

"It's way less than I'd pay for rent."

Hoon scowled. "Aye, but you're no' renting, are you? You had to buy the fucking boat first."

Chuck looked around them again, and looked a touch less impressed this time. "Aye, but... that includes electricity and water."

"Water? You're surrounded by water. You're living in a fucking boat. A lack of water's the least of your problems."

"You can't drink from the Thames. Not unless you want to shit yourself inside out."

Hoon chuckled. "Like in Basra, you mean?"

"Oh, Christ!" Chuck clutched his stomach at the thought of it.

"Them were the days, eh?"

"Yeah. Three of them in a row, if memory serves. I think I shat out a lung at one point."

They shared a laugh about the experience, spent a few

more minutes reminiscing about some of the gorier details, then Chuck addressed the elephant in the room.

"Why are you here, Boggle?" he asked. "Bamber said you weren't coming."

"I'm not," Hoon replied. "I mean... not officially. I don't want him knowing and getting his fucking hopes up. You know what he's like. I'm just poking my nose in. That's all."

Chuck nodded. "Fair enough. You won't be wanting a full report of everything I've found, then?"

Hoon sniffed. "Maybe I'll poke my nose into that, too," he said. "But first thing's first—did you no' mention something about alcohol?"

CHAPTER ELEVEN

SHE PRESSED the button on the side of her phone. Held it, praying the dead battery might find some extra reserve of energy and spring back into life.

It didn't, of course. The screen remained dark. Her contact list unreachable.

"You didn't say it back," said the driver of the car. He was still smiling, still showing too many teeth. They were yellowing, flecked in the gaps with little blobs of food scum.

"Um... say what back?"

"I said you were attractive. You didn't say it back."

"Oh." She looked from him to the road ahead. Other cars were passing, their lights dazzling her through the windscreen. "Sorry. I, eh... You look nice."

"You think?"

"Uh, yeah."

"Thanks! I'm glad you think so. Because I think you're a very pretty girl." He grimaced and poked the middle of his forehead with an angry finger. "Young woman. Not girl. A very pretty young woman. That's what I meant to say. Sorry. Sorry."

She hesitated. "It's fine."

"No, it's not. It's not fine," he snapped, visibly agitated. "You don't say 'girl.' That's sexist. And I'm an ally. I am. I'm a feminist." He took a hand from the wheel and raised two fingers in peace or in victory. "Girl Power! No. Shit. Woman Power!"

She smiled politely. Tried to appear grateful as she pointed to a junction ahead. "I'm round on the right here," she said, but she felt exposed by the words, like they were spilling secrets she'd rather keep to herself. "My, um, my flat-mate's waiting up for me."

"Your flatmate?" The driver laughed. "Lot of help she was waiting up for you! What good would that have done if those men had raped you?"

The bluntness of it made her flinch, but there was nowhere to retreat. Nowhere to draw back to. Nowhere to go.

"Because they would've done, you know?" the driver continued. "Given half a chance. That's exactly what would've happened. Young woman, strutting around dressed like that." He shook his head and gripped the wheel like it was trying to fly out of his hands. "They'd all have taken turns at you. All leering and laughing at you while they pounded and grunted away. What good would your flatmate have done you then? Waiting at home? I mean... Jesus, what a selfish fucking bitch! Where was she when you needed her?"

"Um, could you... I'd like to get out."

"Out? Here? Flaunting yourself like a cheap slut? No. It's not safe. It's far too dangerous."

Hunched in the passenger seat, her breath caught at the back of her throat.

She watched him turn to her. His hand reached out and found her face frozen with fear. A thumb brushed against her cheek, rough and painful. "But don't you worry, princess. You're safe with me. Everything's going to be OK. I've got you," he told her. "I've got you now."

CHAPTER TWELVE

BOOKISH HAD BEEN BUSY. Hoon would give him that.

He wasn't officially a private investigator. It wasn't a title he'd ever claimed, or a service he'd ever advertised, and yet jobs tended to fall into his lap. A decade gathering intelligence for the British Government gave you a certain insight into surveillance and security, and word tended to get around.

The key thing he'd been able to get his hands on was CCTV from the night Caroline was abducted. No single piece of evidence confirmed that she definitely had been taken, which was why the Met hadn't devoted many resources to the case, but Chuck was certain of it, nevertheless.

"Doesn't fit her usual behaviour. Not remotely," he said, discussing the disappearance in general while he waited for his laptop to boot up. "She was in regular contact with her parents prior to that day—three calls a week, Tuesday, Thursday, and a longer one on Sundays. Been doing that for nearly three years, and rarely missed a call. Nobody else has had any contact from her, either. Not her flatmate, none of her friends from uni, nobody."

"And no activity on the bank account?"

"None," Bookish confirmed. He'd managed to get the laptop running, and double-clicked an icon on the desktop. "Here. This is her."

He turned the screen towards Hoon, giving him a clearer view. Grainy footage showed a young woman dressed for a night out. It was late. The housing estate she was walking through was quiet. She was marching on at a fair clip, phone clutched in one hand, bag clasped protectively in the other.

Hoon didn't recognise her, but he knew the body language well enough. She was scared. In a rush, like she was trying to get away from...

Five men. They followed her into frame at the top right corner, as far from the camera as it was possible to be. If Hoon had recognised Caroline's walk, he was even more familiar with theirs. It was menacing. Predatory. A pack on the hunt.

"Do we know them?" Hoon asked, indicating the men with a jab that nudged the screen back a little on its hinges.

"Yes and no," Chuck said. He nodded to the screen, suggesting that Hoon keep watching.

There was a corner visible right at the bottom left of the screen, where the path through the estate joined a street. Hoon could only see a couple of feet of the pavement, but it seemed to be better lit than the area Caroline had been walking through, and the way the shadows moved suggested at least one passing car.

Sensing freedom, she began to walk more quickly. Sensing a missed opportunity, the men did the same, all-but breaking into a run as Caroline drew closer to the corner, then sprinting after her when she vanished out of sight.

"Where's the rest of it?" Hoon asked. "Can we see the other angle?"

"No. Unfortunately not. No CCTV down that way."

"Fuck's sake!"

"There's a camera on a couple of streets after that, but they don't pick her up again." Chuck motioned to the screen again. "But keep watching."

For a long time, nothing seemed to happen. Hoon was about to suggest spooling the footage on before he died of old age, when the five lads came trudging back into view from around the corner. There was no audio, but it looked like they were arguing. A few punches were thrown—dead arms, nothing serious—and Hoon watched as they plodded back up the screen towards where they'd first appeared from.

"They didn't take her."

"No. Doesn't look like it."

"But... what? How? No chance she could've outrun them."

Chuck shrugged. "She goes to the gym. Apparently, she's pretty fast."

"Aye, no' in them fucking shoes. You ever tried running in heels?"

Chuck blinked. "No," he admitted. "Why, have you?"

"More than once, as it happens." He shook his head in a way that made it clear pursuing this further would not be in Bookish's best interests. "And there's no fucking way she outran them."

"Met seemed to think it was possible."

Hoon grimaced. "Aye, but that shower of mangled fuds

wouldn't know a clue if it clawed its way out of their arse-holes head first. She didn't run. She couldn't."

"You think she hid?"

"What, is she six? No. I think she got in a car."

Chuck reached up to a shelf in the little nook above the desk and took down a ring-bound notebook. He flicked hurriedly through the pages, and Hoon's eyes were drawn to all the many pastel colours and patterned strips of tape.

"Is that a fucking scrapbook?" he asked, as Charles rifled through the pages.

"Hmm? No. It's just... I do bullet journalling."

Hoon regarded the man beside him with a sort of bewildered horror. "The fuck's 'bullet journalling' when it's at home?"

Chuck looked down at his notebook and suddenly looked mortified by it. "It's actually an effective way of keeping information organised," he insisted, trying to recover some shred of dignity. "There's a lot of scientific research that says it's a very efficient means of..."

He could see from Hoon's face that no amount of peer-reviewed data was going to make him think any more highly of the coloured headings, subheadings and neatly bulleted lists, and so didn't bother trying any further to convince him.

Instead, he wrote the word 'Car,' on a page near the back, and added a question mark with a flourish of the wrist.

"I can't be the first one to realise she got in a fucking car, surely?" Hoon asked, his gaze performing the full circuit between the notebook, Chuck, and the laptop. "I mean, you said yourself she doesn't show up on the other cameras, so unless she somehow developed the ability to fucking teleport, where else did she go?"

"There's other streets without cameras," Chuck

explained. "The Met's theory was that she might've run off down one of those."

"Aye, well, we've already established what I think of the fucking Met," Hoon said. He pointed to the screen. Chuck had tapped the pause button, freezing five blurry figures at the top right of the frame. "What about these pricks? What are they saying for themselves?"

"Not much," Chuck said. "They were brought in for questioning, I'm told, but didn't give much away. They were pretty hard nuts to crack, by all accounts."

"Oh, they were, were they?" Hoon asked. He interlocked his fingers and stretched them, making the knuckles crack and pop. "Well, we'll soon fucking see about that."

CHAPTER THIRTEEN

"THAT'S THE FLAT. Second row up, fifth along from the stairs."

Hoon sat squashed in the passenger seat of a bright red 1972 MG Midget convertible, his head making a bulge in the fabric of the roof. He had never understood owning a convertible in the UK, where it rained, hailed, or snowed more often than it didn't. If he did ever have to own one, though, this fucking thing would be right at the bottom of the list.

He wasn't a particularly tall man, but even with his seat pushed back all the way, he could've done with another few inches of legroom. The passenger space was narrow, too, with the door pushing in on him from one side, and a raised gearbox pressing his right knee against his left. As a result, his testicles were currently being crushed together, which was doing his mood no favours whatsoever.

Bookish had clearly invested quite a few man-hours polishing up the leather seats, and Hoon had spent the dura-tion of the drive giving his arse friction burns from all the sliding about. That, coupled with the sore back, claustropho-bia, and the testicle situation meant he not only never wanted to travel in this car again, he would ideally like to set it on fire, then push it into the sea.

He ducked to look out through the low windscreen, and muttered darkly when the old-style seatbelt jerked him back. He unfastened it and contorted himself into a position where he could look up to where Chuck had indicated.

The estate was made up of several large buildings on multiple levels, with concrete walkways connecting them on the middle and uppermost floors. The entrances to the indi-vidual flats emerged onto long balconies, with a central stair-well providing access to the floors above and below.

The building directly ahead of them had four storeys. Hoon's gaze traced the route Bookish had given, and settled on a flat whose curtains were drawn.

"Blue door?"

"That's the one," Chuck confirmed. "You, eh, you don't want me coming in, do you? It's just... I can't leave the car here. They'll be away with it."

"Who's going to nick this fucking thing?" Hoon asked, sounding offended by the very suggestion. "There been a big rise in self-loathing masochist car jackers that I haven't heard about?"

"It's a classic!" Chuck protested. "They'll be away with it as soon as my back's turned." He glanced furtively at the estate around them, with its scattered litter and witless graf-fiti. "I shouldn't even hang about here. There's people who'd kill for a car like this."

"Aye, I was tempted to throttle you myself at a corner back there," Hoon said. He opened the door, and let out a sigh of relief as his testicles became unsquashed. "Fine, you stay here and wait. Or circle around, if that'll stop you sitting here shiteing yourself."

"Right, yeah. Good idea," Chuck said. He slipped a hand behind his seat and produced the notebook with its pastel headings. "You want their names?"

"No' if it means carrying that fucking thing," Hoon retorted. "Maybe you could crochet their personal details into a pair of legwarmers for me. Something a bit more masculine than that."

"It's efficient!" Chuck insisted.

"Aye, well, you know what's even more efficient? Texting the names to me." He unfolded himself from the car, put a hand on his lower back, and crunched his spine back into something close to the correct alignment. "Blue door?"

Chuck took a photo of a page in his journal, then tapped to share it. "Blue door," he confirmed. "But be careful. These are dangerous people."

"Good," Hoon said. In his pocket, his phone buzzed to indicate a message received. "Then we should have plenty to fucking talk about."

———

Hoon was pleasantly surprised when the door was answered after the second knock. It saved him the effort of having to kick it in.

A cloud of cannabis smoke accompanied the plooky, pale-faced wee runt who opened the door. The smell of it had been growing stronger the closer Hoon got to the flat, and it came billowing out past the twenty-something in the ill-fitting tracksuit as he looked the new arrival up and down.

"What ya wan'?" he asked. His accent sounded Jamaican. Or a pastiche of it, anyway.

"That's no' your real voice, is it?" Hoon asked, then he shook his head. "Actually, I don't care. I'm looking for..." He checked his phone screen, squinted at the writing, then held the device at arm's length as he tried to focus. "Jesus."

"No Jesus here, mon."

"Fucking cut that out, will you? You sound ridiculous," Hoon said, glancing up just briefly from his phone. "Right. I'm looking for... Fuck. How do you pronounce that? Ghaz... Ghaz*an*fer? *Ghaz*anfer?"

"Who want ta know?"

Hoon frowned. "Well, me. See my fucking lips moving?" He nodded past the lad into the flat beyond, and took a step closer. "Is he in?"

A hand was placed on his chest. The skinny white boy sneered, all spots and spit. "Where ya think ya goin'?"

Hoon caught the hand, twisted. The lad in the doorway had nowhere to go but down. He landed in a heap on a dirty, threadbare carpet, his eyes wide in shock, his thumb bent at an angle nature had never intended it to achieve.

"I'm assuming he's this way," Hoon said, stepping over the fallen fuckwit and continuing into the flat.

The smell inside was richer and more complex than it had appeared from the balcony. Out there, it had been the sickly-sweet aroma of grass, with just a faint hint of tramp's piss around the edges.

In here, there were some more interesting notes to it. An overflowing bin. Some well-matured pizza. An unflushed toilet. The place wasn't so much a treat for the olfactory senses as a full-frontal assault on them.

He found three guys in the living room, where much of

the smell was coming from. Two of them—both black, but wildly different ages—sat on the same big beanbag, thumbs hammering away at the controllers of a games console, a carrot-sized joint burning away in an ashtray between them.

The older of the two was in his early thirties, Hoon estimated, with extensive scarring on his cheeks that suggested his teenage acne had been unusually cruel.

The other man could have been anywhere from ten to fifteen years younger. His skin was in far better condition, but there was enough similarity in their features to mark them out as brothers.

The third man was aged somewhere between the two. He was sitting cross-legged in a lopsided armchair, fixated on the other joint he was rolling for himself. This spliff was longer and thinner—so long, in fact, Hoon wondered if the guy might be going for some sort of record.

He was... Christ, what was the right term these days? Middle-Eastern? Asian? He probably should've paid more attention when Police Scotland was running all those diversity courses.

"Alright, lads?" he asked when they all failed to look his way. He tucked his hands behind his back and rocked on his heels while beanbag brothers looked up and voiced their reactions.

"Shit!"

"Who the fuck are you?"

"Where did you come from?"

"Marty! Fucking Hell, Marty, who'd you let in, you useless piece of shit!"

Hoon checked his screen. *Martin Wilcott. Age 19.*

Tick.

There was a whimper as the lad from the front door came

scuttling into the room, one hand gently gripping the opposite wrist, his thumb still protruding painfully in the wrong direction.

"He... he broke me hand!" Marty babbled, in that same poor parody of Jamaican patois. He shot Hoon a look that was ten percent anger, ninety percent fear. "He broke me damn hand!"

"Let's not get out knickers in a fucking twist here," Hoon said. "I broke your *thumb*, pal. No' your hand. Calm down. You've still got a perfectly functioning one left."

Something about the way Hoon said that last line made Marty stop sobbing. It wasn't so much a reassurance as a warning. *You think it's painful now? Imagine what it'll be like when I break the other one, too...*

The man sitting with his legs crossed in the armchair had not yet spoken. Nor did he seem particularly concerned by the arrival of this stranger in their midst. He was still rolling his joint, his tongue occasionally emerging from the forest of his beard to dampen the paper.

The beanbag brothers had dropped their controllers and were struggling to get up. Each movement from one hindered the progress of the other, though, and it took several seconds of blame and embarrassment before they finally made it to their feet.

They were big lads. The older one more so. He carried himself like someone who knew what he was doing, and Hoon made a mental note to put him on his arse first if things turned ugly.

Hoon thought back to Chuck's list. There had been two names on it with the same surname. African. *Mbarga. Manuwa.* Something like that.

He checked his phone screen. *Mpenza.* That was it.

Pascal and Antoine.

Tick. Tick.

"Who the fuck do you think you are?" the older of the two demanded. The accent was pure *Saarf London*, with no hint of anything more far flung.

Hoon ignored the question and fixed his attention on the fourth man, who was still yet to speak. He checked his phone screen, had a few mental passes at the pronunciation, then went for it.

"You Ghazanfer Abassi?"

"I asked you a fucking question," the older Mpenza brother hissed. He took a couple of steps closer to Hoon—a sort of strut of bravado, all swinging shoulders and outturned knees, that was presumably meant to intimidate all those who saw it.

"You shit yourself or something, son?" Hoon asked, showing absolutely no indication of backing down. "Or are your *Postman Pat* Y-fronts just riding up the crack of your arse?"

The younger Mpenza egged the older one on. "You going to let him talk to you like that, bruv?"

"Aye. He is. Aren't you, sweetheart?" Hoon said, and there was something in the way he spoke the words, and the way he just stood there that made both Mpenzas hesitate. Hoon stepped between them, daring them both with a look to try and stop him. "Ghazanfer?"

There was a hint of something foreign and exotic in the fourth man's reply, but it had been corrupted by the same South London accent as the Mpenza brothers. In fact, of the four of them, it was the blond-haired white guy who sounded the least local, and only because he was playing silly buggers.

"I am," he said, still rolling his joint. He wrinkled his nose like he'd just smelled something bad. Fucking rich, given how badly the flat stunk. "You talk weird. You Scotch, or summink?"

"It's 'Scottish,' actually. 'Scotch,' is a drink," Hoon corrected. "You can have that wee nugget of information on me. We're right into that in Scotland. Free education. It's a cracking place." He gave Ghaznafer a nod. "So, this is your flat?"

"Hoots! 'So, this is your flat?'" one of the Mpenza brothers said, mangling a Scottish accent even worse than the spotty wee jeb-end at the door had mauled the Jamaican.

Laughter cracked like a whip behind him. The bearded lad in the chair didn't join in the hilarity, but he smiled his approval, which only encouraged the others.

"I must say, you're awfully fucking calm, considering a right scary bastard just forced his way into your gaff."

"That's cos you ain't scary, mate," one of the brothers said.

"And it's because we gonna kill you, innit?" added the other.

Hoon turned slowly, addressing the room at large. "I want to make something clear up front. Whatever happens here, I want you all to know that it's not due to any sort of prejudice on my part. I'm what I like to think of as an *equal opportunity bastard*. I don't hate people because of the colour of their skin, which imaginary sky fairy they support, or the gender of the genitals they're driven to mash their own against. I hate people because they are, by and large, all arseholes."

He looked around at the three men surrounding him, and the fourth holding court in the armchair. "And you taco-holed fuckmuppets strike me as no exception."

"What did he just call us?" asked the younger of the two brothers, brow furrowed like he was struggling to decipher these strange foreign utterings.

"Now, if you don't mind me saying, you lads really need to get some fucking fresh air in here," Hoon announced, turning to the window and throwing the curtains wide. The sunlight was thin and grey, but it was enough to draw hisses from at least two of the room's occupants.

"How do I open this window?" Hoon asked. "Because this place is fucking howlin'."

The older and larger of the Mpenza lads clenched his fists, set his jaw, and made his move. "Right, fuck this shit," he announced, springing forward with a surprising turn of speed.

Hoon sidestepped the charge, spun a full three-sixty, and then a hand found the back of the charging man's head.

There was a hollow *thonk* as the attacker's face was introduced to the glass. This was immediately followed by a spray of blood and a cry of pain.

"Shite. You've made a mess of the glass now. Here, I'll wipe it up for you," Hoon said. He smeared the man's face up and down the window pane, painting it in streaks of crimson. "Fuck. That's actually making it worse, if anything."

"Get your facking hands off him!" the younger brother cried. A knife blade flicked open. A lunge was made.

Hoon's foot caught the inside of the lad's knee, inexorably altering the angle and direction of its bend.

It took another half-step for the pain to register, then the younger Mpenza screamed, stumbled, and was met by a right hook. It spun him over the top of the beanbag, launching the ashtray and carrot-sized spliff across the room, and sending him crashing to the floor.

"There was absolutely no fucking need for any of this, by the way," Hoon said, dragging the bloodied older brother away from the window by the hair and depositing him on top of his sobbing sibling. "I came here for a chat. You lot fucking brought this on yourselves."

Over by the door, fake-Jamaican Marty was shifting his weight on the balls of his feet and taking a series of short, sharp breaths as he geared himself up to attack. Hoon raised a beckoning finger, then gave a grunt of disappointment when Marty turned on his heels, ran into the hallway, and went clattering out through the front door.

"Right, then," Hoon said, turning back to the man in the armchair. "Let's try that again. Is this your flat, son?"

Ghazanfer, who had seemed unshakeably calm a few moments ago, appeared decidedly less so now that his three mates were out of action. Two of them were writhing around on the floor, and the look on his face said that he had very little interest in joining them.

"Yeah," he confirmed, the pencil-sized joint trembling in his hands. "But I ain't done nuffink."

"Good. That's good," Hoon said. He stood a few feet from the seated man, his hands crossed neatly behind his back, a smile on his face like he didn't have a care in the world. "Tell me about Caroline Gascoine."

"Who?"

Hoon bent, retrieved the metal ashtray from the floor, and emptied the contents over the Mpenza brothers.

"The lassie you chased a few months back. Just around the corner from here," he said, idly turning the ashtray over and over in his hands.

"I dunno what you's on about, bruv."

The ashtray *whanged* him across the forehead, snapping

his head back. It was made of light aluminium and did very little damage. But it was a pretty effective warning shot.

"Ow! I don't know who that is!"

"Why, is there a big fucking list of women you've chased? Is that the problem? Here, maybe this'll help."

He found the photo he'd taken of the picture Bamber had left for him and held up his phone. Ghazanfer glanced at it, then quickly looked away.

"Aye, that's what I fucking thought," Hoon said, returning the phone to his pocket. "I'm told that you were less than helpful when the polis asked you about her. I'm sure you don't need me to tell you that I'm no' the polis, and believe me, it's in your best fucking interest to answer my questions."

Down on the floor, a hand reached for the dropped knife. Hoon's foot came down on it hard, eliciting a squeal of pain that he seemed to remain oblivious to.

"See, the polis have to follow the rules. They've got all these annoying wee fucking regulations written down, and if they don't stick to them, there's hell to pay. It's a fucking nightmare of red tape," Hoon explained. "But me? I don't have those. *Rules*, I mean. I don't have my hands tied by any of that shite."

He looked back over his shoulder for a moment, then faced front again.

"On an unrelated note, how high is that balcony, would you say?" he asked.

"What? I don't... I don't know."

"Aye, well, unless you want to fucking find out, you'll tell me what happened to Caroline Gascoine," Hoon said. He held up a finger, stopping Ghazanfer before he could start. "But, I'm going to warn you—see me? I've got a built-in radar for bullshit. Lie to me—try and spin me some bollocks—and I will launch you over that fucking balcony and into the most exhilarating two-point-five seconds of your pointless, wasted wee life." He glowered just enough so that he could be sure his point had been made, then lowered his finger and nodded. "Right. Go."

Ghazanfer gave a furtive little shrug. "We didn't... We wasn't going to do nuffink. We was just having a laugh, innit? Nuffink else to do."

"I saw the CCTV. Didn't look to me like Caroline was sharing in the fun."

"We wasn't going to hurt her," Ghazanfer insisted. "We wasn't. We was just chirpsing."

Hoon frowned. "You were what?"

"Chirpsing, bruv."

"The fuck is 'chirpsing?'"

"You know. Like... flirting, innit?"

"Fuck me, is that what passes for flirting these days? Chasing a terrified wee lassie in a fucking pack? And they say romance is dead." He shook his head. "You chased her. Then what?"

"I dunno."

Hoon flared his nostrils. "You *don't know*? How the fuck don't you know?"

"We was well wavey."

Hoon's scowl folded the lines of his face like angry Origami. "Jesus Christ, have you got a fucking *English to Arsehole* dictionary I can borrow? What's 'wavey?'"

"Wasted. We was wasted."

"You couldn't have just fucking said that?" Hoon spat. "What do you remember?"

"I told you, mate, not much!"

Hoon sighed. "We'll try a fucking process of elimination then, will we? Did she fly away on wee magic wings?"

"What? Nah."

"How do you know?"

Ghazanfer blinked. "Well, because... she was human, innit? And because, like, I saw her. Breezing, like. Not flying or nuffink." He caught the look from the man standing over him, and translated before being asked to. "Running. She was running."

"See? Now we're fucking getting somewhere," Hoon said. One of the Mpenza brothers attempted to raise himself up on his arms. Hoon placed a foot on his back and encouraged him to return to the floor. "So, she was running?"

"Uh, yeah. I think so."

"You *think* or you *know*?" Hoon demanded, barking the words out and making Ghazanfer jump in his chair.

"I know! She was running." He twirled his beard around a finger, his eyes narrowing as he thought back. "I think there was a tourist."

"A tourist?"

"Yeah. Just some next man." He nodded. "Yeah. Reckon she went to him." He clicked his fingers, a detail coming back to him. "Wait. He had a whip."

"A whip?" Hoon frowned, processing this. "Who the fuck was he, Indiana Jones?"

"What? Nah, mate. A whip. A car. Real nice one, too. Porsche, or some shit. He was heading for it when she went running up."

"Colour?"

"White. Or... wait? The geezer or the car?"

"Both."

"Right. Well, him, white. The car...? Like... blue. Nah,

wait. Green." Ghazanfer shook his head. "Or, like, what's that colour that's kind of green and kind of blue?"

"Greeny blue," Hoon suggested.

"Yeah. Yeah, like that."

"You get a registration?"

"Mate," said the man in the chair, making it clear that this was a silly question.

"What about this cluster of fucks?" Hoon asked, pointing down at the Mpenzas. "Don't suppose they'll have memorised the number plate? Or your mate who ran away? Albino Bob Marley? Is that no' fucking racist, by the way, him talking like that?"

"Marty don't know nuffink about nuffink."

Hoon nodded. "Aye. I got that impression, right enough," he said. "What about the other fella?"

The look he got back from the man in the chair was one of confusion. "Who?"

"There were five of you that night. Chasing Caroline. He thought back to the list Bookish had given him. "Eduardo something. What about him?"

Sitting in his chair, Ghazanfer stiffened. "What *about* him?"

"Did he see anything?"

"I don't know. Maybe. You'd have to ask him."

Hoon nodded. "Fine. Where is he?"

"He's dead."

"Dead? Since when."

"Since the five-oh took him inside, innit?" Ghazanfer spat back, nervousness momentarily giving way to disgust. "All them rules you say they have? All them regulations about not doing nuffink to no one? Maybe someone wants to try telling them that."

CHAPTER FOURTEEN

HOON WAITED for the MG to reappear after another lap of the estate, then bent to the window as Chuck slowed the car down.

"Thank Christ. You're alive. I was getting close to thinking I might have to come in," Chuck said.

"My fucking hero," Hoon said. "Nothing to worry about, they were a shower of fannies." He gestured to the estate around them. "The street Caroline was taken from. Which one is it?"

"Just round the corner. Hop in, and we'll head round."

Hoon regarded the inside of the car with contempt, then shook his head. "Point the way and I'll meet you there. Want to get a feel for the place. Plus, my balls are enjoying no' being currently pancaked between my thighs."

Bookish looked shocked by the suggestion that anyone might willingly take a stroll through a housing estate like this one, but then rattled off a short list of directions and pointed Hoon on his way.

"I'll meet you round there," he concluded, manually

rolling up the window. He watched in the wing mirror to make sure Hoon wasn't immediately jumped by a gang of hoodies, then pulled away before anyone could start stripping the car for parts.

Hoon shoved his hands down in the pockets of his crumpled combat trousers and went on a meandering walk in the direction Chuck had sent him. A few faces watched him from the windows above. A small knot of lads stood around a souped-up *Volkswagen Golf*, all of them eyeing him up like he was some strange new exhibit at a zoo.

He gave them a nod when he passed, and whistled a tune as he zigzagged through the maze of the estate.

Hoon had never been here before, and yet it was familiar. He didn't know these flats, or these people, but he'd known plenty like them. The one he'd grown up in was a few hundred miles north, yet it had more in common with this place than it had with even the opposite end of Glasgow. Poverty and deprivation didn't care about distance, or borders. It was the same wherever you went.

Despite their fascination with him, nobody moved to intercept as he went about his business. He was glad about that. Mostly.

It was only when he saw the CCTV camera fixed to the side of one of the blocks of flats that he realised where he was. He crossed to the camera, stood directly beneath it, and turned so he could see more or less what it saw.

It matched. This was it. This was the spot he'd seen in the video footage, where Ghazanfer and his crew had set off after Caroline.

Which meant...

He headed for the corner, and heard the rumble of traffic before he'd made the turn. The street was busy. It wasn't nose to tail like a lot of the other areas they'd crawled through in the MG, but the volume of traffic would still be enough to declare a city-wide emergency were it all to suddenly turn up in Inverness.

The pavement ahead of him wasn't exactly quiet, either. There were maybe thirty or forty people within stone-throwing distance—shady-looking youngsters, mostly, plus one or two women in niqabs.

A car horn gave a jolly *poop-poop,* and Chuck's MG pulled up at the side of the road, hazard lights blinking on and off. He leaned his head out of the window, shouted a warning to Hoon that he'd be given a ticket if he hung about, then rolled his eyes and ducked back in when Hoon offered a raised middle finger in response.

The street was a thoroughfare, with nothing of note worth stopping for. No shops, no cash machines, nothing. You couldn't even access the flats without retracing Hoon's steps around the corner and onto the estate.

It was a road on one side, and a big expanse of grey cladding on the other, with nothing much else to write home about.

Which raised questions.

He stepped aside for two Muslim women to pass, then continued on along the pavement, eyes scanning left, right, up, down, for anything that might shed some light on what had happened.

He found no answers. Just another question that he asked out loud when he finally squeezed himself into the MG beside Bookish. "What does that look like to you?"

Chuck followed the extended finger and saw a group of teenage boys and girls necking vodka near some bins. "A load of teenage pregnancies waiting to happen?" he guessed.

"No' them, ye bell-end. Higher," Hoon instructed, and he watched as the other man's eyes crept upwards. "That's a CCTV camera, is it not?"

"Yeah. It is," Chuck said. He turned—not easy, given the narrow confines of the car. "So?"

"So, I thought the Met said there wasn't a camera on this street?"

Chuck's eyes widened. "Shit! Yes, they did. They did say that!"

"Your man in the flat. He said there was some guy hanging around here. A tourist, he reckoned."

"Tourist is just what they say," Chuck explained. "Doesn't mean an actual holidaymaker, just someone from outside the area."

Hoon tutted. "Fuck's sake. Whatever. He says the guy was hanging about here, and gave Caroline a lift."

"Nice! Confirms our theory," Chuck said.

"The fuck d'you mean 'our theory'? You had her hiding somewhere," Hoon said. He shook his head, dismissing the argument before it could start. "Point is... what was he doing?"

Chuck narrowed his eyes. "What was who doing?"

"The guy. The fucking... The guy. The tourist. What's he doing hanging about here for? There's hee-haw here."

Chuck looked out through his side window at the blank grey wall that faced him. "Doesn't exactly strike me as a cavalcade of excitement, right enough," he agreed. "You think he was waiting for her?"

"Weird place to stop and stretch your legs, if no'," Hoon said. "Your man reckoned he was driving something flash. Might have been a Porsche."

"A banker, maybe?"

"I was leaning more towards gay hairdresser, but aye, could be," Hoon agreed. "What happened to that Eduardo fella?"

"Who?"

"From your list. One of the bastards who chased her. Eduardo Gonzales."

"Oh! Right. Um... dunno, why? Wasn't he there?"

"No. No, he wasn't," Hoon said. He sucked in his bottom lip as he gave the street one last look-over, then spat it out again with an audible *pop*. "This contact of yours at the Met," he said, after some thought.

Chuck eyed the other man warily. "What about him?"

"I think it's high fucking time that he and I were introduced."

CHAPTER FIFTEEN

IT WOULD TAKE TIME, Bookish had said, to get hold of his guy. Longer still to convince him that meeting Hoon was a good idea. And so, with nothing else to do, and with absolutely no desire whatsoever to wander the streets of London, Hoon returned to the house on Lampard Grove.

He rang the doorbell, waited, and then was greeted by a broad smile and the smell of something spicy and Caribbean.

"You found your way back, then," Gabriella remarked. "We were wondering if you would. Gwynn reckons you've got a pretty woeful sense of direction."

Hoon looked past her into the hallway. "He said that?"

The slight shift in her smile said that no, he hadn't. But she'd imagined he had—silently spoken his half of a conversation for him as he lay there, mute.

"Dinner's on. Be about twenty minutes." She stepped aside to let him in, then closed the door behind him. "You can go for a shower, if you like."

"I'm fine the now, ta," Hoon replied.

"Go for a shower," she insisted. "You'll be doing us all a favour."

Taking hints had never been one of Hoon's strongpoints, but even he couldn't fail to notice that one. "Right. Aye. Been a long couple of days, right enough."

"Upstairs, first door on the left. There are towels in the basket." Gabriella said. She put a hand on his arm when he moved to go, her fingers soft and warm against his skin. "Oh. But it might not get overly hot. Boiler's been playing up. I need to get someone out to look at it."

"I can have a look at it, if you like," Hoon suggested.

Gabriella's eyes widened hopefully. "Oh. You know about gas boilers?"

"More or less, aye," Hoon said. *Leaning heavily towards the less, mind,* he failed to add. "Just point the way, and I'll see what I can do."

———

There was fuck all he could do. The boiler was fixed to the back wall in the kitchen, and the fact that it had taken Hoon twenty minutes of prising, swearing, and some violent shaking to get the front panel off had not boded well.

Once the front was off, a labyrinth of copper pipes, dials, valves, and an assortment of things he could only describe as 'knobbly bits' had been presented to him, and he'd realised immediately that he was so far out of his depth he could no longer see land in any direction.

Gabriella had provided him with a comprehensive selection of tools, a firm pat on the back, and a hopeful, "Good luck," that had inspired him to get this far without ripping the whole fucking thing off the wall and hurling it to the floor.

Now, though, he'd reached a dead end. He'd worked on the old kerosene boiler back at his house in Inverness a few times. This had largely involved kicking it in a variety of places and calling it a bastard until it had started working again, which wasn't a technique he particularly wanted to use on something connected to the main gas network.

"How's it going?" Gabriella asked. She was standing over the stove, stirring a pot of something that smelled incredible. Clouds of steam rolled from the top of it, before being inhaled by the curved silver cooker hood on the wall above it. "Getting anywhere? Be amazing if you can get it going. I haven't had a hot shower in weeks."

Shite.

Hoon had been about to tell her that he had no idea how to fix it, but how could he disappoint her now? She was counting on him.

There was far too much of that going around at the moment.

"Aye, no' bad," he said. "Just getting the lay of the land."

"Did you get the error code off the front?"

Hoon looked down at the front panel, which now lay on the floor beside him. "Error code?"

"The flashing number," Gabriella said. "With the words 'Error code' above it."

"Oh. That error code. Aye. No. What was it again?"

Gabriella smiled, and it lit up the room. Christ, Welshy was a lucky bastard.

Well, less so these days, obviously, but still.

"Check that drawer. I Googled it and wrote it down," she instructed, pointing to a Spanish style wooden display cabinet that was currently displaying mostly empty wine bottles.

Hoon wiggled the drawer open and found a scrap of paper somewhere near the top. The error code number was 25, apparently. Gabriella's Googling had found out what this meant, and she'd taken the time to write it down.

Squinting a bit at the tiny writing, Hoon read the error details aloud.

"Air in heat exchanger, blocked or restricted primary flow, heat exchanger air flow blocked, flue restriction, flue sensor fault, pump fault, boiler or heating circuit valve closed," he said.

He looked from the note to the inner workings of the boiler.

He looked back at the note, and read it again, silently this time.

What the fuck did all that mean?

He read it out loud again, this time putting emphasis on some apparently random words.

"Air in *heat* exchanger. Blocked or *restricted* primary flow." He looked up at the boiler, then tried again, this time with slightly different emphasis. "Air in heat *exchanger*. Blocked or restricted *primary flow*."

No, that wasn't helping, either.

"Could be a faulty pump," he declared, latching onto the phrase 'pump fault' that was buried near the end of the error description. Hopefully, she wouldn't ask him to point out which part the pump was, or explain in any sort of detail what purpose it served.

"Shit. That sounds expensive. And yet, it's just the hot water. That's weird, isn't it?" Gabriella said. "I can cook fine, and the heating comes on. Bit noisy, and not as hot as it used to get, but it mostly works OK."

Based on her description it didn't sound *too* broken,

Hoon thought. Maybe a couple of solid whacks with a spanner, or a well-placed poke with a screwdriver would be enough to get it fully operational.

Alternatively, he could gas them all, or blow them to bits.

He was about to admit defeat when he spotted a small red button with the letter 'R' printed on it. It was a tiny thing, just a few millimetres in diameter. About the size, shape, and colour of a big plook. It was well tucked away in the workings of the boiler, like whoever had put it there hadn't been keen on the idea of anyone actually pressing it.

He pressed it, anyway.

Something clicked.

Something gasped.

Something spluttered.

He took a cautious step back. He eyed the boiler warily, while simultaneously trying to appear casual so as not to worry the woman currently making dinner just a few feet away. If they had to make a run for it, he reckoned he could get her out through the front door before the fire spread too far. Welshy might prove more problematic, but he'd come up with something.

He was starting to grow a little concerned when the spluttering became a soft, steady hum.

Gabriella's voice came from right behind Hoon, and he had to fight ingrained instinct to elbow her in the face.

"Did you fix it? Is that it working?"

She sounded excited, and before Hoon could urge caution, she hurried over to the sink and turned on the hot tap. There was some more spluttering, a couple of belching sounds, and then the water settled into a steady flow.

Gabriella gave it a moment, then put a hand under the stream of water and quickly whipped it back out again.

"Hot!" she cried, her face—and the room—lighting up even brighter than before. "It's hot! It's properly hot!"

"Fuck me, is it?" Hoon asked, unable to hide his surprise.

Gabriella laughed and shook her head. "No," she said. "Sorry. But thanks for trying." She turned off the tap, dried her hand on her jeans, and returned to the cooker. "Now, go get cleaned up. Dinner's in twenty minutes."

CHAPTER SIXTEEN

THEY ATE in the room with Welshy, a dinner of rice and beans that Gabriella had first eaten when she and Gwynn had visited the Caribbean on their honeymoon. They'd both loved it, and after much experimenting back home, had managed to get somewhere close to the recipe.

"Not quite as good," she'd insisted when she'd told Hoon the story. "But close."

If the original dish had been better, Hoon couldn't imagine how. The ingredients were simple—rice and kidney beans, mostly—but some dark art had been performed to elevate them into something that even his much-abused palate was immediately smitten by.

Of course, he hadn't eaten in a while, and it had been far longer since anyone had actually cooked for him—longer still since it had been an attractive woman—so it was possible that there was some bias creeping in.

Welshy sat propped up, watching them without a word. His own food was on a tray by his bed, Gabriella giving it a few minutes to cool, and taking the opportunity to wolf down some of her own dinner in the meantime.

"Shower OK?" she asked.

She had her bowl clutched in one hand, and was holding it about as close to her face as it was possible to get without it functioning as a nose bag. Her fork was constantly at work, ferrying the rice to her mouth, then returning to scoop up some more as she chewed.

"It was... wet," Hoon said. "I've had worse."

Gabriella paused in her food-shovelling long enough to laugh. "I can imagine. Gwynn's told me some stories."

Hoon glanced over at the man in the bed. "I dread to fucking think."

"How did your day go?" Gabriella asked, then the mechanism restarted and her fork returned to its duties.

"Eh... pass," Hoon said. "I'm not sure yet."

"You said it was work-related?"

"The visit? Aye. Mostly. Sort of." Hoon shrugged. "No' sure. Just... a friend of mine asked me to look into something for him. A friend of ours, actually." He looked over at Welshy. "Bamber. Remember Bamber, Welshy?"

An eye swam. A groan emerged.

"He's not sure," Gabriella said, translating or possibly just guessing.

"Aye, you do. Big Bamber Gascoine. Real name's... Shite. What was it? Elon...? Alvin? Something like that, but we called him Bamber 'cos of the boy off the telly. *University Challenge*. Mind?" Hoon poked at his food, spearing some of the beans. "I think his surname was spelled differently, right enough. Big Bamber."

There was no response from the man in the bed. Nothing

to confirm nor deny that he'd remembered the old friend being spoken about.

Hoon grimaced. He was going to have to go there.

"Lost his legs in a roadside."

There was a grunt at that. A blink. Gabriella didn't need to translate, but did anyway.

"He remembers."

"Good. Aye. Well, he's asked me to help him out with something. A... personal matter."

Gabriella set her empty bowl down on the table with a clunk. "Well, aren't you the man for all the good deeds?" She smiled, then got up from the table and ventured over to the bed. "You hungry, babe? This should've cooled enough."

She took a spoonful and touched it to her lips, then nodded, confirming that it was safe for him to eat. Before she moved to feed him, though, she looked back over her shoulder at the table.

"It can get a bit messy," she said. "You might want to... I don't know if you want to look away, or..."

"He was always a clarty bastard when it came to eating," Hoon said. "Ain't that right, Welshy? I'm sure I'll cope."

Gabriella smiled a *thank you*, then brought the spoon closer to her husband's mouth. It remained firmly shut.

"Here you go, babe. Open wide," she encouraged.

Welshy gave a grunt. His eye swung from his wife to Hoon and back again. His mouth, for its part, did nothing.

"Come on. It's your favourite," Gabriella prompted. Then, when Welshy continued to refuse, she sighed and looked back over her shoulder. "I think maybe... I think he's a bit embarrassed. About you seeing him like this."

Hoon frowned. "Embarrassed? What, in front of *me*?"

"I, eh... I think so, yes."

Hoon sat back on the wooden chair and looked up to the ceiling for a moment, searching through some worn and faded memory banks.

"I'd love to give you the date, but it escapes me," he said, after some thought. "Mid June or July. Ninety-one. We were SCUD-hunting. You know, the missiles? Fucking hopeless things, but they could fair do damage. We're on the lookout for them. Ploughing around in Land Rovers, throwing up dust in the desert. Subtle as fuck."

Propped up in bed, Welshy's eye stopped swimming.

"So, anyway, we're mostly travelling by night, and staying hidden during the day. This one night, I must have eaten something dodgy, because my guts are on fire. I mean, the worst thing I've ever felt. Like everything from the tits down is being dissolved from the inside out. We don't want to stop anywhere, but we've got no choice. We have to so I can have a sh..." He glanced at Gabriella, and felt a sudden urge to sanitise his description. "So I can have a toilet stop, when suddenly gunfire erupts. Just fucking erupts around us. *Crack-crack-crack.* Bullets flying everywhere. Some fucking goat herder or something had clocked us, and grassed us up to the Iraqis."

"Jesus. What happened?" Gabriella asked.

"We fought back. Returned fire," Hoon said.

Welshy grunted. Or laughed, maybe. Something sparkled behind his one good eye, drawing a grin and a point from Hoon.

"Aye, I knew you'd fucking remember this alright, ye big sack of shite!" he said. "So, I come racing out, grab my AR. I'm all tooled up and fucking gung-ho. *Let me at the bastards.* Welshy's already firing. There's bullets buzzing around all over the place like angry fucking wasps. And he looks at me..." Hoon chuckled. "He looks at me, and then he does this double-take. Like in a sitcom or a cartoon, you know? All that's missing is a big fucking question mark floating above his head. So, I look down and I realise my drawers are still around my ankles."

Gabriella bit her bottom lip. "No!"

"That's no' the fucking worst of it. I check behind me, and I've got this tail of bog roll trailing out behind me. Just hanging from my arse like the fuse on a firework. Blowing about in the wind. Bastards didn't let me hear the end of it for months." Hoon shook his head, crossed his arms, and fixed Welshy with a stern glare. "So, don't you talk to me about fucking embarrassment, son, and get your dinner down you before I eat it myself."

Welshy's nose wrinkled. His eye twitched. Then, his mouth opened just a fraction. Just enough.

"Aye, I should fucking think so, too," Hoon said. He gathered up his and Gabriella's bowls. "I'll go do the dishes and leave you to it."

Gabriella called after him as he left the room. "You'll have to boil the kettle..."

"...because the hot water's no' working," Hoon finished. "I'm well aware of my own failures, thanks. You don't have to remind me."

He heard another series of grunts from the man in the bed.

Definitely a laugh this time.

And he smiled as he closed the door.

———

Hoon was elbow deep in tepid water when his mobile rang. He swore below his breath, looked around for a towel, then flicked the worst of the water off when he failed to find one and fished his phone from his pocket with damp hands.

"Bookish?" The phone slipped and he had to sprackle to catch it before it plopped into the sink. "Hello? Aye. No, I dropped you. I'm doing the dishes at Welshy's."

He listened to the reply, then scowled.

"No, they don't have a dishwasher," he said. Then, when Chuck enquired further, "No' even in this day and age, no. At least they don't live on a fucking boat. You're no' one to judge anyone."

He crossed to the kitchen door, pushed it closed, then lowered his voice. "How did you get on? You get a meeting set up?"

He listened. His face darkened.

"What do you mean? Why not?"

Down the line, Chuck offered an apologetic response.

"I don't give a fuck how scared he is, he... Wait, what did you just say?"

He waited while Chuck repeated himself.

"He's a constable? I thought he was someone important? Who the fuck has a constable as their inside man? What information's he been feeding you? The menu in the canteen? Constables don't know shite. Constables know so little they don't even fucking *know* just how little they know. No wonder he doesn't want to talk to me, it's probably past his fucking bedtime." He tutted and shook his head reproachfully. "A constable. Jesus Christ, man. And here I thought you were actually going to be useful for once."

Bookish started to reply, but Hoon cut him off.

"What about that Eduardo guy? Did he know anything?"

Hoon listened. Nodded. "Right, well that's something useful, at least. I'd say 'well done,' but after the disappointment of this phone call, I feel like I'd be insulting your fucking intelligence."

Again, Chuck started to speak, only to be interrupted.

"Look, doesn't matter. Forget it. No point crying over useless bastards, as the saying goes. Leave it with me," he said. "I've still got one or two contacts of my own..."

————

At almost the opposite end of the United Kingdom, what had already been a long and unpleasant day for DCI Jack Logan became incrementally worse when Hoon's name appeared on his phone.

"Bob?" he said, after begrudgingly thumbing the green icon. "You're no' in the jail again, are you?"

"I fucking wish," came the reply. "I'm in London."

Logan pulled his phone from his ear and gave it a look like it was taking the piss. "London?" he asked, once he'd returned it to the side of his head. "What are you doing in London? Are you even allowed in London?"

"Why the fuck wouldn't I be allowed in London?" Hoon asked.

"I don't know. I just sort of assumed there'd be some reason," Logan admitted. "I only saw you yesterday. How'd you get there so fast?"

"Sleeper train. Worst fucking decision I've ever made, by the way," Hoon said.

Logan found that very hard to believe, but chose not to say so. "Right. And why? What are you doing down there?"

There was a moment of silence from the other end. A

noise in the background may have been the sound of a sink gurgling as it emptied. "I'm working a case," Hoon finally said.

Logan's brow furrowed. "I hope you mean a suitcase, Bob," he said. "Because, in case you've forgotten, you're no' in the polis anymore."

"Aye, I'm well fucking aware of that," Hoon said. "It's a... personal thing. For a mate of mine."

Logan took a movement to marvel at this revelation. The idea that Hoon had friends was a novel one. And quite a far-fetched novel it would make for, at that.

"I see. Well... fair enough," the DCI replied, drawing a blank on finding anything better to say. "And you're phoning me because...?"

"You busy?" Hoon asked.

Logan looked down at the plastic evidence bag on his desk, and the note inside it. "You know me. I'm always busy, Bob."

"My arse," Hoon retorted. "Get a pen."

"What for?"

"Because I fucking told you to, that's why!"

Logan sat back in his chair, about as far from his pot of pens as it was possible to get without leaving the room. He said nothing. Waited.

After several seconds of this, Hoon sighed. "Fine. I need you to do me a favour."

Aha. Here we go.

"I told you, Bob, I'm kind of busy right—"

"I'm sure you don't need me to remind you about the less-than-legal favour I did for you recently," Hoon said. "Dangling some bastard off a roof? That's a big fucking ask." He sighed again, and most of the venom drained out of his voice.

"It's a daughter of a mate of mine. She's missing. I think she's been taken, and the polis here are a shower of useless bastards. She's barely out of her teens, Jack. I need to find her."

Logan groaned, pinched the bridge of his nose between finger and thumb, then plucked a pen from the desk tidy. "Fine," he said. "What is it—within reason, mind—that you need me to do?"

CHAPTER SEVENTEEN

HOON HAD GOT off the Tube at Waterloo Station, then had taken a stroll past the London Eye and across Westminster Bridge with the morning commuters. Upon reaching the other side, he had allowed himself a few moments to make some appropriately rude gestures outside the gates of Downing Street, before making his way towards New Scotland Yard, home of the Metropolitan Police Service.

Logan had actually come through for once. Hoon had got the call late the night before, while tossing and turning on Welshy and Gabriella's couch, confirming that a meeting had been set up. Hoon hadn't exactly thanked him, but he hadn't *not* thanked him, either. He'd made it clear that this was the best the DCI was likely to get out of him, and had promptly hung up.

It didn't do to give the bastard too much credit, he'd found. He'd only get used to it.

He'd only been to Scotland Yard once before, in its prior building just off Victoria Street. He hadn't visited the new site that had opened a few years ago, and nor had he had any particular interest in doing so.

As a result, he had very little idea of what he was walking into. He knew the spinning sign out front, of course—everyone knew the spinning sign out front—but everything beyond that was a bit of a mystery.

Still, he went striding in like the entire building was under his direct command, then was immediately stopped by a surly looking bastard at a security checkpoint.

"Can I help you, sir?"

"You're alright, pal," Hoon told him. "I've got a meeting."

The constable waited for further information, then prompted when it wasn't freely given.

"Who with, sir?"

Hoon tutted, then fished around in the many pockets of his combat trousers. Eventually, he found a crumpled scrap of paper he'd torn from a notebook back at Welshy's, and read the name aloud. "Chief Superintendent Bagshaw."

"Oh. I see." The constable looked him up and down in a way that suggested he very much doubted this was the case. "What's your name, sir?"

Hoon briefly entertained the idea of a sarcastic answer, then decided just to play it straight, and gave him his name. Like it or not, this cretinous fucklump was the deciding factor on whether he'd be allowed inside or not, and he looked like just the type to hold a grudge.

"And what's the meeting regarding, sir?" the constable asked, once Hoon had introduced himself.

"None of your fucking business."

The words were out of him before he could stop them. He winced when the officer drew himself up to his full height, and cranked his officiousness all the way up to maximum.

"That came across more harshly than I'd intended," was what Hoon probably should have said. But the look on the constable's face wound him up too much, and he doubled down, instead. "This is a pressing fucking engagement, son, and frankly what a Chief Superintendent chooses to discuss in her private meetings is hee-haw to do with a jumped-up wee prick like you. So, just you get on the fucking phone, let her know I'm here, then point me in the right direction, eh? There's a good lad."

————

In the far north of Scotland, DCI Jack Logan rubbed his forehead, nursing a building tension headache. "What do you mean you need me to call her back?" he asked the man on the other end of the phone.

There was an outburst from down the line. Logan sighed.

"Jesus Christ, Bob. And why, exactly, did they throw you out?"

————

Twenty minutes later, Hoon sat on the wrong side of the desk in an office that was twice the size of the one he'd had in Inverness, with a view that looked across the Thames to the London Eye on the opposite bank. Despite the relatively early hour, each of the big wheel's pods was full of tourists, all marvelling at the expanse of the city spread out below them.

There was something oddly hypnotic about watching its

revolutions. It was no wonder the office's occupant was facing away from the window, otherwise, she'd get no bloody work done.

Hoon had been surprised that Chief Superintendent Bagshaw was a 'she.' It wasn't that he was sexist. Far from it. Some of the least incompetent officers he knew were women. It was just that the institution of the polis still had a long way to go to shake off some pretty deep-rooted misogyny, and despite some high-profile appointments and promotions in recent years, it was still largely a man's game.

He could see why she'd made it this far up the ladder, though. She had an air about her of someone that knew what she wanted, and knew precisely all the ways to go about getting it. Her natural expression was one of stern impatience, like she was barely tolerating the presence of everyone around her.

Or maybe it was just Hoon that brought that out in her.

She wore her uniform like it was something regal and grand, all shiny buttons and polished shoes. She was the kind of person, he thought, who'd be referred to by senior colleagues as 'direct' or 'no-nonsense,' and by those below her as, 'a right nasty bitch.'

Hoon approved. Give him that sort of leadership over some wishy-washy, touchy-feely bollocks any day of the week.

She had told him he had ten minutes. He'd spoken for three—one to tell her who he was, and two to explain why he was there.

He'd told her about Caroline. About the car. About his theory that someone had been waiting for her the night she'd been abducted. He'd told her all of it, condensed down into a manageable, bite-sized chunk.

Her response surprised him.

"And?"

Hoon blinked. Frowned. "Eh?"

"I said, 'And?' What is it you want?"

"Well, I want you to find her," Hoon replied. "How about we make that the starting point and go from there?"

"Do you know how many people go missing in this city every year, Mr Hoon?"

Hoon had to confess that he did not.

"Fifty-five thousand. Give or take. Almost double what it was a decade ago. That's over a thousand people a week, just disappearing into thin air. Poof."

"Aye, but most of them come back in, what? A day?" Hoon said. "Most of the time you don't even get involved."

"We're always involved, Mr Hoon," she retorted. "On some level, we're always involved. And that takes money, and manpower, neither of which are exactly in abundance. Ultimately, we can't look for everyone, much as we would like to."

Hoon leaned forward in his chair. "I'm no' asking you to look for everyone," he said. "I'm asking you to look for her. Then, I can go home, look her old man in the eye, and tell him you're working on it. Tell him she's no' just being forgotten about."

"We never 'forget' about anyone. If what you say is true—and I'm not familiar with her case—then it'll be an ongoing investigation."

Hoon snorted. "I know the lingo, pet. I bet if I looked at those case notes they won't have been updated in months."

"They'll be updated when we have something to update them with," the Chief Superintendent replied. "If there are no updates, there are no updates."

"Because you're no' bothering your arse to find any," Hoon shot back. "She's a young woman. She's no' called anyone, hasn't used her bank cards, and nobody's seen her in months. This isn't some fucking teenage runaway who came back next day with their tail between their legs. Something has happened to this girl, and you're doing fuck all about it."

"OK, Mr Hoon, two things. Firstly, that sort of language is unacceptable, and will not be tolerated in this office. Another outburst, and I'll have you removed. Forcibly." She left her gaze lingering on him for a few moments, giving that a chance to bed in. "Secondly, I'm going to talk to you straight. That's what I do. Apologies if it comes across as overly direct. I have been described as a 'take no prisoners' sort of person."

"You'd think that'd be something of a fucking liability in your job," Hoon muttered, then he folded his arms across his chest and braced himself for whatever was coming next.

"Given what you've told me, I think it's a safe bet that your friend's daughter is dead. While that is, of course, a tragedy, it's just one on a very long list of them. I would dearly love to have the resources to give them all the consideration they deserve, but I don't. Not by a long shot. It might not look it, but it's chaos out there. We're putting out a thousand fires a day, and every day twice as many start burning."

"Are you sure you're no' thinking of the fire brigade?" Hoon asked.

"You're funny," Bagshaw said. It wasn't a compliment, more like the answer to some question she'd been asking herself since he'd arrived. "I wish I had time for funny. But I don't."

The mention of time made her sit back and check the

watch she wore on the inside of her left wrist. "Speaking of which, I need to end this soon."

"ARU?" Hoon asked.

Across the desk, the Chief Superintendent's brow furrowed. "I'm sorry?"

"Armed Response Unit."

"No, I know what it stands for. Why did you say it?"

Hoon gestured to her wrist. "The watch. On the inside. Easier to read when you're holding a sniper rifle."

Bagshaw looked down at her watch and seemed surprised, like she'd never noticed it before.

"I'm ex-military," Hoon said. "Used to do the same."

"Right. Well." She twisted the watch so it was on the opposite side of her wrist. "Yes. ARU. For a few years." She sighed, and seemed to soften slightly. "Look, perhaps if we had some new evidence—a body, some witnesses—then we'd be able to justify the time and expense. For now, though, we've got nothing further to report."

"I gave you new evidence. The car."

"Ah yes. Of course. We're looking for someone who owns, has access to, or possibly stole a car. That narrows it down immensely. Except, of course, we might not be. It could be completely irrelevant."

"Do you have kids?"

She didn't answer right away. When she did, it seemed to be against her better judgement. "No."

Hoon tutted. "Shite. I had a whole guilt trip thing worked out there," he said. "That puts the fucking kybosh on that."

She made a sound at the back of her throat. A dry sort of scraping, like muscles that had lain dormant for years, were now being dragged out of retirement. It sounded even less like a laugh than the sounds Welshy had made, but a minuscule upturn at one corner of her mouth lent the theory some weight.

"I wish I could help you, Mr Hoon. You and your friend have my full sympathies."

"Your sympathies. Great. That'll brighten him right up, that will. He'll be over the fucking moon when I tell him that."

"And what would you have me do, exactly?" Bagshaw asked. She made a weighing motion. "You've sat in a chair not unlike this one. You've got finite resources in one hand—finite and *shrinking* resources, at that—and an apparently infinite number of demands on those resources in the other. How do you balance that? How do you prioritise when *everything* is a priority? Because, if you have some insight, Mr Hoon—some words of Celtic wisdom to share—then I'm all ears."

She waited for him to offer up some sage counsel, then gave a curt nod when he failed to do so.

"No. Thought not. I'm going to have to ask you to leave now. I'm afraid I have another appointment. Please pass on my best wishes to DCI Logan when you next see him." She shot a very deliberate look to the door. "I'm hoping that will be soon."

"It won't," Hoon said. "I'm going to stick around. Sniff about a bit. Poke my nose in where it's not wanted. Cause a bit of trouble."

"I'd advise against that last part, Mr Hoon," Bagshaw warned.

"Why? Limited resources, remember? It's no' like you can spare the manpower to stop me." He stretched, and placed both hands behind his head. "I can make a lot of fucking noise in a short space of time, and all those tit-helmet wearing no-marks you've got parading about out there won't have the first fucking clue what to do about it."

"My officers are more than capable of—"

"And then there's Eduardo Gonzales, of course."

Bagshaw's hesitation was tiny, but unmissable to anyone watching for it.

"Who?"

"Witness to Caroline's disappearance. Died in custody. Terrible tragedy. If I'm no' getting anywhere with the abduction angle, maybe I'll devote some time towards looking into that."

He smiled and opened his hands, like he was presenting her with a gift.

"Or, you could put me in touch with the SIO leading Caroline's case, I can fuck off out of your hair, and you'll never have to see me again." He winked. Grinned. Waggled his eyebrows. "So, Deirdrie, what's it to be?"

CHAPTER EIGHTEEN

THE SECOND OFFICE was far smaller than the first. The view was nowhere near as good, either, largely because of all the many amenities the room was lacking, a window was the most immediately obvious.

While there had been something about Chief Superintendent Bagshaw that Hoon had found himself almost admiring, the very opposite could be said for the jumped-up, suit-wearing, ideas-above-his-fucking station jeb-end who inhabited this office.

His name, to Hoon's delight, was Balls. Detective Chief Inspector Matt Balls, to give him his full title. He had been the Senior Investigating Officer looking into Caroline Gascoine's disappearance, although his recollection of the case appeared to be quite hazy.

His phone had rung four times since Hoon had arrived in the room a few minutes earlier. He had answered it twice, let it go to voicemail once, then just sort of stared at it for a while before lifting the receiver, hanging up, then leaving it off the hook.

His body language was of someone close to the end of their tether, all jerky movements and pained looks. Take a photo of him, though, and he'd look sharp and in control, with his expensive three-piece suit and designer shoes. His hair was cut short, so it would look good without spending time styling it, and while the shape of his frame suggested he'd spent some time in the gym, a chubbiness about his cheeks and jowls said it hadn't been recently.

He was in his early forties, but with the premature stress and worry lines that were more or less handed to you along with your first polis uniform. He had the eyes of a man who didn't sleep as much as he ought to, and the yellowing fingertips of one who smoked far too many cigarettes during those wee small hours.

Unlike Bagshaw's desk, which had been fastidiously well organised, Balls' desk was a veritable clusterfuck of paperwork, notebooks, coffee cups, and takeaway food cartons. It was the sort of desk that could've functioned as an adventure playground for mice. Hoon would've been surprised if the smell emanating from it wasn't luring the rodenty wee bastards into the building like the Pied Piper.

On balance, and despite him putting way too much effort into looking good, Hoon reckoned he should've liked DCI Balls. He saw a lot of himself in the younger man, albeit mostly in the messy desk, and the indignation over people bothering him on the phone.

And yet, he didn't like him. Not one bit.

The similarity between them, Hoon realised, might well have been the reason why.

"Sorry. Right. Where were we?" Balls asked. He had plucked a notepad from a pile, and was rummaging around the desk in search of something to write with.

Hoon found a pen sticking out from beneath a *KFC* brown paper bag, picked it up, and handed it over. "Caroline Gascoine. Age twenty-three. Went missing in February." He waited for Balls to finish writing, before continuing. "Scottish. Here studying at Westminster University."

"That's not that far away," Balls remarked, still writing.

"I wouldn't know," Hoon replied.

"And you are...?" Balls quickly looked the man on the other side of the desk up and down. He was sitting back in a chair, picking small stones out of the tread of his boot with a thumb. "Parent?"

Hoon shook his head. "I'm an... outside investigator," he said. "Former Detective Super for Police Scotland."

"And you're now what? Freelance?"

"One time only," Hoon said. "Helping out a friend. I'm sure you got word from Deirdrie—Chief Superintendent Bagshaw to you, I'd imagine—that you're to help me clarify a few things about the case."

Balls did not look particularly impressed with this, but he nodded. "Well, that's the only reason we're both sitting here. What do you need to know?"

He studied the other man for a moment, then sucked in his bottom lip, scraping his top teeth against his stubble. "You don't remember her, do you? You don't have a clue."

"We get a lot of missing people..."

"Aye. So I heard," Hoon said. He took out his phone, found Caroline's picture, then held it up for the man on the other side of the desk. "This is her. Ring any bells?"

Balls squinted and beckoned for the phone to be brought closer. When Hoon leaned over with it, the DCI examined the picture on-screen, eyebrows almost meeting in the middle as he concentrated. "Hmm. I don't..." He tilted his head, rubbed his chin, then made a popping sound with his tongue against the roof of his mouth. "She's not... Was she the one that was chased by a group of lads?"

"Aye! Aye, that's her," Hoon said. "Five of the bastards. Right pack of fucking jackals."

"Right. Right. Yes. They didn't give us anything much to go on, if I remember rightly," Balls said, thinking back. "We brought them in, but couldn't keep them. CCTV more or less cleared them of any involvement, and their stories all matched. That's if it's the same case I'm thinking of, of course. I'd have to check."

"Sounds like it," Hoon said. "I had a wee word with some of those lads myself. I think I maybe managed to jog a memory or two. They reckon they saw Caroline getting into a car."

"A car?" Balls leaned back, additional lines forming on his brow. "Don't remember anyone mentioning a car. Although, it did strike me as a possibility. Did they get a registration?"

Hoon shook his head. "A colour and a possible make. Greeny-blue. Maybe a Porsche. Something expensive, anyway."

"And this came from those lads?"

"Aye," Hoon confirmed. "They saw a guy there, too. Only description they could give me was that he was white. He was outside the car when Caroline approached."

"Outside?" Balls drummed his fingers on one of the few expanses of bare desk available. "Side street in Walworth, wasn't it? What's someone doing hanging around there with a flash motor? There's nothing there. Not at that time of night.

"I thought the same thing," Hoon said. "There's something else, too. We got access to the CCTV from the estate—"

"What? How?"

"Doesn't matter. The point is, we were told there were no cameras on the street where the actual abduction took place."

"We don't know for sure it was..." Balls began, but he lost all conviction midway through the sentence and the whole thing fell away into silence.

"Aye we do," said Hoon. "And there is a camera on that street. Perfect angle. It would've seen the whole fucking thing. Seems a hell of a coincidence if there's no footage."

"I mean... I can look into it. Maybe make a few calls. But you've got to understand, we're rushed off our feet here. You know how many missing women I've had reported this week? Four. Just this week. And it's still a long way to the weekend. But I can ask about the CCTV. Maybe something was just logged incorrectly."

Hoon grunted. It was a grunt that said, 'Aye, that's the least you can fucking do, pal,' only without resorting to actual words.

"In the meantime, if you hear anything else, give me a call," Balls said. He flicked his gaze to the door and clicked the top of his pen to remind his visitor of just how busy he was.

"You got a card?" Hoon asked.

DCI Balls tried hard to hide his disappointment, but needed more warning to be able to truly pull it off. "Yes," he conceded, reaching into the uppermost drawer of his desk. He rummaged around in the drawer for a few moments, then frowned. "Oh, actually, I'm all out. Sorry."

"No bother. I'll just write your details down," Hoon said.

The squeak of the drawer closing very nearly hid Balls' sigh. "Yes, do that."

"You got a bit of paper?" Hoon asked.

The DCI's lips moved like he was about to say something, but then he ripped a page from a small flip-open notebook and passed it over the top of the cluttered desk.

"And a pen?" holding eye contact.

Balls stared back for a long, drawn-out moment, then pulled his desk drawer open again. "Actually, yes, I've got loads of them. Get them for all these training events we get dragged to. Promotional things."

He fished around until he found a sleek silver-coloured retractable ballpoint. "Have this one. I've got dozens of the bloody things."

Hoon took the pen and turned it over in his hands. The name of what he presumed was a hotel of some sort was printed discreetly onto the barrel, but otherwise, it was a pretty standard-looking *Parker*. "Nice one. Cheers. Right, go for it."

"Go for...? Oh. Right." He recited his phone number. "But please, only use it if you absolutely have to, eh? I'm flat out as it is. Only call if it's something concrete. If I find anything out at my end, I'll call you."

He smiled politely and indicated the door again. Hoon didn't move, other than to pocket the paper and pen.

"So, you'll be needing my number, then," he said.

"What? Oh. Yes. We'll need that." He picked up his own pen again. "Fire away."

After a couple of false starts at reciting the number from memory, Hoon took out his phone and read it out loud. Balls scribbled the details down, nodded to indicate 'job done,' then set the pen down and crossed his hands on his pad.

"Thanks. Got it. Thank you for coming in. I'll be in touch."

Hoon's chair dragged on the carpet tiles as he pushed it back and got to his feet. "One last thing. Caroline's flatmate. I'm going to go and have a word with her."

"Are you? Why?"

"Just checking in. Making sure the poor lassie's OK."

"That's very kind of you."

"And maybe asking her a couple of questions. About Caroline's mood. Boyfriends. Whatever. See if she can shed some light."

"Right, well..."

"You got her name and address?"

Balls' eyebrows both rose in surprise. "Her name and address?"

"Aye. The flatmate's address. I need that."

The DCI shook his head. "I can't give you that, and you know it."

Hoon leaned both fists on the desk, like a silverback asserting his dominance. "Aye, you can, son. Go on. I won't tell if you don't."

Balls stood up. He was a little taller than Hoon, and while it might have softened a bit, there was still a bulk of muscle there. "No. I can't. And I won't."

"I can make it worth your while," Hoon said. "Chuck a few bob your way."

"Absolutely not," Balls replied. "Now, Mr Hoon, I suggest that you piss off out of my office before I have you charged under the Bribery Act."

Hoon grinned, and eased back on the confrontational body language. "Just testing. I already know her name and address. But well done, Ballsy. Congratulations."

"For what?" the DCI asked.

Hoon stopped at the door, looked the detective up and down, then gave him a nod. "You passed."

CHAPTER NINETEEN

HOON SAT SQUASHED in the MG across the road from another block of flats. This one was different to the estate he'd visited earlier, though. That one had been a testament to functionality over style, all drab concrete and square corners.

This block *flowed*. There were curves and bends, with a few twiddly bits added here and there for no other purpose other than to make the prospect of living in the middle of a stack of strangers seem a smidgeon less grim.

It was early afternoon, and the street was a thunder of chaos. There were more buses on this one stretch of road than in the whole of Inverness, Hoon reckoned. And, if the city centre congestion charge was reducing the number of cars knocking about, it must've been absolute carnage before.

"Which one is it?" he asked, ducking to look out beneath the convertible's closed roof.

"Third floor, left-hand side," said Chuck, pointing the way. "Yellow curtains."

"I see it," Hoon said.

"Flatmate's name is Yui. Japanese. Hot as fuck. Bit young-looking. But still. Proper tasty."

"Aye, very good." Hoon unfastened his seatbelt, and Chuck did the same. "The fuck you doing?" Hoon asked.

Chuck looked down at his seatbelt buckle. "Coming in."

"No, you're no'," Hoon said.

"Why not?"

"Because you just used the phrase, 'Bit young-looking, but proper tasty.' And because you're a creepy-looking bastard who'll only give her the heebie-jeebies," Hoon pointed out. He shrugged. "No offence, like."

"How am I meant to not take offence at that?" Chuck asked. He regarded himself in the mirror, swept back a strand of hair, then ran a hand down his face. "There's nothing wrong with me. I look fine."

Hoon snorted. "Aye," he said, patting the other man on the leg. "You keep telling yourself that." He pointed back over his shoulder. "There's a coffee shop back there. Away and get yourself a Unicorn Juice, or whatever that pink shite was you were drinking. I'll call you when I'm done."

Bookish looked from Hoon to the window of the flat and grimaced. "You're just going to talk to her, aren't you? You're not going to do anything stupid?"

"What do you take me for?" Hoon spat. He opened the door, and was met by a blaring of horns and a screeching of brakes.

He quickly closed it again, returned the rude gesture of the driver of the van that went speeding past, then shot Bookish a sideways look.

"Totally fucking meant that, by the way," he muttered.

Then, with a check of the wing mirror and a glance over

his shoulder, he exited the car and ran across the road between gaps in the fast-moving traffic.

———

Yui Nakamura was not prepared for Bob Hoon. Very few people were, when it came down to it, but Yui even less so than most.

She had studied him via the camera built into the outside intercom at first, then through the peephole in the door, then through the small gap allowed by the thick security chain.

Even once he'd explained who he was, what he was there for, given full details of Caroline's parents, and shown her a remarkably authentic copy he'd made of his old polis ID before it had been taken off him, she seemed uncertain, and had suggested phoning Bamber—Mr Gascoine, she called him—to check.

"I'd rather you didn't," Hoon said. "They don't know that I'm here. In London, I mean. I don't want to get their hopes up."

"Do you think you can find her?" Yui asked through the gap in the door.

"Honestly? I don't know," Hoon admitted. He shrugged. "But I'm here, and I'm looking. And I wouldn't be doing that if I didn't think there was a chance."

She bit her lip and looked back into the flat. "My boyfriend is here. He's asleep. In my bedroom," she said.

It was a warning. Almost certainly not true. Hoon played along with it, anyway.

"If you want me to wait out here until you wake him up, that's fine. Otherwise, I'll keep my voice down, and be out of your hair before you know it."

"Best not to wake him," Yui said. "He doesn't like being woken up. And he's a big guy. He plays rugby. And does karate."

The look on Hoon's face suggested he was simultaneously impressed and alarmed. It was, all in all, one of his more convincing performances, given that everything the young woman had just told him was a load of old bollocks.

"God, right, aye. I'll keep it down, in that case. Wouldn't want to poke the bear." He smiled hopefully, crossed his hands in front of himself, and waited.

Yui gave him another once over—the fourth or fifth, he'd lost count—then closed the door. Hoon listened to the scratching of the chain being undone, then nodded his thanks when the door was opened again, and stepped past Yui into the flat's hallway.

He almost recoiled at the way the decor assaulted his eyeballs. The hall had been painted in vibrant yellows and bubblegum pinks, with hanging banners of cartoon schoolgirls winking out from the walls.

Matching coloured shelves were crammed with an assortment of small statues and action figures, each more extravagantly detailed than the last.

There were a lot of soft toys shaped like frogs. A *lot*. Far too many than might reasonably be considered normal, in Hoon's opinion. Although, to be fair, the same could be said for any number that wasn't zero.

The carpet was green. Very possibly the only shade of green that didn't exist anywhere in nature, in fact. It practically squealed, '*HEY! YOU! FUCKING LOOK AT ME!!!*' as he stepped through the door, and while he refused to give it the satisfaction of looking directly at it, even being in its presence made the lower half of his eyeballs ache.

A rope of multi-coloured LED lights ran along the top of the walls, right below where they met the ceiling. It lent the place either a festive charm, or a nauseating absurdity. Hoon couldn't quite decide on which, although he had a pretty good idea of which way he was leaning.

Just as Chuck had said, Yui looked much younger than her twenty-six years. She was a post-graduate student, Bookish had told him on the drive over. Something to do with chemistry that Bookish might be able to explain, but Hoon would never be able to understand.

She could've passed for sixteen, though. In fact, with her bobbed blue hair and painted-on freckles, Hoon half expected to look around and find one of the cartoon school-girl banners missing its star.

"Cheers for letting me in," Hoon told her. "Like I say, I won't take up too much of your time."

Yui looked very deliberately at what Hoon assumed was her bedroom door, really hamming up the act. "We can talk in the front room," she said, steering him through a different door and into a room even more over the top than the hallway.

The walls were painted in stripes of pink and purple, with the same violently green carpet that had ambushed him when he'd first entered the flat.

Every surface was covered by cuddly toy versions of those wee cartoon bastards. *Pokey Monsters*. Some nonsense like that. They huddled together on shelves, on the couch and coffee table, and hanging in hammocks at the corners of the room.

Not as Japanese, but equally pop-culture inspired, the room's single light shade was in the shape of the Death Star from the *Star Wars* movies—or, as Hoon always chose to refer to it, 'That magic space shite with the asthmatic robot and the teddy bears.'

One wall of the room was taken up by some kitchen cabinets, a sink, and a fridge that buzzed like a queen bee in heat. The cabinets were bog-standard browns, but had been decorated with stickers of unicorns, and kittens, and Christ alone knew what else.

"You can... You can sit down," Yui told him, indicating the one available space on the couch.

Hoon hadn't really planned to sit, but he could tell his standing was making her nervous, so he relented. The moment he did, a stack of hideously garish plush toys toppled over and landed in his lap like overly excitable pets.

"Sorry, I keep meaning to move them," Yui said. "Just push them onto the floor."

Hoon manhandled the soft toys back into their pile. "No bother. It all gives the place a bit of character," he said, although he neglected to add that it was the character of a five-year-old lunatic.

"They're all Caroline's," Yui said. She gestured around at the room. "Most of this stuff is, in fact. When I moved in I thought it was all some really elaborate, slightly racist wind-up, but no. I mean, we both liked Kawaii and Otaku culture, don't get me wrong, but Caroline was really into it."

"Was?" Hoon asked, latching onto that one word and expertly glossing over all the other bits he didn't understand. "You think she's dead?"

"No. I meant before I moved in. She loved it before she even met me."

Hoon finished restacking the soft toys and removed his hands from the pile. He kept them close to it, though, ready to make a grab if any of the bastarding things fell again.

"You do think she's dead, though," he pressed. "Don't you?"

Yui lowered her head, like she was ashamed. "I mean... No. I hope not. I just... It's been such a long time, and I haven't heard anything, and..." She shrugged. "But I hope not. She was—is—really nice." She bit a glossy lip. "Do you think she's OK?"

Hoon gave the question some thought before replying. He considered sanitising the response, but he wanted Yui to help him, and the cold, hard truth would be a better motivator than some cosy lie.

"If you'd asked me if I thought she was alive, I'd have said maybe," he told her. "But is she *OK*? No. No, I doubt it. I think someone took her. And the fact she hasn't yet turned up means that, aye, she might still be alive, but she's being held somewhere, most likely against her will. And that's never a barrel of laughs. So, is she dead? Not necessarily. Does she wish she was?" He nodded. "Very possibly."

"Oh... God. Oh, God. Caroline. That's so... I can't even..." Yui pulled a cheaply made computer chair out from beneath a ramshackle desk, spun it around, then took a seat. "I feel sick. I actually feel sick."

"Aye. You and me both. You can imagine what her parents are going through," Hoon said. "And why I'm so keen to get her back."

Yui was staring at the floor, so lost in her fears that the overpoweringly vibrant shade of green didn't appear to bother her.

"You OK?" Hoon asked.

"What? Oh. Yes. Sorry. I was just...:

"Letting your imagination run away with you?"

Yui nodded. "Yes. I suppose I was a bit. God. Poor Caroline. It's so awful. So horrible." She cleared her throat and straightened up, like she was reporting for duty. "What can I do to help? Is there something? There must be something I can do."

Hoon took out the scrap of paper and the pen that DCI Balls had given him. "How about you go over what you told the police?" he suggested. "And we can take it from there."

———

There wasn't much to tell. So little, in fact, that less than five minutes later they were going over it all for a second time.

It had been the birthday of one of Caroline's friends from her part-time job at a local *Five Guys* restaurant, and a few of the staff had headed out after their shift. Caroline hadn't been working that night, but had got dolled up and headed out to meet them around nine-thirty.

"And you didn't go?" Hoon asked.

"No."

"Why not?"

"I didn't know them. Not really. It was a work thing," Yui said. "And..."

She fell silent, until two raised eyebrows and a couple of nods from Hoon prompted her to finish.

"I mean, Caroline and I always got on great. She's really nice, and everything. But we're not really *friends* exactly. We just shared a flat. Share. Shared. God. I don't know."

She winced, like the words sounded much harsher out loud than she'd intended them to. "We were *friendly* and everything. We hung out, and we did go out together some-times, don't get me wrong. We just weren't that close, if you know what I mean? She did her stuff and had her mates, and I had mine."

"Do you have their details?" Hoon asked. "The people she was out with?"

Yui shook her head. "No. But didn't you get in touch with them via her work?"

"Me?"

"The police."

"Oh. Right. Aye. We may have done. I've, eh, I've been brought in from up north. At her parents' request, like I say."

Yui's otherwise perfectly smooth brow formed a single crease. "But they don't know that you're here?"

"No, not..." Hoon shrugged. "It's complicated."

He looked down at the single scrap of paper he'd been writing on, mostly to buy himself some time. It had been a while since he'd done this face-to-face interviewing stuff, and the first time ever while only pretending to be an officer of the law. It was taking him a little longer than expected to find his feet.

The torn notepad page was a mess of text, like the whole alphabet had got together for one big orgy, and things had got seriously out of hand.

"Do you want a pad?"

Hoon looked up. "A what?"

"A notepad. I've got loads."

"Oh. Aye. That'd be handy, actually," Hoon said. "Thanks."

He watched as she crossed to an antique writing bureau that had been desecrated with chalky lavender coloured paint, pulled open the door, and reached inside.

Hoon didn't want to appear ungrateful for the thing that

was offered to him. He didn't want to, but he was powerless to prevent it.

"What the fuck is that?" he asked.

Yui brushed her fingers against the shiny pink sequins that made up the cover of the hardback book. "It's a notebook."

She passed it over. Hoon contemplated it for a moment, then took it from her with the air of someone who'd just been handed a wafer-thin transparent bag filled with human excrement.

"It transforms," Yui announced, which caused Hoon some further consternation.

"Fuck," he muttered, holding the thing at arm's length. "Into what? It's no' one of them robot things, is it?"

Yui giggled. Actually giggled, like people in cartoons did, and nobody in real life would ever seriously contemplate.

"No, silly. Look." She brushed a hand across the sequins. They turned over to reveal a drawing of a winking girl holding up two fingers and sticking out her tongue.

It was a decent enough drawing. Not really Hoon's cup of tea, though. Without a word, he brushed the sequins over again, hiding the picture from view.

"Thanks," he said, and he made a mental note to bin the fucking atrocity the first chance he got.

For now, though, it would do the job.

They went over things for a third time, Hoon scribbling the information on his newly acquired pad. The same winking girl from the cover appeared in the bottom corner of every right-hand page, and a quick flick through confirmed his fears that the drawings were part of a flip-book style animation, the finale of which was the image on the book's front.

Christ, he hoped nobody else ever saw him with this thing. He'd never live it down.

Once the recap had been done, and his questions asked, he invited himself to look in Caroline's room. He'd expected some resistance, but Yui gave her blessing right away, on the proviso that Hoon didn't wake up her sleeping boyfriend.

She was still keeping up the act, bless her. So, she didn't trust him yet.

Good for her. Trusting people, in his experience, got you nowhere.

"Her parents keep paying her share of the rent," Yui explained, as they stood in the doorway of the room. "It's the only way I can afford to keep the place on. They want all her stuff to be waiting here for her when she gets back, just as it was."

"So, you've not moved anything?" Hoon asked.

Yui shook her head. "The police poked around. They took away her laptop, but I don't think they touched anything else."

"Right. OK. Thanks," Hoon said. He stole a look back at the room they'd just left. "How about you stick the kettle on, and I'll crack on here?"

Yui nodded enthusiastically, relieved to have been given permission to leave. Hoon waited for her to return to the front room, and listened for the sound of the kettle being filled, then turned to the door of Caroline's bedroom, nudged it open, and stepped inside.

CHAPTER TWENTY

IT WAS A CHILD'S BEDROOM. That was Hoon's first instinct when he was standing there alone in it. It was all pastels and pinks, with a frilly veil hanging from the ceiling around the single bed, giving it the feel of a four-poster. Glow-in-the-dark stars were dotted around the ceiling, and the furniture—from the bedside table to the wall-hanging mirror—was all old stuff that had either been cleverly upcycled or completely ruined, depending on your tastes.

It was the sort of room that a five-year-old fairy princess would slit your fucking throat for, but it made the skin pull back from Hoon's fingernails and the hair in his nostrils shrivel up and die.

"Jesus. Fucking. Christ," he muttered. It was almost a reprimand of the room itself. A, '*Look at the bloody state of you. Don't you even think you're going anywhere dressed like that,*' aimed at all four walls and the ceiling.

At least the green carpet hadn't followed him in. That was something. Instead, the floor here was a sensible grey laminate, albeit with a fluffy yellow rug concealing most of it.

Storage space was limited to a single small wardrobe and a slightly wonky-looking chest of drawers, both of which had been covered in stickers.

Four shelves held an assortment of toys and statues, all with oversized heads, cartoonishly huge eyes, and a range of costumes designed for everything from dragon slaying to double maths.

He checked out the wardrobe first. It was a cheap, flat-packed thing, and opened with a wobble. Fewer clothes than he would've expected were hung on the rail inside—two black dresses and a couple of semi-formal jackets. There were also three of what he assumed had to be some sort of costume. They were garish, multi-coloured things that quite closely resembled the outfits worn by the toys on the shelves. A wig in a net was attached to the hanger for each costume— one purple, one yellow, and another a brilliant shade of blue.

The bottom of the wardrobe was like a nest of shoes, belts, and bags. He checked through the bags, but found nothing of note.

If the wardrobe was fairly sparse, the chest of drawers was anything but. Each drawer had to be forcibly heaved open, jammed as they were by items of clothing. The bottom two drawers exclusively contained folded t-shirts, all with various logos and slogans emblazoned across the front.

The drawer above held jumpers in pinks, purples, yellows, and greens, with sparkly accents attached here and there.

Jesus. She was a child. A child in a woman's body, maybe, but a child all the same.

He tried not to think about what might have happened to her.

Or what might be happening still.

The top drawer was filled with pyjamas and underwear. Usually a good hiding place for diaries and other personal items, in his experience.

He had a rummage around until his fingers brushed against something hard, then gave a triumphant *a-ha* and pulled out a small, discreet vibrator.

"Shite!"

He was about to return it to its hiding place when a floorboard creaked behind him. He heard a male voice eject a, "What the fuck?" This was closely followed by the sound of running footsteps.

Turning, Hoon caught a glimpse of a large, angry, and completely naked man charging towards him, cock and balls flapping like the tail of an excited dog. Before he could react, a flying kick sent him stumbling into the wardrobe.

He crashed through the flimsy wood, got tangled in a Japanese schoolgirl outfit, then landed badly on his shoulder. The vibrator, which he'd still managed to hold onto, suddenly kicked into life, jumped out of his hand, and buzzed noisily where it fell on the laminate flooring.

For a moment, he watched it wiggle off towards the bed, then he twisted. Grimaced. Pain tearing through his shoulder.

The big naked bastard dropped onto him, knees first, knocking the wind out of him. The smell of the guy assaulted Hoon almost as much as the kick had—sweat, and sex, and personal hygiene that was lacklustre at best.

A hand caught Hoon's throat. A fist drew back. It was on the wrong side for him to be able to block, thanks to the fire of pain now consuming his shoulder and the top of his left arm.

He wouldn't be able to avoid the punch. Couldn't stop it, either.

Only one thing for it, then.

He went for the goolies. Grabbed, twisted, nails digging in. The attacker's eyes bulged. He howled, hesitating just long enough for Hoon to land a finger-strike to the throat, then a glancing knee to the ribs.

They rolled together through the wreckage of the wardrobe and the clothes that had been contained within. The heel of a shoe sent a bullet of agony through Hoon's hip as his weight came down on it, but then he was rolling on again, still crushing the other man's crown jewels with one hand, while punching and gouging with the other, until—

"Stop! Stop it! Leave him alone!"

Yui flew at Hoon just as he got the upper hand. She grabbed him by the face, her fingers finding purchase in his mouth and nostrils, and dragged him backwards.

"Stop fighting! Cut it out!"

Hoon shrugged her off and jumped clear. He raised both fists, ignoring the pain that one of them brought along for the ride.

Down on the floor, the attacker grabbed tenderly at his testicles and curled himself up into a ball, affording Hoon a view of his hairy bare arse that would've made a proctologist blush.

"You've hurt him!" Yui yelped, dropping to her knees and putting her hands on the whimpering man's chest as he rocked from side to side on the floor.

"It's no' my fucking fault!" Hoon protested. "I was minding my own business, then fucking Kung-Fu Panda there comes flying at me in the buff. I hurt my fucking shoulder there, by the way, if anyone cares." He pointed to the sobbing mess of a man on the floor. "Who the hell is he, anyway?"

"I told you, he's my boyfriend!" Yui told him. "He was asleep. I said not to wake him!"

"Your boyfriend?" Hoon looked from the young woman to the naked man. "I thought you'd made that up."

"What? Why would I make it up?"

"I mean... I thought maybe you were worried I was a rapist or something," he explained. "I thought you were trying to warn me off from trying anything."

"*What*?! No! Of course not!"

"Well, don't blame me! You weren't exactly convincing," Hoon said, then he bent, picked up the vibrator, and pressed the button to turn it off. "That buzzing was getting on my tits," he explained.

Yui ignored that last part and focused on the sentences before. "I wasn't trying to be convincing! I was just telling you that Richard was sleeping and that..." She sighed, clutched her head, then pointed to the bedroom door. "You need to go. You need to get out."

Hoon raised his hands in a calming gesture. "Look, let's not get too upset here. It's just a misunderstanding."

"You nearly ripped my bollocks off," Richard whimpered.

"Well, you're the one who put the fucking things within grabbing range, son, coming at me like Bruce Lee at a fucking nudist beach. So, I think there's plenty of blame to go around, don't you?"

"Out!" Yui barked, pointing to the door again. It had been thrown all the way open before the attack, and was now slowly inching closed again from the rebound. "I mean it, get out before I call the police."

"I am the—"

"The proper police!" Yui snapped. "And I'll call Caroline's parents and tell them you've been here."

"Rummaging around in her underwear drawer," Richard groaned.

Was his voice always that falsetto, Hoon wondered?

Probably not.

He tried the calming gesture again, but with the same lack of results. Before he could even offer any soothing words, Yui got up and slapped at him, forcing him to either fight back or retreat.

For once, he chose the latter.

"Fine, fine, I'm going," he told her. He snatched the notebook from where he'd sat it on the bed. "But I'm fucking having this."

"I don't care. Go! Get out!"

She gave Hoon a shove. He tutted, did an about-turn, and almost walked into the door, which had swung most of the way closed.

He stopped when he saw a corkboard hanging from a single hook on the back of the door. It was a treasure trove of Polaroid photos, notes, lists, and inspirational quotes urging the reader to *be the change they wanted to see in the world,* and other similarly inane bullshit.

One Polaroid overlapped everything below it, suggesting it was a recent addition. It showed about half of Caroline's face on the left, and two-thirds of a man's face on the right. Caroline was grinning goofily, whereas the guy was playing it more cool. His eyes were narrowed, his jaw was clenched, and one eyebrow was raised. It was unconvincing, though, like he was playing some suave hardman in a school play.

"Who's this?" Hoon asked.

Yui dished out a few more slaps, then stopped when she realised they were no longer having the desired effect. She followed his gaze to the photo, then shook her head. "I don't... I'm not sure. Probably a friend from work."

Hoon pulled the photo free, sending the pin pinging across the room. "I'm going to take this," he announced, in a way that made it clear it wasn't open to debate. He tucked the photo into his notebook. "Now, remind me again where she worked."

"Five Guys in Clapham," Yui said. "Now, go. Out!"

Hoon relented, and allowed himself to be escorted out of the flat.

After locking the door and sliding the chain across, Yui returned to Caroline's bedroom and helped her nobbled boyfriend up onto his feet.

"Come on, let's get you back to bed," she soothed, supporting his weight.

"I could've kicked his arse, babe," Richard insisted, limping. "If you hadn't interfered, I would have totally kicked that old bastard's—"

He stopped talking. His eyes widened. He lifted a foot to reveal a drawing pin buried in his heel.

One flight down in the stairwell, Hoon listened to the scream and smiled.

CHAPTER TWENTY-ONE

HOON AND CHUCK sat at a table in the Clapham *Five Guys*, munching their way through burgers so expensive they had drawn a gasped, "Holy fuck!" at the point of payment. Hoon had immediately downgraded the order to one portion of fries instead of two, and swapped Chuck's Banana and Oreo milkshake for a cup of lukewarm tap water.

"What kind of meat do they use at that price?" Hoon wondered while waiting for the order to be called. "Haunch of fucking centaur or something? They should all be wearing masks, the robbing bastards."

"They use special potatoes, I think," Chuck said.

Hoon scowled. "In what? The burger?"

"No, the chips."

"How special are we talking?" Hoon asked. "Because unless they grant fucking immortality, they're no' special enough to justify that price."

When their number was eventually shouted, Chuck headed up to collect the food, saving the server from another angry ear-bashing.

As they ate, Hoon had to begrudgingly concede that the burgers were actually pretty good. The chips were decent, too, and the portion size generous. Too generous, if anything. He'd have happily traded two-thirds for even half of his money back.

They'd both memorised the face of the man in the photo, and Hoon had paced up and down in front of the kitchen area, watching the staff working away preparing the food. They were all hidden under bright red baseball caps, which made it trickier, but by the time his cups of tap water had been deposited in front of him, he was fairly certain the man they were looking for wasn't there.

They were heading into the early evening rush, but Hoon had managed to persuade a young couple to give up their table near the centre of the sitting area. He sat there now with his back to the door so that he could continue to watch the counter area, while Chuck, sitting opposite, could cover the rest of the place.

The young couple, for their part, hovered around at the edges of the room, waiting for another table to become available. Judging by the look on the girl's face, this would be their final ever date.

So far, Hoon had seen two other members of staff emerge from a door at the back of the kitchen. Neither one was the man in the photo. Not unless he'd changed race or gender in the time since the Polaroid was taken, anyway.

"Oi. Bookish. You're meant to be fucking looking," Hoon muttered, shooting Chuck a dirty look. Chuck was slumped back against the wooden bench-style seating, idly scrolling through his phone. "Eyes peeled."

"I am, I am," Chuck insisted, raising his head and making a show of looking around. "Nothing this side. You?"

"Not a thing," Hoon grunted. He took another bite of his burger, then muttered below his breath when half a pound of onions, cheese, and ketchup slithered out of the other side and splattered onto the table.

Chuck watched in horror as he scooped the mush back up between his fingers and forcibly reinserted it under the top of the bun.

"The fuck are you looking at?" Hoon demanded. "You know how much this cost? That's three quid there. I'm no' letting that go to waste."

He took another bite. The same squidgy dollop of toppings was immediately ejected back onto the table.

"Jesus fuck," Hoon spat. This time, rather than shoving it back onto the burger, he tipped his head back and deposited the cheese and onion sludge straight into his mouth.

Across the table, Chuck shuddered in horror. "Are you sure that table was even clean?" he asked, then he turned his attention back to his phone.

"I might have to ask someone," Hoon said.

Chuck raised his eyes. "What, about the table?"

"No. About the guy," Hoon said. "In the photo. I might have to ask if anyone knows him."

"Oh. Right. Aye."

Hoon tutted and turned his attention back to the kitchen. He'd hoped he might be able to clock the man Caroline had been photographed with so he could follow him without his knowing. If he asked someone and they did know him, they were bound to report back, which meant he'd be on his guard.

Not ideal, but needs must. The man in the photo was currently his best lead.

Which, when he thought about it, was a pretty desperate state of affairs.

Hoon polished off the rest of his burger, scrunched the wrapper into a ball, then fished a couple of chips from the miniature mountain of the things that sat on the tray between them.

He opened the notebook that Yui had given him, and which had been a source of much hilarity for Chuck when he'd clapped eyes on it, then took out the Polaroid.

"Right, I'm going to see if anyone knows him. Can't afford to sit around here all fucking night. Literally, I mean, with the price these bastards charge."

His phone buzzed in his pocket, letting him know he had a text. He took it out, saw Bamber's name on the screen, then braced himself as he thumbed the message icon.

'Thank you,' it read.

With a grunt, Hoon returned the phone to his pocket and stood up.

"Right, I'm going to find this bastard."

"Got him."

Hoon sat down again. "What?"

"The guy in the photo. I've got him," Chuck said.

Hoon turned his head, surveying the restaurant behind him. There were a dozen or more diners at various tables, but the only member of staff was an Asian woman in her forties who was mopping a spilled drink off the floor.

"Christ, he looks a fair bit different in his photo, doesn't he?" Hoon remarked, then he turned back with a scowl. "Clearly, that's no' him."

"Not there, you dick," Chuck said. He held up his phone to reveal a social media profile. A young man with a lopsided smile and a raised eyebrow smarmed out from the screen. "On Facebook. I've got all his details."

Hoon gawped at the phone like it had magical powers. "How the fuck did you manage that?"

"Because I'm a clever bastard," Chuck said, then he threw in the phrase 'reverse image search,' like it should mean something to the Luddite sitting opposite.

It didn't.

"His profile's locked down, but I've sent him a friend request," Chuck continued.

"He's hardly going to accept a friend request from a random stranger," Hoon said.

"You'd be surprised. A lot of people accept anyone."

"Aye, but no' a sad old fat fucker like you. There's a line, surely?"

"Cheers for that," Chuck replied. "But you're right. He probably wouldn't accept me. However, I didn't invite him. She did."

He turned the screen to show an attractive twenty-something female with long dark hair tumbling down her bare back, and a swimming costume that left very little to the imagination.

"Who's the bird?" Hoon asked.

"Allow me to introduce you to Ms Ailsa Scarrow. Aged twenty-three, currently studying at City University, London, single and looking for a bit of no-strings-attached fun."

Hoon leaned closer, studying the photograph in more detail. "And who the fuck's she when she's at home?"

"No one. She's not real. It's a stock photo. I made her up," Chuck said.

Hoon looked him up and down, nostrils flaring. "You creepy bastard."

"For *investigative purposes*," Chuck stressed. "It's a great way of getting access to locked-down profiles. You add them as a friend, they let you in, and boom, you've got access to everything they've posted. Every status update, every photo, every time they've checked in somewhere and tagged their location—it all opens up. I've got a few different profiles I use, just change the photos and interests to match whoever I'm targeting."

"Aye, but a photo of a fit lassie in a bikini looking for 'no-strings-attached fun'? Way too obvious. No chance that's going to work," Hoon sneered. "No bastard's going to fall for—"

The phone buzzed in Chuck's hand. A notification announced that his recent friend request had been accepted.

He smirked, picked up a chip, and dunked it in a little paper cup of tomato sauce. "Sorry, Boggle, what was that you were saying...?"

CHAPTER TWENTY-TWO

BRADLEIGH COMBES WAS GETTING his end away tonight. He'd put good money on it.

In a sense, he *had* put money on it. The restaurant—an Italian place in the more gentrified end of Peckham—was bloody expensive. The meal itself had taken a sixty quid chunk out of his student loan, and then it had taken three large glasses of their cheapest plonk just to get his date warmed up.

But warmed up she now was. He recognised the twinkling eyes and goofy smile. The constant hand contact across the table. The slight delay in her words and movements as her alcohol-dulled brain struggled to process all the various inputs.

She wasn't quite pissed, but she was well on the way, and her critical faculties were swirling around at the bottom of the empty bottle of house red.

She was younger than he was. First year student from some godforsaken town up north, still finding her feet in the big city. Still naive and full of wonder.

Up for anything, girls like her, once you'd got them *relaxed* enough.

She was talking at him about her course—marketing or some shit. He nodded, smiled, and did his best to look interested, all the while tracing his fingertips up and down the inside of her bare arm, and thinking of all the things he was going to do to her back at his place.

Another drink first, maybe. Blast those inhibitions away until the morning. Get the bitch firing on all cylinders.

He caught the eye of a waitress, clicked his fingers, and pointed to the two almost empty glasses on the table. She nodded her understanding and went scuttling off towards the bar. Hopefully, she'd be bright enough to realise he only wanted top-ups, and not another bottle. No point going overboard. Another glass would be the sweet spot. Any more than that and she'd be comatose.

Not that this would necessarily be a problem, of course, except that it'd be a nightmare getting her up the stairs.

"Ooh. I'm drunk. Are you drunk?" she asked. "Everything's, like, whooshing. *Whoom. Whoom.* Like that." She ran her hand through her hair. It bounced attractively around her shoulders. "I'm really drunk. Are you drunk?"

"I'm really drunk," Bradleigh lied.

"I should probably go home." She hiccupped, looked surprised by it, then closed one eye. "Should I go home?"

"Maybe. If that's what you want." He ran his fingertips further up her arm, and she shuddered when they reached the crook of her elbow. "Do you want to go home?" he asked in a low murmur.

She hiccupped again, let out a little laugh, then shook her head. "No. Do you?"

"Yes, actually," Bradleigh said.

After a moment, the girl's features contorted into a rubbery frown. "Oh. Right."

"But I want you to come with me," he added.

Another pause while her brain processed this, then she pulled a mock-serious face and pointed to him. "OK. But no funny business. Y'hear?" She hiccupped again, put a hand to her mouth like she might be sick, then relaxed. "Well, maybe a *little* bit of funny business, but that's it."

"What you need is more wine! Where's that bloody waitress?" Bradleigh said, grinning.

He had a good grin. All the girls said so. And so he should. He had cultivated the thing for long enough, practising, rehearsing, getting just the right mix of *cheeky schoolboy* and *sex god*. He had honed it over the past couple of years, too, developing and improving it over countless drunken conquests.

It was as natural now as a real smile, and effective enough to more than justify all those hours spent in front of the mirror. It had the first and second year girls eating out of his hand in no time, and him eating *them* out in not a whole lot longer.

It was proving particularly effective on tonight's victim. She gave an audible happy sigh, her eyes glazing over for a moment as they refocused themselves on his mouth. He deployed the big guns by biting gently on his bottom lip, then flicking his tongue out a tiny fraction and moistening the front of his polished white teeth.

After that, she was putty in his hands. Suddenly, the extra glasses of wine felt unnecessary.

"Want to get out of here?" he suggested.

She nodded, apparently so smitten—or possibly so hammered—that speech was no longer an option.

Bradleigh felt a twitch of excitement in his crotch, and turned to look for the waitress to cancel the drink order and ask for the bill.

When he looked around, a man was there. He was an older guy, hair cut short, face like a bulldog licking piss off a nettle. He stared... or *glowered* more like, as if trying to start a fight.

Bradleigh's smile turned to one of confusion. "Can I help you?"

"You Brad?"

Bradleigh said nothing, so his date answered for him. "He is," she said, slurring her S's. She put a hand on his. "He's my boyfriend."

"Aye, well, I wouldn't be so sure about that, sweetheart," the stranger said. "My friend and I just spent an interesting twenty minutes going through his Facebook. You're the third bird he's been out with this week. Posted some pretty fucking intimate photos of the other two. One was just last night, wasn't it, Brad?"

"What? No. That's bollocks."

Bradleigh glanced around the restaurant. A couple of people at the closer tables were idly eyeing the scene, but for the most part, everyone was being intensely British about the whole thing and robustly ignoring it all.

"Bookish," the newcomer said, and another man came hurrying over.

This one was more portly and redder in the face, and apologised quietly as he squeezed between the tables, bumping the occasional chair.

"Show the lady what her 'boyfriend' has been up to."

The man who'd answered to Bookish walked over to where Bradleigh's date was sitting, bent low, and showed her the screen of his phone. He scrolled through it slowly, and the drunken smile that had been a permanent fixture on her face since the last glass of wine fell away into something sadder and more solemn.

"He posts their photos on Facebook," Chuck explained. "Clothed, I mean. Not naked. From there, though, it's fairly easy to find them on sites like these."

"What the fuck are you doing? What is this? Get away from her," Bradleigh warned. "This is bullshit, Emma. It's bullshit. I don't know who these guys are, but—"

"Ella."

Bradleigh felt his rectum constrict. *Shit.*

"Ella. That's what I said."

She shook her head, the movement exaggerated by the alcohol. "You didn't. You said 'Emma.'"

"You did say 'Emma,'" the fat man across the table confirmed.

"How about we get you home, sweetheart? Let you sleep it off," the other guy suggested. "Bookish here will get you a taxi." He rolled his neck from side to side, making the bones go *crick*. "This butter-faced cock goblin and me are going to have ourselves a nice wee chat."

CHAPTER TWENTY-THREE

HOON WAITED until Ella had gathered up her things, and Chuck had led her through the restaurant before sliding onto the chair she had just vacated. Bradleigh had an incredulous look fixed to his face, but he had made no attempt to stop her, or to get up and leave himself.

A sensible move, Hoon thought. Safer here, surrounded by people, than on the darkening streets outside.

A waitress chose that moment to arrive with two glasses of red wine. She appeared confused by the date substitution, but Hoon helped her decide her next move by pushing aside the empty glass, tapping the table, and offering a warm, "Cheers, pet."

She set both glasses down, took a step back, then asked if they needed anything else.

"We're fine the now, thanks," Hoon said. He glared at the younger man, daring him to argue.

"Nothing for now," Bradleigh said, trying very hard to hold Hoon's gaze without blinking.

Hoon let the waitress head off, then took a gulp of his

wine and winced. "Fuck me, that's rough," he said. "You on the vinegar, or something, Brad? Mind you, got to keep costs down with a social life like yours, I suppose."

"Who are you?"

"Who am I? That's a very good question, actually," Hoon said. "I like to think I'm different things to different people. To some, I'm a wise fucking mentor, guiding them through these challenging times we find ourselves in. Like yon wee green homeless bastard in *Star Trek,* or whatever. Wi' the ears and the funny voice."

Hoon took another sip of his wine. This time, the flinch was less pronounced as he warmed up to the taste.

"To others, I'm a much-loved friend and colleague, bringing a wee fucking touch of joy to their day. A wee sprinkle of magic to their otherwise drab and pointless little lives," Hoon said. He shrugged. "But, I suppose what you're really asking here, Braddy-boy, is who am I to *you*?"

"Look, mate, I don't know what—"

Hoon slapped a hand down, pinning Bradleigh's to the table. His eyes blazed as he leaned sharply forward. "To you, son, I'm the cold north wind that'll cut you in fucking two. I'm the big angry bastard that'll huff, and puff, and blow your house down, your world apart, and your balls out through your arsehole.

"I am every fucking moment of every fucking nightmare that's ever popped into that rapey wee head o' yours, and the only reason I haven't already cut your bollocks off with this glass is that I need you to answer some questions, and mid-fucking-castration would feel like a somewhat awkward time to start asking them."

He gave that a moment to sink in. Bradleigh tried to remove his hand, but Hoon's grip on it was too tight, and the younger man clearly decided that pretending not to be too bothered about it was a better look than struggling to pull away and failing.

"Alright. Alright, I'm listening."

Hoon's whole face twitched. "Listening? You're *listening*? Aye, you'd better be fucking listening, son, or it'll no' be my hand pinning you to the table, it'll be a fucking fork. And it'll no' be your hand I stick it through, it'll be your tongue, your cock, and both of your fucking elbows, all with one well-aimed stabbing action. Is that clear?"

Across the table, Bradleigh swallowed, but didn't utter a sound.

"If you don't give me every last fucking *ounce* of your attention, I won't just break every bone in your body, I'll find all new bones and I'll break those, too. I'll defy fucking medical science. Years from now, scientists will dig you up and think they've stumbled upon a new species. That's how much I'll mess you up, son. That understood?"

This time, Bradleigh nodded.

"Good lad," Hoon said, patting the hand, then drawing back a little so he wasn't leaning halfway across the table. "Caroline Gascoine. Tell me about her."

"Who?"

Hoon picked up his fork, twirled it around two fingers, then gripped it so the prongs were pointing down.

"Caroline. Gascoine," he repeated through gritted teeth. "Scottish lassie. Dark hair. Student. Into all that Japanese bollocks. This ringing any bells for you?"

Bradleigh's face remained mostly blank. Not all the way, though. Not quite. He knew more than he was letting on.

Hoon produced the photograph from one of his many

trouser pockets and placed it on the table between them. "Her," he said. "That's her there. With you."

Bradleigh reached for the photograph, then stopped when Hoon hissed at him.

"Don't fucking touch it until I tell you you can touch it," he warned. He eyeballed the younger man until his hand retreated, then flicked his gaze briefly to the picture. "Right. You can touch it."

Bradleigh hesitated, like he was afraid this might be some sort of test. His hand crept slowly across the table, pinned a finger at the edge of the Polaroid, then dragged it back towards him.

"Well?" Hoon barked, approximately three-fifths of a second later. "Jogging any memories?"

"Uh... Yes. Yes. Caroline. Of course. We, uh, we went out a couple of times."

"And?"

"Uh, and... nothing. That was it. We had a couple of dates. Went out for a meal. And then, I think, just the pub. It was a few months back, and it was nothing serious."

"Then what?" Hoon demanded.

"I don't... What do you mean?"

"Did you get her pissed and shag her, like with all those other girls you plaster all over Facebook?"

"How do you know about my Facebook?"

A fist came down, smashing Bradleigh's fingers against the tabletop, and drawing a yelp of pain.

"Answer the fucking question, son," Hoon instructed withdrawing his fist. "Did you get her drunk, take her back to your place, and work the old rapist charms on her?"

Bradleigh had his hand jammed under his armpit. He

leaned closer, dropping his voice into a whisper. "I'm not... I'm not a rapist! Stop saying that!"

"I'll say what I like, you sloppy-boxed wee fuck," Hoon spat back. Anger raised the volume of his voice, and a few of the closer tables began muttering in concern or condemnation. "Is that what happened? With Caroline?"

"No! No, nothing like..." Bradleigh's face went pale. "Wait. Are you her dad?"

"Lucky for you, Braddy-boy, no. I'm not. If I was... Jesus, your head'd be so far up your arse by now you'd be doing your own fucking colonoscopy. I'm just a friend of the family, here trying to find out what happened to her."

Bradleigh frowned. "What do you mean?"

"Don't try and play fucking dumb with me, son," Hoon seethed. "Or *dumber*, anyway."

"I'm... I'm not. What do you mean? What happened to her?"

"Why don't you tell me?"

"Well, because... I don't know. I don't know what you're talking about," Bradleigh insisted. "I haven't heard from her in months. She stopped answering my texts."

"And what? You didn't think of phoning?"

Bradleigh gave a half-chuckle, before concluding that Hoon was serious. "Oh. Right. Um, no. I mean, who phones these days? I got a couple of texts one night, inviting me out, but I was..." He glanced away, just for a second. "...busy."

"Doing what?"

"Just... I was with a friend."

"Aye, I fucking bet you were. When was this?"

Before Bradleigh could reply, Hoon became aware of someone standing behind him. At first, he thought it was Chuck coming back, but then a deep baritone spoke.

"Excuse me, sir, I'm going to have to ask you to leave."

Hoon turned in his chair, and found himself facing the navel of a black bomber jacket. He looked up.

And up.

And up, until he eventually met the eye of one of the largest men he'd ever clapped eyes on. The guy was black, bald, and bearded, and had a Bluetooth earpiece blinking away in one ear. He chewed a piece of gum with what could only be described as 'malevolent intent.'

"What's the problem?" Hoon asked. "My friend and I are just having a wee catch up."

"You're upsetting the other customers, sir," the bouncer said, in a timbre so low the empty wine bottle on the table *hummed* in harmony with it. "They don't like what you're saying."

"Is it the accent?" Hoon asked, glaring around at the other diners, almost all of whom were doing their best to pretend he didn't exist. "Can we maybe arrange fucking subtitles for them? Would that help?"

"I'm going to have to ask you to leave," the bouncer reiterated. "*Now*, sir."

"Tell you what, I'll just sit here and finish my wine first," Hoon said, turning back to face Bradleigh. "And I'll keep the swearing to an absolute minimum, so these fudge-nosed uppity pricks don't get all teary-fucking-eyed on us. How about that?"

A hand was placed on his shoulder. It was a big hand. Strong. The sort of hand custom-built for hurting people.

"I'm going to have to ask you to leave," the bouncer said for the third time. By the tone of it, it would also be the last.

Hoon took a sip of his wine, stuck his tongue out at the taste, then regarded the hand. When he spoke, his voice was devoid of anything resembling emotion. "And I'm going to have to ask you no' to touch me."

"I'm not with him," Bradleigh said, seeing his opportunity to escape this situation. "He just sat down. I was here with my girlfriend. I don't even know who this guy is!"

"Outside, sir. Now."

"Take your hand off me."

"He came in here threatening me," Bradleigh continued. "He tried to break my fingers. I think you should call the police."

A woman chipped in from a nearby table. "I saw him hit the young lad's hand. He's been really aggressive."

"Take. Your hand. Off me," Hoon instructed.

"See? Thank you!" Bradleigh said to the woman at the other table. He clasped his hands together as if in prayer, nodded his gratitude, then flashed her his well rehearsed smile. It wasn't his best performance by a long shot, but she blushed and smiled back, then studiously avoided eye contact with her husband who sat across from her.

The hand still hadn't moved from Hoon's shoulder, and his patience with it was rapidly running out.

"He's a psycho," Bradleigh continued. "He threatened to stab me."

"That wasn't a fucking threat, son, that was a promise," Hoon told him.

"Right, that's it. You're leaving," the bouncer intoned, and an arm was suddenly around Hoon's throat, heaving him up off the chair, smashing his legs against the underside of the table.

Jesus, the guy was strong. He hoisted Hoon up without any obvious effort, his arm like an iron bar across Hoon's throat.

"Alright, folks," he said, his voice like the tolling of a funeral bell. "Nothing to see here, just enjoy your meals."

He was just doing his job, Hoon knew. Management would've pointed him to the table, and instructed him to do whatever was necessary to remove the angry, swearing Scottish bastard as quickly and with as little fuss as possible.

It wasn't his fault. Which made Hoon feel almost guilty for what he did next.

The sound the fork made as it was buried in the bouncer's thigh was not a particularly pleasant one. Nor, for that matter, was the howl of pain that followed, or the scream from the interfering, *poking-her-fucking-nose-in* woman at the next table.

Hoon rubbed his throat, then held his hands up, pre-emptively trying to calm the restaurant before the whole place descended into chaos. "I repeatedly asked him to take his hand off me," he said, as if this somehow justified impaling the poor bastard on a fork. "This was an act of self-defence. I was in no way the aggressor. If anything, I'm the fucking victim in all this, and so I think we should all just—"

"Oi!"

It occurred to Hoon that the bouncer's howling had stopped almost as abruptly as it had started. He managed to turn just enough to catch sight of a small metal canister being aimed squarely in his direction.

There was a hiss.

There was a spray.

And then, a moment before the pain and the blindness set in, Hoon's legs were kicked out from under him, his jaw met the floor with a *thud*, and the restaurant, South London, and the whole wide world beyond it, slid sideways into the dark.

CHAPTER TWENTY-FOUR

THE CELL HOON eventually found himself in was even less glamorous than the one he'd been thrown in back in Inverness. A few bits of makeshift graffiti had been etched into the painted brickwork, none with enough literary merit for him to bother paying attention to.

There was a powerful aroma of piss hanging around the place, which the cell in Inverness had been lacking. Similarly, the mattress of the bed up there in the Highlands had been notable for its lack of faded yellow staining. Certainly in comparison to this one, anyway.

He'd been knocked out for only a few seconds, but long enough for his hands to be bound behind his back with cable ties, and for Bradleigh Combes to do a runner.

The substance that had been blasted into his face was not the illegal pepper spray that he had braced himself for, but some watered down legal alternative that left a foul smell and a UV trace for later identification, but did very little in the way of damage. The idea was that, while you might still be mugged, raped, murdered, or some combination of the three, you'd at least make the polis's job that much easier for them, which would hopefully come as some consolation.

He had been given a phone call. He had used this call like he'd used the last one—to ring up a Detective Chief Inspector. This DCI, however, was not the same as the previous one. If anything—and incredibly as that sounded— he was even more of an arsehole.

"Alright, Balls?" Hoon asked, getting up from where he'd been sitting on the piss-stained mattress. "Took your fucking time."

DCI Balls didn't even bother drawing the thin veil over his impatience like Logan had. Instead, his response was a scowl, a shake of the head, and a barked, "What the hell did you do?"

Hoon shrugged. "Your job, pal. That's what I did," Hoon said. "I dug around. Went to see Caroline's flatmate."

"God." Balls massaged his temples. For a moment, he managed to resist asking the question, but it found its way out in the end. "And?"

"And I found something very interesting."

"Wasn't the carpet, was it?"

"No, but Jesus Christ. What were they thinking there?"

Balls shook his head and stared into the middle distance, like the colour of the carpet had left some lingering PTSD type aftereffects.

"She was seeing someone," Hoon said.

A couple of lines furrowed Balls' brow. "Who? Caroline?"

"Aye. Right slimy wee bawbag. Seems to specialise in getting lassies blootered and then firing into them when they're out of the game."

The DCI's lips moved like his brain was running some

sort of translation protocol. "He gets them drunk and has sex with them?"

"Is that no' what I just said?" Hoon asked. "Aye. Takes photos and videos of them, too, which I highly fucking doubt he's got their permission for."

"Right. And what's that got to do with you being in here, exactly?"

"Oh. That. Aye, I went and had a chat with him in a restaurant that he'd... I don't know, tagged himself in on Facebook, or some shite."

"You 'had a chat'?"

"Aye. More or less," Hoon said. "I may have threatened to put a fork through his cock at one point, but it was light-hearted. It was banter."

"Right. So you wouldn't have actually done it, then?"

"Realistically? No. I'd have gone for the eyes," Hoon said. "But, that's no' the point."

"What's the point?" Balls asked.

"The point is that he's a fucking lead, isn't he? Rapey wee bastard like that? Him and Caroline were going out around the time she went missing. Two days later, he's out shagging some other poor lassie, and plastering her bare arse all over the fucking internet."

Balls sighed. "Right. Fine. I'll look into it. Do you have a name?"

"I do," Hoon confirmed. "Got an address, too."

The DCI waited. "So, what is it?"

"You'll get hee-haw out of me on that score, pal," Hoon said.

There was a moment of silence while Balls attempted to process this, before he eventually gave up. "No. You've lost me on that one."

"Jesus Christ, son, It's no' like I'm talking fucking Martian," Hoon spat. "I mean, I'm no' going to give you the address. But I can take you to it."

Balls gave a dry laugh, pointed to Hoon like he'd just made a humorous statement, then turned to the door and shouted for the guard to come let him out.

"You're missing a trick here," Hoon told him. "Not only do I think this bastard knows something about what happened to Caroline, but he's a dirty fucking predator who needs taken off the streets. Think of all the women you can protect if you nick him. 'Serial Date Rapist Behind Bars'? That's a fucking good collar, son. That's going to put you in the good books with Joe Public *and* the big boys upstairs."

"Then give me his address," Balls said.

Hoon shook his head. "Get me out of here, and I'll take you right to the prick."

There was a clunk and a creak, and the cell door swung open at the DCI's back. Balls blew a long, slow jet of air out through both nostrils, gave his forehead another rub, then conceded with a nod.

"Fine," he said. "But you stay in the car when we get there."

"Whatever you say, Ballsy," Hoon replied. "Whatever you say."

———

Neither the restaurant nor the bouncer had chosen to press charges, so getting Hoon out didn't take much effort. A couple of forms and a few signatures later, and Hoon was being handed his personal effects in a clear plastic bag, which

he carried out to the car park with him until they reached
DCI Balls' car.

"Volvo. Classic," Hoon observed, as the lights flashed and
the alarm was deactivated on the shiny blue SUV. "Want me
to drive?"

"Absolutely not," Balls replied. "I want you to sit there
and keep quiet."

They climbed into the car, and Balls pulled on his seatbelt. "And try not to touch anything with your face. That
stuff they sprayed on you stinks."

Hoon frowned. "What the fuck would I be touching with
my face?"

"I don't know. Just anything."

"Aye, but I mean... what? It's no' like I'm going to be
winding the fucking window down with my forehead."

"Just... shut up and put your belt on," Balls said, sounding
for all the world like a man already regretting his decision.

He waited until Hoon had belted up, then watched him
open the plastic bag he'd been handed after being checked
out. Hoon's mobile, wallet, and keys all slid out first, followed
closely by a notebook and pen.

"That's not yours, is it?" Balls asked, eyeing the pink-
sequinned monstrosity with a mixture of suspicion and
disgust.

"Sadly, aye," Hoon said. "Temporarily, until I can get a
new one."

"And that's the pen I gave you," the DCI remarked. He
looked down at the book it was being used to write in, and
practically shuddered at the indignity. "Is it too late to take it
back?"

"Aye. Afraid so," Hoon said, slipping the pen into his

pocket. "Now, come on. Straight ahead out of the car park, and take the first right."

"Is that the way to the guy's address?"

"No. But I think I saw a petrol station on the way in," Hoon told him, shuffling uncomfortably on the leather seat. "And I am *bursting* for a pish."

————

Hoon stood at one of the *McDonald's* urinals, enjoying the unique sense of relief that can only come from an emptying bladder, while simultaneously talking into his phone.

"Where the fuck did you get to?" he demanded, drawing a worried look from an older fella washing his hands in a sink. "I ended up getting lifted."

Chuck's reply was drowned out by the roaring of the hand drier. Hoon shot the old man a glare, then pulled off an impressive mid-stream hand swap, moving the phone into his left hand while juggling his genitalia over to the right.

"I didn't hear that. What did you say?"

"I said there were no taxis. She lived just down the road, so I dropped her off," Chuck explained. "When I got back, you'd already gone. I've been phoning around trying to find out where you were taken. Although, I have to say, I assumed I'd be your phone call."

He sounded almost hurt by the fact that he hadn't been the one Hoon had contacted. Hoon gently suggested that he 'dry his fucking eyes,' and then had finished his piss and zipped himself up, one-handed.

"That wee bawbag, Bradleigh. We got a home address for him?"

"Eh... I don't think so," Chuck replied, earning himself an

outburst of swearing that sent the old man scurrying out of the bathroom in fright. "I can get it. If you give me fifteen, twenty minutes or so. I can call you back."

"Text it to me," Hoon instructed. "In fact, you know that map thing that Google does?"

"Google Maps."

"Whatever the fuck it's called—"

"Google Maps."

"Jesus fuck. Fine. Google Maps, then. I don't care. Can you send me one of them links that'll open in that?" Hoon asked. "So it'll give me step-by-step directions?"

"Aye. No problem. Shouldn't be an issue," Chuck replied. "Want me to meet you there?"

"Nah, you're fine," Hoon told him. He turned on the tap above one of the bathroom sinks. "I've found someone new to play with."

————

Seventeen minutes, two double cheeseburgers, and a regular *Coke* later, Hoon returned to Balls' car, clambered in, then gave the DCI the nod.

"Right, that's me," he announced.

Balls' teeth were clamped together, suggesting he'd been sitting there seething for quite some time.

"Queue, was there?" he asked.

"Aye, something like that," Hoon replied, then he rapped his knuckles on the dashboard and indicated the darkening street ahead. "Right, chop-chop," he urged. "We're no' going to catch this bastard sitting here twiddling our thumbs."

CHAPTER TWENTY-FIVE

THE JOURNEY PASSED UNEVENTFULLY ENOUGH.
Balls had insisted all the windows remained open so that the
smell of the spray Hoon had been tagged with didn't forever
permeate the materials of the Volvo's cabin. The cold had
swirled in, bringing with it all the other smells that made up
London, and which were, in Hoon's opinion, far worse than
his own.

Chuck had come good with the address, and Google
Maps had also performed its role admirably, guiding them
through the streets of South London until they arrived
outside a large, modern-looking building on New Kent Road,
dozens of windows lit up like beacons in the night.

Right away, Hoon could tell from the hordes of lazy,
workshy, hippie-looking bastards malingering around outside
that this was student accommodation. He spent several
seconds pointing out the worst haircuts and outfits, and
quietly despairing about the youth of today.

He tried to use Bradleigh's room number as leverage so
that Balls would let him tag along, but the DCI seemed confi-

dent that a member of staff would be able to provide the necessary details, and so had once again insisted that Hoon stay put.

After a brief, half-hearted argument, Hoon had agreed to wait in the car.

He did not, however, agree to a timescale.

Approximately seven seconds after Balls had vanished through the building's front door, Hoon got out of the Volvo, took a set of external side-stairs up to the first floor, then set off in search of Bradleigh's room.

After a bit of wandering, and a few pointers from a daft-haired bastard with a twirly moustache, he found the room at the end of a long corridor. He listened at the door until he heard music and movement from within, then backtracked a bit until he found a couple of young women heading off on a night out.

"Excuse me, ladies," he said, calling to them. "Any chance you two could do me a quick favour?"

The women, barely out of their teens, huddled a little closer together and stared at him like he was wearing a blood-soaked apron with a *Jack the Ripper* name badge fixed to it.

"It's nothing dodgy," Hoon insisted. "And there's twenty quid in it for you."

The women exchanged glances. One of them shrugged.

"What?" asked the other. "Each?"

———

Bradleigh lay on his couch, one hand down the front of his jeans, the other arm tucked behind his head. He had got himself worked up at the thought of yet another conquest, and his frustration was evident in the bulge that he was now idly stroking away at.

What a fucking day. What a fucking *waste*. He had the camera all set up and ready. The ropes all under his bed, within easy reaching distance.

Come on, it'll be fun. Live a little.

He could almost picture how unsure she'd be. The uncertainty she'd have looked up at him with, lying there with her eyes glazed, and her legs open. The whole lot on show. She'd have been worried. Nervous. But he'd have talked her round. He always did.

One way or another.

He removed his hand from his jeans and started working the button just as a *rat-a-tat-tat* sounded at the front door.

He froze, mid-unbuttoning, the throbbing of his crotch stopping like it was holding its breath.

Slowly, quietly, he got up off the couch, secured his jeans, and crept over to the door. He brought one eye close to the peephole, then both eyebrows rose in surprise when he saw two of the girls from along the corridor standing on the other side.

Shit. What were their names? He'd been introduced to them at one point. They were both on his list of targets, in fact, although he hadn't quite gotten that far yet.

The tension returned to the front of his jeans. Maybe the night wouldn't be a total write-off, after all.

He opened the door, leaned an elbow against the frame, and flashed that perfectly crafted smile. "Ladies," he said. "To what do I owe this—"

He let out a little yelp when the women stepped aside and the same boggle-eyed bastard who'd challenged him in the restaurant moved in to take their place.

A single shove from Hoon sent Bradleigh stumbling backwards into his room. He hit the back of the couch, flipped over it, and went crashing to the floor on the other side.

"Nice one, girls," Hoon said, producing two crumpled twenty-pound notes from his wallet. He handed them over, and both women studied them with suspicion.

"What's this? That's not real money," one of them objected.

"What? Aye it is. It's forty quid."

"But it's not proper money."

"The fuck do you mean, 'proper money'?"

"It's Scottish money. What are we meant to do with Scottish money?"

Hoon frowned. "What do you think you do with it? Make wee hats? Wipe your arse? Fucking spend it."

"How can we spend it? We're not in Scotland, are we?"

"Why would you have to...? You don't have to be in..." Hoon's annoyance brought flecks of foam to the corners of his mouth. "That's legal fucking tender, I'll have you know. You can spend that anywhere." Out of the corner of his eye, he saw Bradleigh scrabbling back to his feet. "Don't you fucking move," he warned, then he turned his attention to the women again. "I'll have it back, if you're no' wanting it."

They whipped the money away before Hoon could take it. "It's fine, I suppose," one of them said.

The other nodded into the room. "You're not going to hurt him, are you?"

"Well, he's basically a serial rapist who tries to ruin lassies' lives by posting pictures and videos of them on the internet without their say-so." He made a weighing motion with both hands and shrugged. "So, who knows?" He stepped inside the flat, then gave them a wink. "We'll wait and see where the mood takes me."

And with that, he closed the door, turned around, and found the studio flat empty. A door leading through to an adjoining room stood open. Hoon approached it, making a soft whistling sound like he was calling a cat.

"Here, Braddy-Braddy," he sang. "Heeeere, Braddy-Braddy."

Reaching the door, he peeked his head inside, wary that some blunt implement might come crashing down on it.

Instead of the bedroom or bathroom he'd been expecting, he found himself peering into a mirror image of the room he was currently standing in. The door didn't divide two rooms in the same student flat, it divided two student flats, each with its own front door.

Hoon's head snapped to the right. He saw the front door of this second flat standing open, ejected a "Bastard!" then charged into the room, vaulted the couch, and went racing out through the door.

He made it into the corridor in time to see the back end of Bradleigh disappear around a corner. Not a massive head-start, but a headstart all the same. The student was younger, fitter, had longer legs, and knew his way around the place far better than Hoon did. Chasing him was pointless.

"Fuck it."

He chased him, anyway.

The two women who'd helped lure Bradleigh out jumped in opposite directions to escape the path of the charging Hoon. He gave them a nod as he went thundering along the corridor and flung himself around the corner.

The next corridor was long and straight, and contained maybe a dozen students dotted along its length. They were all watching Bradleigh sprinting past, and most of them didn't notice Hoon until he came pounding up behind them, all sweat and rage.

"Out of the fucking road!" he bellowed, sending teenagers and twenty-somethings scattering. "Someone stop that bastard!"

Nobody moved to stop the bastard in question. If anything, they further facilitated his escape by getting out of his way, and getting *in* Hoon's as much as they dared. Which, fortunately, wasn't much at all.

By the time Bradleigh reached the end of the corridor, though, he had pulled further ahead, and there was a cockiness to his stride that drove Hoon to summon some long-buried reserves of speed and pick up his pace.

He was going to catch him. One way or another, he was going to fucking catch him.

———

It had taken almost five minutes for DCI Balls to track down a staff member, and the same again to convince them to give him the information he needed.

Now, he wandered through the maze of corridors, trying to make sense of the numbering system. It had started with odd numbers counting upwards on the left and even numbers counting down on the right, but somewhere in the last four-way junction, that had flipped around the other way.

Even more annoyingly, the room he was looking for was somewhere in the chunk of missing numbers that had been lost in the switchover.

He backtracked to the junction, followed the corridor to

the left until he was sure he'd gone the wrong way, then doubled-back and took the turning on the right, instead.

This was more promising, he thought. The numbers were now at least in the right ballpark, and they were climbing in the right direction. Assuming no more crossroads-related chaos, finding Bradleigh Combes' room should be relatively straightforward.

He turned a corner, found himself at another four-way junction, and mumbled a couple of curse words under his breath.

Just as he was about to pick a direction, two young women came hurrying down the corridor on the left, both chattering excitedly about money. He blocked their paths with his warrant card.

"Sorry, ladies. Detective Chief Inspector Balls."

"*Balls*?" one of the women practically sniggered. "Seriously?"

It was not the first time that DCI Balls' name had elicited mirth, and he had long-since accepted that there would never be a last time, either. He smiled politely, gave a nod, then continued.

"I'm looking for room one-eight-two. Any ideas?

The women made eye contact. Something passed between them. "Down that way," one of them said, throwing a thumb back over her shoulder. "Right at the end."

"Your partner's already chasing him, though," said the other.

Balls frowned. "Partner? Chasing who? What do you—?"

"Here, you're the police. Do you know if Scottish money's legal?" asked the first woman. "Your mate said it was, but we don't know if we should believe him."

"Scottish...?" The lines on Balls' forehead became

smooth, then creased again when his eyebrows flipped from being all the way down to all the way up. "Oh," he muttered. "Fuck!"

And with that, he ran.

———

When Hoon finally went skidding into the next corridor, he found it full of students, but notably lacking in Bradleigh Combes. It was another long passageway, lined with doors on each side. Unless there was a junction of some sort, the bastard must've summoned an impossible turn of speed to get himself all the way to the end before Hoon reached the start.

Hoon jogged to a stop, his chest rising and falling as he swallowed down big gulps of air. Reaching into his pocket, he produced his fake polis ID and held it above his head. "I'm looking for the man who came running down this way a few seconds ago," he announced. "Who saw where he went?"

Of the twenty or more obscenely fresh-faced students currently stopped in the corridor, nobody volunteered the information. Not on purpose, anyway.

About a third of the way along, a short, squat lad in a turban shot a sideways look at the closest door. Keeping his counterfeit warrant card raised in front of him like a shield, Hoon quietly approached, forcing the man back with a glare and a mouthed, "Fuck off."

Once at the door, he stopped. Listened.

There was whispering inside. Hissed. Urgent. He couldn't make out the words, but he didn't have to. The words didn't matter.

Got the bastard.

Turning and pocketing his ID, he made a series of

shooing motions, dispersing the scattered crowd of onlookers. They turned in opposite directions and all set off away from him, some walking quickly, others sauntering backwards, hoping to catch sight of something exciting.

He waited until they'd all left the corridor, then stepped back, took a breath, and exploded forwards with a kick that landed right below the door's handle.

Wood splintered. Metal squeaked. The door flew inwards like a hangman's trapdoor, swinging until it *banged* against the wall on the other side.

Hoon shuffled several steps to his right, and enjoyed the moment of raw terror on Bradleigh's face when he tried to make his escape through the neighbouring door, only to find his path blocked by a scary smiling man with a sheen of sweat coating his forehead.

"Alright, Braddy-ma-boy?" Hoon asked. His hand went around the lad's throat. His voice came as a low, animal growl. "Where were we?"

CHAPTER TWENTY-SIX

BRADLEIGH WAS CRYING. Proper, red-faced, snotter-nosed crying. His features were all scrunched up, and the sounds coming out of him were high-pitched warbles which were, quite frankly, music to Hoon's ears.

He was sitting on the couch back in the room with the broken door. The room's regular occupant—a plump blonde girl in sweatpants and a baggy t-shirt—stood by the window, her eyes wide, her hand positioned like it was still holding the phone Hoon had slapped out of it.

"Jesus fuck, son. Stop greetin'," Hoon barked, which—as he knew fine well it would—only made Bradleigh worse.

Leaving the lad to his sobbing, Hoon looked back over his shoulder at the lassie by the window. The colour of her face was somewhere between tangerine and *Tango*. She had drawn on her eyebrows with what was presumably some sort of make-up pencil, but could equally have been a black *Sharpie*. Whatever she'd used, she'd gone way overboard, and was mere millimetres away from qualifying as an honorary Marx Brother.

"You friends with this guy?" he asked her.

She nodded, then shook her head, then deviated into a sort of diagonal zig-zag pattern that failed to answer his question.

"You didn't go out with him, did you?"

"What? No. No. I mean... Sort of. Once. I just..." She finally realised that she was no longer holding her phone, and wrung her hands together. "Please, don't hurt me."

"Hurt you? Don't worry, sweetheart, the last thing I'm going to do is hurt you. Him?" He pointed to the weeping mess on the couch. "That's another story. See, Brad here has been a very naughty boy. He's been picking up lassies left, right, and centre, getting them too drunk to know what they're doing, then taking them back to his room and having his grubby little way with them, whether they're conscious or not."

The blonde looked from Hoon to Bradleigh and back again. "What?"

"Oh, aye. He gets them absolutely fucking lashed, then he films himself pumping away on them, and sticks it on one of them revenge porn sites. He's stuck hours of footage on there. Haven't you, Braddy-boy?"

He shook his head, denying it. Of course he did.

"Don't you fucking lie to me, son," Hoon growled. "We've found your accounts. We've seen the stuff you've put up there. And, well, let's just say I hope you haven't bought your big black dress and hat for your graduation, because that's right out the fucking window."

Behind Hoon, the room's owner stepped forward. "Am... am I on there?"

"I don't know," Hoon said. "Sorry."

"I wasn't asking you. Bradleigh?" When she got no

response, she shouted his name, snapping him out of his teary-eyed daze. "*Brad!* Am I on there?"

The lad on the couch buried his face in his hands, avoiding her eye. She inhaled sharply and stumbled back, one hand going to her mouth.

"Don't tell me you shagged this shite-fingered doughnut hole?" Hoon asked, with perhaps a touch less tact than he might have.

She shook her head. "No. I mean... He said he just took me back here. He told me he just put me to bed, but..." She swallowed back something hot and sour. "When I woke up, it felt... I just... I thought..."

With a sudden cry of anguish, she threw herself at him, hands slapping at his covered head, pulling at his hair, clawing at his arms.

Hoon gave her a few seconds to work through it, then caught her by the arm and gently but firmly pulled her away. "You're alright. He's going to get what's coming to him. He's going away for a long fucking time."

Bradleigh was curled up on his side on the couch now, a heaving, choking mess of facial fluids. It was all very disappointing, really. Hoon had hoped the prick would've at least taken a swing. Ideally, he'd have pulled a knife, and given Hoon the excuse to break a bone or two in self-defence.

Instead, he was a snivelling wreck, barely worthy of a slap, let alone a solid kicking.

Hoon squatted beside him, drawing another breathless whimper of fear.

"First, though, before you get carted off to jail to spend the next two decades being arse-banged every hour on the hour by a man twice your age and three times your size, you're going to help me out with something," he said. "Caroline Gascoine. What happened to her?"

Bradleigh shook his head. Sobbed some more. Christ, he cried ugly, his mouth contorted, his eyes scrunched up, his nostrils all flared. If only all those lassies he'd charmed could see him now.

In fact...

Hoon took out his phone, spent several seconds trying to remember where the camera app was, then snapped off a couple of pictures of Bradleigh's crying face.

That done, he handed the phone back to the young woman with the cartoon eyebrows, and told her to send herself the photos and to share them as widely as she liked.

Bradleigh's bloodshot, red-ringed eyes shot her a pleading look, but Hoon moved to block his line of sight. "I asked you a fucking question, you girnin'-faced clown. Caroline Gascoine. What happened to her?" He pointed a finger right up in Bradleigh's face. "That's the second time I've asked now. You won't enjoy the situation you find yourself in if I have to ask you again. You'll hate every agonising fucking moment of it, in fact, so I suggest you hurry up and spit it out."

"I don't... I don't know. I don't know, I swear, I don't know," Bradleigh babbled. "I never... Her and me, we never..." He choked on his own snot, gagged, then carried on. "She just stopped contacting me. Just out of nowhere. I promise. She'd asked me to go out with her to some work night out thing, but I didn't want to go."

"Too many witnesses?" Hoon asked. "Was that it?"

Bradleigh shook his head urgently, sending tears tumbling onto the faded fabric of the couch. "I was... I was seeing someone else. It was nothing serious. None of it. With anyone. It was nothing serious. But... I was out. I couldn't go. She texted me a couple of times. Left me a couple of voice-mails. Flirty stuff. Nothing serious."

"What then?"

Bradleigh sniffed and wiped his eyes. Pretty prematurely, Hoon thought, given that there'd be plenty of tears left to come. "What do you mean?"

"I mean exactly what I fucking said," Hoon hissed. "Did you talk to her again?"

"No."

"Messages? Emails?"

"No. No, nothing. She sent one last message late on, but I didn't get it until next day. I was..." He cleared his throat. "...busy."

"Aye, I bet you were, you rabbit-knobbed wee fuck," Hoon spat. "The last message. What was it? What did it say?"

"I can't... I don't remember," Bradleigh said, then he gave a yelp as Hoon's hand clamped down on his head like the claw of a fairground grabbing machine.

"You'd better try and jog your fucking memory then, son, or I'll have to do it for you. And let's just say that my methods are crude, but effective. No' to mention outlawed by the fucking Geneva Convention." He clicked his fingers a few millimetres from the younger man's face, distracting him before he could descend back into sobbing and tears. "So, text message. What was it?"

Bradleigh's voice was a full-on vibrato, like he was talking while sitting on a fast-spinning washing machine. "It was nothing. An accident, I think. Just weird, like string of letters and numbers. I thought she was probably just drunk."

"Show me," Hoon instructed.

"I might've deleted it," Bradleigh whimpered. "I'm not sure, but I might have deleted it."

Hoon leaned in closer, bringing his face close enough to Bradleigh's that they were sharing the same stale, whisky-tainted breath. "Well, son," he uttered. "Let's just hope that for your sake, you haven't."

———

A few minutes later, DCI Balls was halfway along a corridor he was reasonably certain he'd already been down when he spotted a partly open door and a fully broken doorframe, and heard the sound of a grown adult male crying.

He nudged the door open a little further, and was met with a hearty smile, and the open arms of the man he quite clearly remembered telling to wait in the car.

"Finally!" Hoon boomed. "What kept you?"

"What the hell is all this?" the DCI demanded. "What's going on? What did you do?"

"Your job, that's what I did. Again," Hoon told him. He held a hand out to the woman with the *Tango* tan, and gave her a nod of thanks when she handed him his phone back. "I'd say Bradleigh's about ready to confess everything he's done. And if not, I reckon this young lady will be able to tell you some interesting stories, and I'll have a mate of mine fire over links to all the video nasties Braddy-boy here produced. I'm sure, given all your resources, you'll be able to find the women in the footage, and this daft bastard's face is plastered all over them, so should be a pretty open and shut case."

He patted the DCI on the shoulder on his way to the door. "So, congratulations, Detective Chief Inspector. You've

taken a really fucking horrible piece of work off the streets."
He winked. "You're welcome, by the way."

Balls looked at the other occupants of the room in turn,
like he was trying to figure out exactly what had happened
here, but failing.

"What did he tell you?" Balls asked, indicating Bradleigh
with a nod. "About your friend's daughter. Did he know
anything?"

Hoon sighed. He shot a glare back at Bradleigh. Even
though the younger man still had his face hidden behind his
hands, he somehow sensed the look, and tightened further
into a protective ball.

"No. Sadly not," Hoon said. "He's a dead end."

"Sorry to hear that," Balls replied. And, to his credit, it
seemed genuine. He glanced back at the broken door, then to
the sobbing man on the couch. "You know I should probably
arrest you for this, don't you?"

Hoon gave a nod. "I do, aye," he confirmed. He headed
for the door, and the DCI made no move to stop him. "You've
got my number," he said, pausing in the doorway. "If you
need me, just give me a call."

And then, without waiting for a response, Hoon shoved
his hands into the pockets of his combats, and whistled tune-
lessly as he set off along the corridor.

Once down the stairs and back outside, Hoon raised a
hand and tried to flag down a taxi. While he waited for one to
stop, he took his notebook from the large side pocket of his
trousers, flipped to the page he'd written on while he'd been
upstairs, and muttered his disapproval.

A taxi came trundling to a halt in front of him, the illumi-
nated sign dimming as Hoon opened the door. He clambered

in, gave the address for Welshy and Gabriella's house, then sat back and took out his phone.

"Nice notebook," the driver remarked. Hoon saw his smirk reflected in the rearview mirror.

"Tell you what, pal, how about you don't critique my choice of stationery, and I'll no' share my views on the offensiveness of your fucking body odour? How does that sound?"

The driver's smile fell away. He cleared his throat, turned his full attention to the road ahead, and pulled them away from the kerb without another word.

Hoon tapped at his phone, then placed it to his ear and listened to the *burring* from the speaker.

It was answered six rings later, and six hundred miles away.

"Bob? What the hell is it this time?" groaned the man on the other end of the line.

"That's a charming way to greet an old pal, Jack," Hoon retorted.

"What are you talking about? I literally spoke to you a few hours ago," DCI Logan reminded him. "It's no' like we're being reunited on *Surprise, Surprise.*"

"Still an' all, a wee bit of common fucking courtesy wouldn't go amiss," Hoon said. He sniffed indignantly. "Anyway, I'm calling for a favour."

"Surprise, surprise," Logan said again, though with different emphasis this time. "What do you want now?"

Hoon looked down at the details of the text message he'd copied onto the page of his notebook and shook his head.

A string of letters and numbers indeed.

"I need you to run a car number plate for me," Hoon continued. "And I need you to do it pronto."

CHAPTER TWENTY-SEVEN

IT WAS late by the time the cab had made its way across the river and back to Lampard Grove, and Hoon had been expecting Gabriella to be asleep.

Instead, she was curled up on the couch, wrapped in a dressing gown and half-covered with a fluffy tartan blanket. She had a glass of white wine in one hand, and one of those ebook reader things in the other, her hair pinned up and back to avoid interfering with either.

She looked up when Hoon entered, exaggeratedly wiped the back of one hand across her forehead, then gave a sigh of relief. "You're not dead!" she announced, like this might come as some surprise to him.

"Not so far," Hoon confirmed. He shrugged off his jacket, looked for somewhere to hang it, then settled for the back of an armchair. "How's himself doing?"

"He's sleeping," Gabriella said. "I told him you'd go in and say hello in the morning."

"Aye. Aye, of course," Hoon confirmed.

Truth be told, he was disappointed that Welshy wasn't

awake now. While it wasn't pleasant seeing his old pal like that, there was something relaxing about being in his company. It was nice just to hang out with him, shoot the shit, hold his hand. Give him comfort.

"How are you doing?" he asked, and Gabriella responded by taking a sip of her wine, then raising it in a toast.

"You?" she asked. "How's the mission going?"

Hoon chuckled. "It's, eh, it's progressing, aye," he said.

The only light from the room came from a lamp in the corner, turned down low. As Hoon took a seat on the armchair across from the couch, a flicker of concern crossed Gabriella's face.

"What happened? You're hurt."

Hoon touched his jaw and felt a jolt of pain rattle up into his teeth. "Oh. That. Aye. I think that happened somewhere between a bouncer's fist and a solid wood floor."

"Jesus." She sat forward, studying his face. There was a flash of cleavage through the opening in the dressing gown. Hoon forced his eyes to the ceiling and presented the purple bruise on his jaw for examination. "Looks painful."

"No' really," he lied.

"You want some ice?"

Hoon shook his head. "I'm grand, thanks."

Gabriella sat back and motioned to the open bottle of white. "You want some wine?"

Hoon hesitated. Wine was not a favourite drink of his. He'd take a cheeky red, if it was going, but as far as he was concerned, white wine was exclusively for women, children, and sexually ambiguous footballers from the 1980s.

Still, *some* alcohol trumped *no* alcohol, any day of the week, and since there was apparently nothing else on offer, he accepted.

Gabriella shrugged off her blanket and stood up.

Legs.

The word burst into Hoon's mind like an over-caffeinated SWAT team, sending all other thoughts scrambling for cover.

The dressing gown was short, barely reaching halfway down Gabriella's thighs. Hoon had never been a leg man, but that was mostly because he'd never seen legs like these.

Or, maybe the reason they had the effect on him they did was because he *had* seen legs like these before. These very legs, many years earlier. They hadn't changed much, despite the time and the mileage, and the sight of them again after all this time made him feel younger. Fitter. More alive.

Also, all that aside, they were just fucking marvellous legs in their own right.

He fixed his gaze on the window and stared at the street outside. Considering the curtains were closed, this only drew attention to the fact that he was desperately trying not to look anywhere else.

He finally turned when a glass of sparkling white was offered to him. He took it. Their fingers brushed against each other, then Gabriella returned to the couch and tucked one leg up beneath her.

To Hoon's joy and horror, she didn't pull the blanket back over herself.

"Cheers," she said, raising her glass.

Hoon matched her, took a sip, then tried not to spit the liquid out again.

Fucking white wine.

"You sure you don't need me to ice that for you?" Gabriella asked.

Hoon's eyes very briefly flitted down before he realised

what she was talking about. He touched his jaw again. "This? No. No, it's fine. I've had worse."

"I've developed some pretty kick-ass nursing skills over the last few years," she said. "Feel like I should get myself one of the outfits."

"Heh. Aye. I can imagine," Hoon said.

He tried not to.

They sipped their drinks in silence. Gabriella glanced at the screen of her *Kindle*, then pressed the button that made it go dark.

"Reading anything interesting?" he asked, trying to distract himself from the legs, and the cleavage, and the whole of the woman sitting across from him.

Gabriella shrugged. "Not really. Trashy romance stuff. Living vicariously, and all that."

Hoon said, "Heh," for the second time in as many minutes. It was also, he thought, only the second time in his entire life to date. Where the fuck was, "Heh," coming from? He'd never been a, "Heh," type of guy before.

"You read much?" Gabriella asked.

"No' really. I read exactly one book a year," Hoon replied. "*The Broons* or *Oor Wullie*, depending on what one's out."

"Right. I see. I've never heard of them. What are they about?" Gabriella asked.

"They're Scotland's happy family that makes every family happy," Hoon offered by way of an explanation. "*The Broons* are, I mean. *Oor Wullie's* just some cheeky wee prick with a bucket fetish."

This led to some nodding, and another spell of silence. Hoon sipped his wine, which was becoming marginally more palatable each time the glass touched his lips.

"How's—"

"Do you—"

They both smiled.

"Sorry. You go," Gabriella said.

Hoon shook his head. "No. Please. Fire away."

She took a drink. Her eyes were sparkling in the low light. Like the wine, but presumably without the vinegary aftertaste.

"I was just going to ask if you think you'll find her," Gabriella said. "The girl. Caroline, was it?"

"Caroline, aye." Hoon drew in a breath and held it for a moment, then let it back out. "Honestly? I don't know. Don't get me wrong, I want the happy ending here. I want to carry her back home with her sitting on my fucking shoulder, safe and sound."

"But...?"

"But it's the real world. When did that ever give us a happy ending? I'd love to find her. Fucking love to," Hoon said. "But I don't have any control over that. It might be too late. She might've been dead weeks ago. She might've died the night she vanished."

More wine. Almost enjoyable now.

"What I do have control over is finding out what happened to her," Hoon continued. "Who took her. What they did. *That*, I can find out. *That*, I can do. And I'm going to. Whatever it fucking takes, whatever I have to do, I'm going to find out what happened to that lassie."

Another sip. Bloody hell, this stuff was good.

"And then God help whoever took her, because He's the only chance they've got of stopping me coming after them."

"She must mean a lot to you."

"Caroline? No. Barely know the lassie. Her old man, though? Bamber? Him and me—Welshy, too—go way back."

"Quite a friendship you must have," Gabriella said.

"Aye. I suppose," Hoon agreed. "Although, it's no' just that."

Gabriella brought her other leg up beneath her like she was settling in for a story. "What, then?"

Hoon swirled his glass and watched the bubbles spin around in the semi-clear liquid. He must've sat that way for longer than he thought, because it was Gabriella's, "Sorry, if you don't want to talk about it..." that brought him back to the present.

"No. It's fine," Hoon said. He stopped swirling, and the wine settled again in the bottom of the glass. "It was late nineteen-ninety. About three months before that drawers-around-the-ankles incident I told you about before. We were leading a convoy, headed north. There'd been a few skirmishes, but nothing major. Convoy was small, and we were managing to stay pretty low key.

"We were using back roads. Dirt tracks, basically. Often not even that. If we came across anything iffy, one of us would go ahead, scope it out, and make sure it was safe to pass. This day, it was my turn to be on point."

He drained the glass, swirled it around his mouth like he was washing away a bad taste, then swallowed. Without a word, Gabriella nudged the bottle across the table towards him.

"Except, I'd had a few drinks the night before. We weren't meant to, but it was my birthday, and we'd got our hands on this fucking awful home brew rum stuff from Christ knows where. Like paint stripper, it was, but it did the job.

"So, anyway, I'm dog rough next morning. Hands shaking. It's thirty-five degrees in the sun, and I can't get warm. Throat as dry as a granny's chuff, and this sharp pain between my eyes like my brain's trying to drill its way out through my forehead."

"Sounds grim," Gabriella said.

"Aye. No' pleasant, put it that way. Anyway, we spot what looks like a collapsed roadblock up ahead. Load of junk scattered around, blocking the way. By complete chance, we've got air support in the region, and they do a flyover—all clear. No one lurking about waiting to ambush us," Hoon continued. "So, I start hauling myself up to go check it out, and Bamber takes one look at me and gently points out that I look like I've been carved out of a block of shite."

Hoon cleared his throat. Refilled his glass. Cleared his throat. Drank. Cleared his throat, and spoke.

"'Tell you what, Boggle,' he says. 'You sit this one out, eh? I'll get this one. You can get the next one.'"

His top teeth scraped over his bottom lip, like some self-preservation instinct was trying to stop himself saying any more, trying to fend off the memory of it. His eyes were locked on something far away beyond the living room wall.

"And I said, 'Aye. Nice one. Cheers, pal.' And then, I put my head back. Eyes shut. Arm across my face. I sat there, waiting for the world to stop spinning."

His voice became a croak. Another swig of wine did nothing to help it.

"Must've nodded off. It was the blast that woke me up," he said in a whisper. "Two hundred yards away, and it shook everything. Punched a hole in the desert and threw the fucking sand at us. We get out. Blind. It's like a wall of fog, turning everything dark and quiet. Soft, like. Muffled, you know?"

He looked to her for confirmation that she understood, and when she nodded he nodded back.

"But then, through it, we hear Bamber. He sounds far off. Miles away. And he's making this noise. Not a scream. Not exactly. Just this... this *noise*, like nothing I'd ever heard before. No' from a person, anyway."

Hoon's breathing became more laboured. He'd been mostly still until then, but now his upper body rocked slightly back and forth, his eyes returning to staring at nothing at all.

"Welshy found him, actually. Or found the bit that mattered, anyway. It was an IED. Big one. The blast had..."

He swallowed, shook his head, then drained the entire contents of his glass in one gulp.

"Anyway, point is, it should've been me out there. No' him. So, the way I see it, I'm his fucking substitute down here. If it hadn't been for me, he'd be here himself. And would he stop hunting until he found the bastards who took his wee girl?" Hoon snorted. "Never. So, neither will I."

Gabriella offered a sympathetic smile. "You're a good man, Bob."

Hoon laughed. It was short and sharp, like the fire of a machine gun. "No. No, I am not. I'm a long fucking way from being a good man," he said. "But we do the best we can with what we've got."

Gabriella drained her own glass, rubbed the back of her hand across her mouth, then stood up.

"Yes, we do," she agreed. "And who wants to be good all the time?"

Hoon watched as her hands went to the belt of her dressing gown, then his eyes widened when the robe fell away, revealing the curves and lines of her naked body.

"Gabriella," he said, but she was straddling him before he

could react, plucking the empty glass from his hand and placing it on the table behind her.

It was an unexpected turn of events, that was for sure, the result of which was that he was no longer thinking 'Legs.'

Sure, the memory of them was still rattling around in his head somewhere, but the naked breasts hovering just a few inches from his face had successfully vied for supremacy, and were leaving very little room for any other thoughts.

She felt warm. Soft. Smelled of freshly cut strawberries, ripe watermelon, and just a hint of *Head & Shoulders* shampoo.

Her mouth was on his. Her hands on his chest, on his ribs, on his stomach. She writhed, wriggling her weight on his crotch. The hands crept further down until they found his belt buckle.

He wanted her. God, he wanted her. He had done since the first moment he'd met her all those years ago, and had been reminded of it the second he'd stepped through the door yesterday.

She was gorgeous. Elegant. Stunning. Everything he could ever want in a woman.

But she wasn't his. And she never would be.

He caught her arms and pushed her back. Not hard, but firmly enough to break the contact of their lips.

"We can't," he told her.

Couldn't they?

No. No, they couldn't.

Fuck.

"Come on, you know you want to," she said, hitting him with a smile that made him feel twenty years younger.

He relented enough for her to lean in again, until guilt

got the better of him and he tensed his arms, preventing contact at the last moment.

She stayed close. Her expression became pained, and Hoon thought for a moment that his grip must be hurting her arms, then he realised the pain wasn't physical.

"Do you know how long it's been since I've been touched like this?" she pleaded. "Do you have any idea what it's been like?"

"I don't. I mean, I'm sure it's been hard."

"Feels pretty hard right now," Gabriella whispered, and that smile returned as she rocked her weight forward and back in his lap, building the heat between them.

She moved closer. Tried to, anyway. Hoon held fast, despite the full-blown conflict currently ripping through his insides.

"He won't know," she told him, shooting a look at the door. "Gwynn. He's sleeping. He won't know."

And that was that. The fire that he'd been battling to keep under control spluttered and died.

"It's not happening," he told her. "I can't. I'm sorry."

She recoiled like he'd slapped her, then slid off him and onto her feet. She looked down and saw herself, naked and exposed, and looked shocked by it. He looked away as she grabbed for the blanket that lay piled up on the couch and hurriedly covered herself with it.

"You need to go," she told him, a wobble in her voice. "I'm sorry, you can't... I shouldn't... You need to go."

"Gabriella, you don't have to... I get it. I do," he said. "I'm an extremely desirable man."

The joke didn't just fail to land, it exploded on take-off. She wrapped the blanket around herself, clutching it to her chest like it was a part of her she couldn't bear to lose. Like it was the only thing shielding her from being violated by this man's prying gaze.

"I said you need to go. Get out," she told him, her volume rising. She stamped a foot, as if shooing away an overly inquisitive animal. "Just... go. Fucking *go*, will you?"

Hoon got up, nodded, then retrieved his jacket. "I'll grab my bag. If that's what you want."

"It is. Go. I want you out," she urged.

"Right. Aye. Fair enough," he conceded. "Tell Welshy I said cheerio, will you?"

"I will, just... Go. Please. Just go."

Hoon pulled on his jacket, fetched his bag, and left without saying another word.

Gabriella waited until she heard the door click and the gate swing closed, then dropped onto her knees on the floor, buried her face in the couch cushion, and sobbed her shame away.

————

Chuck peeled open one eye, gave it a few seconds to adjust to the darkness, then yelped, "Jesus Christ!" when he saw the man sitting on the end of his bed. "Don't kill me! Please, don't kill me!"

"Fuck me, calm down, Bookish," Hoon said. "Who do you think I am, your dietician? I bring good news, my friend!"

"Good...? What? Jesus. What time is it?" Chuck asked, sitting up. "What do you mean? What good news?"

"It's going to be just like old times," Hoon declared. He slapped Chuck's knee and gave it a friendly rub through the bedcovers. "Cos you, ya lucky bastard, just got yourself a new roommate!"

Chuck made a sound that might well have been a groan. "Shipmate," he corrected.

Hoon tutted. "Let's no' be arseholes about it," he suggested. "Just you budge up, because it's been a long fucking day, and some of us need our beauty sleep."

CHAPTER TWENTY-EIGHT

NEXT MORNING, Hoon and Chuck sat in one of the many, many *Starbucks* around Canary Wharf, swigging coffee and munching their way through some sort of ham pastry that was the closest thing to a bacon roll that had been available.

It was alright, as pig-based pastry products went. Bit bland, but a couple of sachets of salt and a wee squirt of brown sauce had helped immensely on that front.

"You look like a half shut knife," Hoon said.

"Aye? I wonder why that is?" Chuck replied with a hint of venom. "Could it have been some big sweaty bastard crawling into my bed at two in the morning and keeping me awake with his farting and snoring?"

"Fucking hell, seriously?" Hoon asked through a mouthful of pastry. "Who was that? I must've slept right through it. You should've woken me up and I'd have sorted the bastard out."

He swallowed, washed it down with a gulp of coffee, then let out a lip-smacking *aaah*.

"They let you out of the jail alright, then?" Chuck asked.

"Aye. No charges pressed. All good. Balls got me out."

Chuck frowned. "What, the DCI from Caroline's case?"

Hoon nodded, while his tongue explored around inside his mouth, searching for any errant bits of ham or pastry. "He gave me his number when I went into Scotland Yard. Used him as my phone call. Talked him into taking me to visit Bradleigh Combes."

"Smooth," said Chuck, impressed. "And?"

"And Bradleigh and I had a few words. Found him hiding in some lassie's room. Reckon he'd worked his mojo on her at some point. She was not fucking happy when she found out. Balls—excellent fucking name, by the way—was going to arrest him when I left."

"Name's even better than you know," Chuck said. "It's Michael Terence Balls."

He sat back, waiting for the penny to drop. Hoon's mouth moved silently, then he spluttered into his coffee cup.

"Fuck off! It is not!"

"It is."

"MT? *Empty* Balls? No way."

"I swear to God."

"Jesus. What do you reckon? Did his parents hate him, or were they just a pair o' cretins?" He shook his head. "MT Balls. Christ on a bike. No wonder he joined the polis. It was probably that or blow his brains out in a sketchy fucking motel room somewhere."

"Yeah, it's a good one," Chuck agreed, then he rerouted the conversation back to more pressing matters. "I take it you didn't get anything useful off Bradleigh, though? About Caroline, I mean?"

Hoon knocked back his coffee, burped into a paper napkin, then scrunched it up and dropped it onto his plate. "That's where you'd be wrong. Turns out our Brad's no' just a repeat predatory sex offender, he's a veritable wealth of information, too."

Chuck's eyebrows raised and his head lowered as he leaned in closer. "Oh? Like what? Did he know what happened to her?"

"Sadly not. But Caroline sent him a text late on the night she went missing."

"Saying?"

"Not much. Just a car reg."

Chuck's look of surprise became one of confusion. "Like a number plate?"

"Naw, I mean a mechanic named Reginald," Hoon retorted. "Aye, a fucking number plate. What else would it be?"

He half-stood so he could reach into his side pocket, pulled out the notebook Yui had given him, and then sat back down again.

"You're not still using that bloody thing, are you?" Chuck asked.

"It's actually growing on me," Hoon said. "Shows my fucking what do you call it? My playful side." He flipped through the pages until he found the note he'd made the night before, and turned the book around. "That's it."

Chuck pulled the notebook closer and ran his fingertips across the page, like a blind man reading braile. "Looks like a private plate," he said.

"The sort of thing you'd get on a big fancy Porsche, you mean?" Hoon asked. "Aye, that crossed my mind, too. So I plugged it into one of them insurance price comparison sites.

It tells me it's a Porsche Cayenne E-Hybrid. Worth north of seventy grand new."

Chuck whistled quietly. "Nice car. Hybrids are good, too. Most of the benefits of electric, but with the fossil fuel back-up."

"Aye, he's got excellent green credentials for a kidnapper, right enough. I'll be sure to congratulate him before I set him on fire."

Chuck gave a laugh, but only a small one. "You're not... You're not actually going to set him on fire, are you?"

"Not sure, yet," Hoon said. "Still considering all the options. I'll play it by ear when I track the bastard down."

Chuck remained visibly concerned about this, but chose not to enquire any further, for fear of being labelled an accomplice. He tapped a finger on the page beside where the registration number had been written.

"Want me to get onto my guy? See if he can trace this for us?"

"No need. I've got my best man working on it," Hoon said. "And that's no' a compliment to him, by the way, it's a criticism of everyone else I've ever worked with. But I do want your man checking something for us."

"Oh yeah? What's that?"

Hoon glanced around, then leaned in closer and dropped his voice. "Something's no' adding up. Bradleigh said something last night, just before Balls turned up. I need to know if he's lying."

Chuck mirrored Hoon's body language and shuffled in closer. "What did he say?"

"He said the polis already questioned him. Week or two after Caroline went missing. Said they'd run her phone records and seen that she'd texted him on the night she disappeared. He claims he showed them all the messages."

"Wait, but... I thought Balls hadn't heard of him?"

"He hadn't," Hoon confirmed. "But big caseload, one missing girl out of a hundred, chances are he wasn't on top of everything." He shrugged. "I didn't give him Bradleigh's name until we pulled up outside the student digs. He wouldn't have had a chance to look him up, or go back over the notes."

"Suppose," Chuck conceded.

"But something about it doesn't feel right. If that rapey wee fuck handed over the text messages, was there any follow-up done on the plate? If not, why not? I want to know who took the statement. If it was Balls himself, there's something very fucking shady going on."

Chuck nodded in agreement. "Yeah. Coupled with the missing CCTV footage, it's all a bit sketchy. I'll give my guy a call. Sure you don't want me to get him to run the plate while—"

"Hold on." Hoon half-stood again, and this time pulled a buzzing phone from his pocket. "Here's the very man I've been waiting for."

He flopped back down onto the padded bench and pressed the mobile against his ear.

"About fucking time," he said, drawing judgemental looks from all the many Macbook typists at the nearby tables. "What were you doing, going door to door asking if anyone knew whose car it was?"

From the other end of the line, Jack Logan's voice bristled with indignation. "No, Bob. I told you I'd check it in the morning when I was back in the office."

"I assumed that was your usual woeful attempt at

humour," Hoon told him. He dragged the notebook back across the table, and fished DCI Balls' pen from another pocket. "But forget it. Better late than never. What did you get?"

He started writing what he thought would be a name and address, then stopped again almost immediately.

"It was reported stolen three days before your lassie went missing," Logan said.

"Stolen? What do you mean it was stolen?"

"I mean it was taken without permission. What else would I mean?"

"Fuck's sake, Jack!

"Here, it's no' my fault!"

"Have they any idea who nicked it?" Hoon asked, and he could almost hear the DCI's head shake.

"No. I can give you the address of the registered keeper at the time, but I had a quick shifty at his details. The vehicle was taken the day before him and his girlfriend flew out to Jamaica for a month, so can't see how he could be involved in your case. The car's since been claimed on his insurance, so technically they own it now."

"Bollocks." Hoon seethed quietly for a moment, then shook the disappointment off. "What about related cases? The registration showing up anywhere else?"

There was a sound of a computer keyboard being prodded. "Not that I can see. Why?"

Hoon shot Chuck a meaningful look across the table. As the other man had no idea what was being said at the other end of the line, though, he didn't quite know what to make of it.

"Doesn't matter," Hoon said. "And no sign of the car itself turning up anywhere, I take it?"

"None," Logan confirmed. "I'd imagine it's been stripped down and sold off. You know what it's like with these expensive motors and classic cars. Probably a gang dealing in them."

"Aye, probably," Hoon agreed. He sighed. He'd really thought he was onto something with the number plate. He'd kidded himself that he might actually be getting somewhere. But now he was back to square...

Wait.

"Hold on, what did you say?" Hoon asked.

There was a moment of silence from the other end. "When?"

"A minute ago. About gangs."

"Oh. Well, I mean it's London, isn't it? Park a fancy motor in the wrong place, and you might as well kiss it goodbye."

Hoon smacked a hand down on the table, making everyone within earshot jump. Especially Chuck, whose expression suggested he'd come dangerously close to soiling himself.

"Jack, you're a fucking genius," Hoon cried, then he shook his head and reined himself in. "No, that's too far. You're smarter than you look. How about that?"

"Too kind, Bob."

"Aye, you're probably right. You're a fucking dunce with the occasional flash of inspiration. That better?"

Logan tutted. "You remember I'm putting my neck on the line here to do you a favour?" he asked.

"No, you're putting your neck on the line to do the right fucking thing and find a missing lassie. This isn't a favour to me. Don't you even think about holding this over my head," Hoon told him. "Do you know where it was nicked from?"

"I do," Logan said. He sounded tired—far more so than he'd done at the start of the call. "Got the details here. Do you want me to send them over?"

"No, I want you to keep them to yourself," Hoon replied, then he worried the DCI might not catch the sarcasm, and clarified. "Yes, of course I want you to send them over."

"Right. Fine. I'll text them," Logan said. "But that's me done, Bob. I've got my own case to worry about."

"Aye, fine," Hoon said, then he hung up without saying goodbye. "Car's not linked to Caroline's case," he announced, as he returned the phone to his pocket. "So, either Bradleigh Combes is full of shite, or someone somewhere didn't follow up on that text."

Chuck nodded. "I'll get onto my guy in a minute. See what we can find out."

"Good. Aye. Do that," Hoon said. He stroked his chin, his fingertips rasping across his greying stubble. "Bookish, you were always a man who could get his hands on stuff."

"For the right price, aye," Chuck confirmed.

"You still able to do that?"

"For the right price," he said again, then he winced at how it sounded. "But, I mean, given the circumstances... yeah. Course. What do you need?"

"Two things," Hoon said. "Firstly, a blunt, heavy implement, ideally with a nail through it about that long." He held his index fingers six inches apart, then reconsidered and moved them two inches further. "Wait, no. About *that* long."

Chuck frowned. "What do you mean, like a baseball bat?"

"Aye. Like a baseball bat. That'd be just the very dab," Hoon said.

"What's the other thing?"

Something inside Chuck tensed when he saw the smile spreading across Hoon's face. He knew that grin, and he didn't much care for it.

"Secondly..." Hoon checked his watch. "...in about thirteen hours, I'm going to need to borrow your car."

CHAPTER TWENTY-NINE

HOON SAT on the bow of Chuck's boat, listening to the slow, solemn creaking of the woodwork. His legs dangled through the railings like they were reaching to soak in the gently lapping waves five or six feet below.

The Thames was particularly ripe today, the smell of the black water thick enough to coat the back of his throat. Technically, the boat wasn't actually on the Thames, but in a little marina just off it instead. It was the same water, with the same smell as the stuff beyond the locks, though, so he wasn't about to split hairs.

The marina was surrounded by towers of orange brick and silvery grey glass, and yet it felt far away from the city, somehow. A tranquil oasis, removed from the traffic, and the impatience, and the noise. Things were slower here. Calmer. You could feel it in the air, and hear it in the murmuring of the water.

It had been four hours since breakfast. Three-and-a-half since Chuck had headed off on his mission. The nail-enhanced baseball bat was going to be the easy part, he'd reckoned. Getting his contact at the Met to give out the details of who had taken Bradleigh Combes' original statement would likely take some more doing.

"There could be a cost involved," he'd warned. Hoon had told him to keep the receipt.

As he'd sat there on the boat, watching the sun blinking in and out from behind wispy grey clouds, Hoon had taken his phone out of his pocket on four separate occasions. Once, he'd made it as far as bringing up the contact number he had stored for Welshy, but had aborted the call before the first ring.

What would he say to her? What was there *to* say?

In an ideal world, they'd gloss right over it. Pretend none of it had happened. Put it behind them, and move right on. For Welshy's sake, if not their own.

But, she'd looked mortified, both by her actions and his rejection of them, and he had a feeling it was going to take her a long time to get over that.

He pushed her from his mind and devoted the space to the bigger picture.

Where was he with the investigation? What did he know?

Very little.

What did he *believe*, then?

He believed that a man driving a stolen Porsche had waited for Caroline that night.

He believed she had got into the car willingly, terrified of the men chasing her.

After that... He had no idea.

He'd like to say he believed she was OK.

That he believed she was safe, and that all this was going to have a happy ending.

He wanted to believe that he was looking for Caroline, and not just for answers.

Not just for revenge.

He wanted to believe those things. He did. And he tried.

Dear God, he tried.

The water beneath his feet had been crying out to have stones *plopped* into it. With none available to hand, he'd gone hunting through the cabin until he'd found a stash of loose change—coppers, mostly—and had nabbed a handful.

Over the last couple of hours, he'd tossed a good pound fifty into the tar-like liquid, and watched the coins be sucked down one-by-one into the darkness.

He had just flipped a particularly shiny two pence piece into the air, when he heard the thud of a footstep behind him. He swung his legs out from under the railing and turned just as the coin sploshed into the water, then gave a nod of approval at the wooden baseball bat that Chuck was holding.

Approximately one-fifth of the bat was contained within a plastic carrier bag so thin it was bordering on invisible. As a means of transporting an almost three-feet-long piece of wood, the bag was utterly impractical. Judging by the way Chuck had one hand clamped around the carrier, pinning it to the bat, it had proven more of a hindrance than a help.

"What's with the fucking bag?" Hoon asked.

"Well, I can't just walk the streets of London carrying a baseball bat, can I?" Chuck pointed out. "I'd get lifted."

"Isn't that exactly what you're doing?"

"No. I'm carrying a baseball bat *in a bag*." Chuck rustled the bag to demonstrate. "So people can see I've just bought it."

It made sense, Hoon admitted, in a very London sort of way.

"Did you get the nails?" he asked.

"I did. Big eight-inchers, like you asked for."

"Nice one. Did you get a hammer."

Chuck raised a finger like he was about to make an important point, but whatever words he'd intended to say dried up in his throat. He winced, and looked at the boats around them.

"Maybe we can borrow one," he suggested.

"Or maybe we can knock it in with your fucking forehead," Hoon countered. "Jesus Christ, Bookish. You had one job."

"Bollocks I did! I had a number of jobs," Chuck reminded him. He began counting on his fingers. "Baseball bat. Nails. Police source. There's no mention of a hammer anywhere on that list." He rocked back on his heels, looking quite pleased with himself. "And I'm three for three, by the way."

Hoon's eyebrows raised. "You got hold of your polis guy?"

Chuck nodded, then indicated they go below deck, away from any prying ears.

Once in the main living quarters, with the parallel lines of its wooden beams running overhead, Chuck set the baseball bat and a small bag of nails down on the coffee table with a clunk and a rattle. He knelt on the floor and activated a small blow heater to take some of the chill from both the air and his bones.

"Well?" Hoon asked, perching himself on the edge of the couch. "What did you find out?"

"It was a detective who took Bradleigh's statement originally. A DC Randhir Khatri."

"That a man or a woman?" Hoon asked.

"It's a man," Chuck said, like this should be obvious. "Balls was the senior officer on Caroline's case, but a lot was delegated to Khatri. Looks like Balls' own involvement was relatively minor."

"Explains why he knows fuck all about it," Hoon muttered. "What else did your man know?"

"There's no mention of a registration number in the official report."

"It was missed off?"

"Worse. It was made-up," Chuck said. "According to the report, the last text Caroline sent Bradleigh said, 'I'll see you tomorrow!'"

Hoon frowned. "That's bollocks. I've seen the text."

"I know. That's what I'm saying. Someone made that up for the report. Someone wanted to hide the registration number. Same someone who claimed there was no CCTV camera on that street, I'm guessing."

"And the report was written up by...?"

"DC Khatri," Chuck said. "He did the whole thing."

"Right, then I need to talk to him," announced Hoon, standing up.

Down on the floor in front of the heater, Chuck winced. "I'm not sure that's such a good idea, Boggle. If they're changing details in reports, you don't know how deep this goes. This might be bigger than we thought."

"All the more reason to get stuck in."

"Yeah. I mean... maybe. But it might be bigger than you can deal with. I don't want you ending up dead over this," Chuck told him. "We should take some time. Dig around a bit more. See what we can find, then take it up the chain. Get your old contacts up in Scotland involved, maybe. Just to cover yourself, you know?"

"Who are you, my mother?" Hoon asked.

Chuck smiled, but it was an anxious, unconvincing thing.

"Thankfully not. But... I just... This could be major, Boggle. I'm worried that the deeper you dig, the more likely it is I'm going to see you floating past here face-down in a day or two. And, despite your snoring, I don't actually want you getting yourself killed."

"That was a fucking heartwarming wee moment there, so it was," Hoon retorted. "But plenty of folk have tried to kill the pair of us before now, and nobody's managed yet. I don't plan letting some no mark from the Met be the one to finally do it. Just get me that DC's home address, and leave the rest to me."

Chuck sighed, groaned, and made various other noises of complaint, then finally relented with a nod. "Right. OK," he said, dragging himself to his feet. "Give me ten minutes. I'll make some more phone calls."

"Good lad," Hoon said, giving him a slap on his ample back. "But before you do..." He picked up the baseball bat and gave it an experimental *swish*. "Gonnae find out about getting me that hammer?"

———

The hammer was procured relatively easily, a cheerful older couple from the next boat over happily providing the use of a small toolset in a battered baby-pink bag.

The couple watched in a sombre sort of silence while Hoon sat on the top deck, battering four large nails through the thickest part of the baseball bat. He thanked them as he leaned over to return the hammer and the other tools, which they accepted with a wary nod and an uncertain smile, before scurrying back into the cabin of their canal boat, out of sight.

The four nails were all angled in different directions, like the points of a compass. It balanced the weight this way, as well as making the weapon that much more efficient.

He might not need to use it, of course. In fact, that was one of the reasons for the extra nails. Over the years, he'd identified an inverse correlation between the number of nails in a baseball bat, and a person's desire to be smashed in the face with it. Four nails, he'd found, was the point of diminishing returns.

Very few people would try their luck against a scary bastard wielding a baseball bat with four big nails sticking out of it. The handful who were prepared to take on a four-nailer were unlikely to be put off by the addition of further nails. If anything, it would only encourage the bastards. That was just the sort of people they were.

Hoon took a few minutes to get used to the change to the bat's weight and balance, then set the weapon aside for later. He returned to the cabin below in time to hear Chuck bringing a telephone conversation to an end.

"Right. Yes. Got it. Thanks. I owe you one." Chuck flinched at the earbashing he received from the other end of the line. "OK. Yes. More than... *Considerably* more than one. Yes. Good point. Right. Thanks. Bye."

He hurriedly jabbed the button that ended the call, puffed out his cheeks, then turned and presented Hoon with the sequin covered notebook. It was open to an apparently random page, where an address with a North London postcode had been scribbled.

"This that DC's place?" he asked, taking the book.

"It is. Although, he's not a DC anymore. He's a DS now."

"Good for him," Hoon said. "He still working under Balls?"

Chuck gave a little snigger at that, then stopped when he

saw that Hoon wasn't joining in. "Eh, not directly, no. Sort of a diagonal step. Reports elsewhere."

"Right. Fair enough." Hoon looked down at the address, considering his next move. "Do we know his shift pattern?"

"He's on the sick, actually," Chuck replied. "Went home yesterday evening."

"What's wrong with him?"

"I don't know. My guy didn't say, though he thinks it might be stress related."

Hoon grunted. "Aye, well, his life's about to get a whole lot more fucking stressful."

"Look, Boggle, are you sure this is a good idea?" Chuck asked. "You always told us to trust our gut, and my gut's telling me this is off."

"Aye, well, you've plenty of gut to trust," Hoon said, patting him on the stomach. "It's going to be fine. I'm just going to ask him a few questions, that's all."

Chuck's eyes crept down to the baseball bat on the table. "What about that?"

"That? On, no. That's no' for him. That's for later," Hoon said.

For a moment, this seemed to set Chuck at ease, until it occurred to him that this meant 'later' was going to be even more of a concern than 'now' was shaping up to be.

Spotting the worried look, Hoon had a bash at setting his old friend's mind at rest. "Look, why would there be a big polis conspiracy to abduct Caroline Gascoine?" he asked. "What's so special about her?"

Chuck shrugged and shook his head. "I don't know. Nothing."

"Nothing. Exactly," Hoon said. "She's just an average, everyday lassie. So, chances are the text message thing? It's a mistake. That's all. Cock-ups happen. On a daily basis with some of the fud-footed fannybangles I've had to work with over the years, in fact. It'll be a wee mistake that we'll sort out over a nice chat."

"And if it isn't?"

"If it isn't?" Hoon blew out his cheeks. "If it isn't, then it means there's something bigger happening here."

"Like what?" Chuck asked.

"How the fuck should I know?" Hoon replied. "I'm not into the guts of it yet. But, I don't know. Balls said there's a lot of people go missing. Lassies, mostly, and worse than usual of late. Maybe they're connected. Maybe... I don't know. But I'm going to find out."

He snapped the notebook closed, then tucked it into the side pocket of his trousers alongside his pen.

"And I'm going to start with that wee chat with Detective Sergeant..." He clicked his fingers a few times.

"Khatri," Chuck said.

"Bingo. That's the boy," Hoon said. "Now, are you coming with me?" he asked. "Or are you going to sit here whinging into your tits?"

CHAPTER THIRTY

DETECTIVE SERGEANT RANDHIR KHATRI'S house was in one of the leafier parts of North London, tucked away from the main thoroughfares at the end of a rectangular garden that was generous in length, but short-changed on the width front.

Still, a garden of any sort this close to Central London was usually the reserve of the mega-rich, even if this one only really lent itself to conga lines and queuing.

The owner—either past or present—had done their best with what was available, though, and most of the garden was a long strip of well-tended lawn, broken up near the house end by a small patio. From a bird's eye view, the whole thing would've looked like a lower case letter 'i,' with the seating area forming the gap between the body of the letter and the dot above.

Hoon had Chuck drive past the place a couple of times, then park a few streets away. After instructing him to wait in the car, he'd set off for Khatri's house, walked by it a few more times, then wandered up the path for a nosy.

He had found the front door standing ajar, the thin gap between door and frame giving him a glimpse of an old-fashioned hallway with floral ceiling coving, some well-aged pine panelling, and a stripe of yellowing flocked wallpaper.

Hoon inched the door open wider. The floor was covered in a carpet so outdated it made the rest of the place look like some sort of modern art installation. It was a hypnotist's swirl of browns and greens, as nauseating as it was mesmerising.

It had to be a rented place. Or a parent's house, maybe. One of the two. No self-respecting adult male in the twenty-first century would even contemplate such design choices himself, surely?

The half-open door was a bit of a surprise. As areas of London went, this one didn't seem too bad, but it wasn't 'leave your door unlocked' territory. Not by a long shot.

He knocked, rapping a knuckle against one of the door's glass panels. There was a lead rose trapped beneath the panes, mirroring the design of the coving. Moisture bloomed alongside it, indicating a failure in the double glazing at some point in the past.

When nobody responded to the knock, Hoon opened the door all the way and called into the musty hallway. "Hello? Detective Sergeant..." He sighed, muttered a, "Fuck," then took out his notebook. "*Khatri*? You there?"

There was no sound from within the house.

Or... wait. There was something. A faint rumbling from somewhere upstairs, like an old heating system chugging and gurgling into life.

Stealing a quick glance back over his shoulder, Hoon stepped into the hall, and the carpet squelched beneath his feet.

He walked on the spot, rocking his weight and pressing his feet against the flooring. Water pooled around them.

"What the fuck's this?" he wondered, then he jumped as a drip hit him on the back of the head.

Wiping it away, he looked up, just in time for a second drip to *sploot* into one of his eyes, momentàrily blinding it.

The water was tepid, not cold. Not all the way. Hoon watched another drip running across a slight slope in the ceiling, then wobbling and teetering when it reached the lowest point.

He stepped aside and watched it plummet to the floor, where it was immediately consumed by the waterlogged carpet.

Directly above him, the rumbling continued.

Running water.

A tap.

"Shite!"

He ran to the stairs, took them two at a time, already calculating the upstairs floor plan based on the hallway below.

The carpet outside the bathroom was sodden, too, a puddle stretching across the hallway to the wall opposite. The door was locked. Hoon opened it with a shoulder. A wave crashed over his shoes as he ran in, and he was forced to windmill his arms as the slippery lino threatened to throw him off balance.

There was a body in the bath. Dead. Very much dead, in fact, judging by the blood on the tiles, and on the porcelain, and on the floor. It had bled out through gashes in both wrists, turning the water into a graduating cocktail of reds and pinks.

A few packets of pills floated on the floor, the foil strips empty, the bubbles all popped.

DS Khatri was clothed, and yet, lying there in a soup of his own blood and bowel contents, likely more exposed than he had ever been before. His eyes were half-closed, like he was trying to remember where he recognised the ceiling from. His mouth hung open, a wad of vomit sitting on his t-shirt just above the tide line.

One arm hung down over the side of the bath. The other was at his side in the water, the open blade of a razor clutched between fingers that were plump and wrinkled from their time beneath the surface.

Hoon checked for a pulse, knowing full well that he wouldn't find one. Some habits, though, were hard to break.

The body wasn't fully cold to the touch, but then the water flowing from the tap was warm, which made it difficult to tell how long he'd been dead for. Could've been two hours, could've been twenty. A pathologist would have to determine that, and it was highly unlikely they'd send him a copy of the report, no matter how nicely he asked.

He backed out of the bathroom and sent Chuck a text.

'*Dead*'.

There was a lengthy pause, and then the reply came back.

'*what?*'

'FFS,' Hoon replied. '*He's dead. Suicide.*'

Another pause. Another few seconds wasted.

'*what??*'

"Jesus fucking Christ," Hoon muttered, then he rattled off a message instructing Chuck to stay where he was, and went for a quick poke around the house.

There were two bedrooms, although one was barely more

than a walk-in wardrobe with big dreams. Hoon had a peek in there, but beyond a foldaway bed and some black bags filled with bedding, found nothing worth taking note of.

The other bedroom was larger, though still not exactly generous in its dimensions. This was the one where the dead DS had presumably slept, given the piles of dirty washing, the half-empty coffee cups, and the unmade bed. The curtains—more old-fashioned things with an unflattering pelmet at the top—were closed, trapping most of the darkness from the night before. Hoon pulled his sleeve up so it covered his hand, then clicked the lightswitch so he could better see what he was dealing with.

A laptop lay on the bed, the power cable stretching across the untidy mound of the covers and into an extension cable that was tucked down beside the bedside table. Still keeping his hand inside his sleeve, Hoon prodded one of the keys, fully expecting the darkened screen to stay that way.

Instead, the hard drive whirred and clunked, and the screen lit-up with a cheerful sounding *da-daa* like it had just performed some great magic trick.

There was a *Microsoft Word* document open on-screen. Rows of typed text filled as much of the page as Hoon could see without scrolling.

'*I'm sorry,*' the first line announced. '*I'm so sorry for what I have done.*'

With the sound of running water rumbling from across the hallway, and a dead policeman relaxing in the bath, Hoon squatted down to get a better view of the laptop, blinked a few times to help focus his eyesight, and began to read.

———

The ambulance arrived first. Hoon stood back at the end of the garden, watching them go charging in. He moved closer and listened to the evidence being contaminated—the tap being turned off, the body being moved.

The paramedics at least knew enough not to bag the corpse yet, though. They returned downstairs, took a breath of the early evening air, then went in opposite directions— one heading back to the ambulance, the other making a beeline for Hoon.

"You family?" the paramedic asked. Hoon shook his head. "Friend?"

"No."

"Neighbour?"

"No."

The paramedic, a prematurely greying man with the frame of a long-distance runner, looked him up and down. "So... what are you, then?"

"Just a nosy bastard," Hoon said with a shrug.

"Right. Fair enough," the ambulance man said, a touch warily. "You'd better hang on. The police will want to talk to you."

"No worries on that front, son," Hoon told him. "I've got a few choice words for them, too."

The conversation petered out then. The paramedic gave a nod, then retreated to the ambulance to wait with his partner. Hoon sat on the wall, took out his phone, and responded to the fifth text from Chuck in the last three minutes.

He sent a reply confirming that he was OK, and that he still wanted Chuck to wait where he was, then found DCI Balls' number and gave him a call.

It went to voicemail after three rings. That wasn't long enough for the call to have rung out, nor short enough for the phone to be switched off. Balls had dinghied the call, then. Cheeky bastard.

"Alright, Empty Balls?" Hoon said, once the recorded greeting had finished playing. "Just thought you should know that there's been a big fucking development in your case. You might want to get yourself over to the house of DS... *Fuck*." He checked his notebook again. "...Randhir Khatri. Seems he's done himself in, and left a note that you're going to want to read."

He removed the phone from his ear to hang up, then returned it long enough to spit out a, "You're fucking welcome, by the way."

After ending the call, he opened up his phone's photo app, zoomed in on the picture he'd taken of the note, and scribbled it into his shimmering pink notebook. The words felt heavy, like the pen was resisting. Like it didn't want to commit those words to paper, for fear of confirming they were true.

Hoon knew how it felt. He didn't want to believe it, either.

Because if the words were true, then Caroline Gascoine was dead, and any chance of payback had bled out onto that flooded bathroom floor.

CHAPTER THIRTY-ONE

HOON WENT ROUND in circles with an assortment of
constables, then sergeants, then lower ranking detectives,
saying the same thing over and over again until DCI Balls
finally screeched up outside and came marching towards him
with the gait and demeanour of some vengeful god.

"What in the name of Christ are you doing here?" he
demanded. "What have you done?"

"I've no' done fuck all," Hoon replied.

Balls glossed over the double negative and pointed to the
house. "What are you doing here? Why the hell are you
sniffing around the house of a serving officer? You've got no
right being here."

"Alright, alright, keep your fucking hair on, Empty."

One of the DCI's eyes twitched. He knew exactly what
his new nickname was referring to, and it clearly wasn't the
first time he'd heard it.

"You've got ten seconds to explain yourself, or I'm
arresting you," Balls told him. "Starting now. One."

"He killed Caroline Gascoine."

"Tw—" Ball's forehead became a washboard of ridges. "What? What are you talking about?"

"So he says, anyway."

Balls looked from Hoon up to the house. Half a dozen Uniforms were standing outside the front door, managing to look purposeful without having much in the way of actual purpose. The pathologist had turned up shortly before Balls had, and had been swiftly escorted into the house by a female detective constable with severe hair.

"What do you mean?" Balls asked. "I thought he was dead."

"Aye. He is." Hoon presented his notebook, open to the page where he'd transcribed the Word document from the laptop. "But he left a note."

Balls accepted the book, gave the drawing of the little Japanese lassie in the corner a look that bordered on concern, then scanned the page.

This took him a couple of minutes. Hoon's hand-writing had been described as many things over the years, but 'challenging' was one that kept coming up. He'd started off taking some care over his transcription of the suicide note, but had soon lost patience and the whole thing had quickly deteriorated into his usual artless scrawl.

"What is...? I don't..." Balls looked up from the page, his eyes wide, then returned his attention to the drunken spidery lines on the paper. He finally reached the end, muttered something downright blasphemous, then met Hoon's eye again.

"And this was where?"

"Laptop in his bedroom," Hoon said.

"And you were in his bedroom *why*?"

"Front door was open. Hall carpet was soaked. Being a concerned citizen, I went to investigate."

"I mean what were you doing here in the first place?" Balls demanded.

Hoon lowered himself onto the wall again. "How did you get on with Bradleigh Combes?" he asked.

"Personally? We didn't really click," Balls said. "Professionally, I had the night of my life. That little bastard's going away. I'm going to make sure of it."

"Good stuff," Hoon said. "I meant about Caroline. What did he tell you?"

Balls frowned. "Not much. Not yet. We were getting to that. Turns out there are a lot of women he's been working his charms on. It's quite a list."

Hoon nodded. Caroline wasn't the Met's priority. He'd be surprised if her name had even come up during the interview.

"Aye, well, he told me a thing or two," Hoon said. "He was interviewed before. Shortly after Caroline went missing." He pointed up the narrow garden to the house. "Your man in there took his statement."

"DS Khatri?"

"Well, he was a DC at the time, I'm told, but aye, him. In his report he said the last text was some shite about meeting up soon, or whatever. But it wasn't."

Balls' eyebrows, which were already so knotted they looked to be partially obscuring his field of vision, somehow lowered further. "What was it?"

"A car registration. Can't say for sure, of course, but I reckon it was the car she got into that night. It's one of the bits of advice we always give lassies, isn't it? Let someone know where you are at all times, because men are sick, predatory bastards, and you're never fucking safe." He shrugged. "I mean, we don't word it like that, obviously, but that's the gist of it."

"Why didn't I hear about this?" Balls asked.

"Because, like I said, your man in the bathtub up there made sure it didn't go into the case file. He covered it up. I came here to ask him why."

Balls sighed and put his hands on his hips, pushing open his suit jacket. "You shouldn't have. You should have called me. You can't just go running around like you're the Sheriff of London. Whatever you were in the past, Mr Hoon, you're a civilian now. Even when you weren't, you had no jurisdiction here, and now you're just—"

"Doing your job for you?" Hoon ventured. "I mean, how the fuck did you not know this fella was up to something? That's your job, son, to be aware of these things. He was on your team. You should've known every-fucking-thing about him."

"It's a big team," Balls said. "I can't possibly know everything about every DC on it."

"Well, high time you got fucking working on that, then. When I was in charge—higher up than you, mind—I knew all my DCs better than they knew themselves." Hoon started counting on his fingers. "The haircut one. The Indian fella. The woman." He half-extended a fourth finger and waggled it for a moment. "There might have been another one. Can't remember. But, the point is..." His eyes narrowed. He bit his lip. "Actually, I can't remember what my point was, either, but I'm sure it was fucking excellent, whatever it was."

"Jesus," Balls whispered. He ran a hand down his face. "Has anyone ever told you you're a pain in the arse, Mr Hoon?"

"One or two people might have mentioned it," Hoon said. "All fucking dead now, of course."

"I'm not going to arrest you," Balls announced, in a tone that suggested he was already regretting the decision. "But you're done. No more of this. You know what happened now. You've got what you came for."

Hoon looked up to the house and let his gaze linger there on the frosted glass of the bathroom window.

Finally, he nodded. "Aye. I got what I came for," he confirmed.

"You don't get to keep this," the DCI said, tearing the handwritten copy of the suicide note from the notebook.

"That's going to have totally ruined the flipbook effect," Hoon complained. "But fair, I suppose."

He stood up and tucked the notebook back into his pocket. Balls beckoned over another plainclothes officer—a big fella who looked more like the bouncer of a back alley bar than a detective.

"DS Powell, escort Mr Hoon past the perimeter, will you? And make sure he keeps going."

The surly DS touched an imaginary cap in deference, then loomed over Hoon in what was presumably meant to be an intimidating manner.

"Aye, nice try, son," Hoon sneered. "Maybe start cracking your knuckles for added effect, eh? If you can stop dragging them on the fucking ground long enough, I mean."

"Goodbye, Mr Hoon. It has been... an education," Balls said, stepping aside and motioning to the gate.

"One favour," Hoon said, which drew a sharp laugh of surprise from the DCI.

"Bloody hell, you're persistent."

"Don't tell her parents," Hoon said, and there was a rare

and fleeting vulnerability to the request. "I know you'll have to, but let me tell them first. Just give me until tomorrow. They'll take it better from me."

Balls ran his tongue around the inside of his mouth a few times while he considered this. "Fine," he conceded. "It'll take a few hours to get everything processed anyway. I'll call them at lunchtime tomorrow. You have until then."

He stuck out a hand. Hoon peered at it like it was something toxic or explosive, then relented and shook it.

"Good luck, Mr Hoon," Balls told him. "For both our sakes, I hope we never meet each other again."

―――

Night was in the process of sweeping across London. Ironically, it was now, with the blanket of darkness descending, that the city started to wake up, becoming alive with lights, and laughter, and—if you knew where to look, and had the cash—love.

From a nearby bar, a decent cover version of Take That's *Back For Good* drifted across the water until it found Hoon sitting on the bow of Chuck's boat, his bare arms goosebumping in the cool evening air.

How long had he been sitting there now? Twenty minutes? An hour? He'd lost track of time, his mind running over and over the day's events, picking them apart and putting them back together again.

Better to think of what had happened than to consider what came next.

He remembered Bamber's face when he'd asked Hoon for help. The desperation. The hope.

Hoon drove the thought away, and went back to going

over everything that had happened in the past twenty-four hours.

The rocking and creaking of the boat, the faint lullaby of the music, and the adrenaline crash from the day's grisly discoveries had made his eyelids heavy. He let the metal railing take his weight, and was about to surrender fully to sleep when the door leading up from below opened, and Chuck came clumping up the steps.

"Jesus Christ," he said, holding Hoon's phone at arm's length like he didn't want anything to do with it. "That's... that's mental. He killed her. That fucking... that cop. He killed her."

Hoon's eyes flicked open. He inhaled sharply through his nose—a mistake, given his proximity to the Thames—then swung himself around to face the other man.

"Aye," he said. "It's all there."

And it was. All of it. How he'd killed Caroline and dumped her body. How he'd been racked with guilt ever since. How, when he'd discovered that someone from outside was looking into the case, he'd known it was only a matter of time before the truth came out.

It told how he couldn't face the consequences of what he'd done.

Couldn't face his parents.

Couldn't face hers.

Couldn't face the justice he knew was snapping at his heels.

He covered everything. The stolen car. The missing CCTV. The changing of Bradleigh's statement. The works.

It was, Hoon thought, the most complete confession he had ever seen.

"So... that's it, then?" Chuck asked, flopping down next to

Hoon. "After everything, it's over just like that?" He rubbed his forehead and handed Hoon back his phone. "Bamber's going to be broken."

"Thorough, isn't it?" Hoon said, indicating the photograph of the suicide note. "Really fucking crosses the t's and dots the i's."

Chuck shrugged. "Suppose, yeah."

"Impressive, really. Given he must've been a touch on the fucking emotional side when he wrote it. You think, if you're going to take a big heap of pills and slit your wrists, you might no' be at peak mental performance, but he's wrapped it all up very nicely for us."

Chuck shuffled a few inches further away so he could get a better look at the man sitting beside him. "I mean, yeah. What are you saying? You don't believe it?"

Hoon sighed and looked out across the water. The lights of the surrounding buildings danced on the black surface, like gold shimmering on the riverbed below.

"I don't know," he admitted. "It's convenient. I don't like convenient. Things are rarely fucking convenient, I find."

"But sometimes?"

Hoon grunted. "Aye. Sometimes. And it fits. It's all there in black and white."

"You should sleep on it," Chuck suggested. "Take a look with fresh eyes. No offence, Boggle, but you look like shit. A good night's kip will help. I'll even let you have my bed. I'll take the fold-out." He smiled. "Wasn't much fancying sharing again, anyway."

"Aye, maybe." Hoon nodded, then shook his head. He sat straighter, shoulders back, like he'd been in low power mode and was now coming back online. "I mean, no. What time is it?" He checked his watch before Chuck had fully registered the question. "Half nine. Right, we need to crack on."

Chuck blinked, and watched as Hoon jumped to his feet and started marching across the deck. "Crack on? With what? I thought we were done?"

"No' quite," Hoon told him. "No' yet."

He went skipping down the steps and ducked through the door. Chuck listened to the thudding of his feet in the cabin below, then got up and met him as he came hurrying back up the steps.

The baseball bat was in his hand, raised straight up in front of him like he was a swordsman preparing to duel.

"What are you going to do with that?" Chuck asked, shooting the weapon an anxious look. "You know you could get arrested for carrying that thing, yes?"

"Aye, but nobody's going to see me," Hoon said.

"Because you're staying here?" Chuck asked with a hopeful note.

"Because I'm going to be in your car," Hoon corrected.

"My car?"

"Aye. Your car," Hoon confirmed, and his grin turned Chuck's blood to ice. "Specifically, I'm going to be in the boot."

CHAPTER THIRTY-TWO

HOON WISHED, more than anything, that he'd thought to go for a piss.

It was safe to say that the boot of a 1972 MG Midget was never meant to accommodate a fully grown adult man, particularly one armed with a long piece of wood with nails through the end.

And yet, with some effort, and against his better judgement, Chuck had helped Hoon wedge himself into the short, narrow space, and somehow found a way to successfully shut the lid.

The drive had not been the most pleasant of Hoon's life, mostly thanks to his chin bumping against his knees, and an eight inch nail poking him repeatedly in the shoulder. Nor, though, was it the least pleasant car journey he'd ever had. At least this time, he didn't have a bag over his head, a bullet in his thigh, and nobody was screaming at him in Arabic.

Compared to that one, this trip was like a relaxing day out in the country.

The evening traffic was much thinner, and progress was

made relatively quickly. Hoon had held his breath when the car came to a stop, felt the shudder of the engine cutting off, then heard the mumbled warning from Bookish that he'd better know what he was fucking doing.

Then, there had been a jingle of keys, the scuffing of footsteps, and Hoon had been left alone in the cramped, oil-scented darkness.

That had been a couple of hours ago. He'd nodded off for a while, then cramp, claustrophobia, and an urgent need to pee had all combined to wake him up.

It had taken a bit of fiddling to fix the boot release so he could open it from the inside. He contemplated doing it now, popping the lid open, and jumping out for a stretch of the legs, a breath of fresh air, and a much-needed slash.

What were the chances of anyone being around? Slim, he thought. He could be out and back in before anyone noticed. With a wee break, he could comfortably go the rest of the night. And, if anything happened, he'd be in a much better state to tackle it.

His bladder was firmly in agreement with this plan, and positively hummed with excitement at the thought of the imminent easing of pressure.

The latch was fiddly in the dark. He muttered quietly to himself as he struggled with it, then let out a little sigh of relief when the mechanism gave a clunk and the boot lid raised.

The urge to pee now overwhelming, he didn't waste any time in extricating himself from the boot via its narrow opening. His legs, having been locked in the same position for hours, refused to support him, and he folded to the ground like a puppet whose strings had all been cut.

It was at this point that he noticed the three men staring at him.

It was a moment later that he realised the car was not, as he had assumed, still parked on the same side street where the Porsche used in Caroline's abduction had been stolen from. It was instead parked in a large, cluttered garage.

"Shite," he muttered. "That must've been a deeper sleep than I thought."

The three men hadn't yet moved, and had just stood there staring, wondering what the hell was going on. Hoon sized them up while attempting to shake some life back into his legs.

Their ages varied, ranging from a skinny kid in his late teens to a much heavier-set guy in his mid-thirties. The third man was towards the lower end of that range, hovering somewhere around twenty-two or twenty-five, Hoon estimated. He was of significantly less interest than the other two at the moment, though, being the only one not currently clutching a large metal tool in a threatening manner.

"The fuck?" the youngest man asked, not really aiming the question at anyone in particular.

Hoon's plan—a word he now realised was quite a generous descriptor—had relied largely on the element of surprise. That was now right out the window, however, given that he was probably the most surprised of any of them.

It didn't help that his legs weren't working, and that the contents of his bladder had backed up to somewhere around his ribcage. He heaved himself up on the MG until he could prop himself against the back of it.

The trio of bastards had started to get over their initial shock now. The one not currently tooled up crossed to a roll-up garage door, watching Hoon every step of the way. He gave a tug on a hanging chain, closing the door with a *clang* and cutting off the escape route to what had looked like some sort of works yard out front.

Hoon had to act fast before they fully got their wits about them. Assuming they had any.

"Fuck me, if it's no' the Three Bears," he announced, in a voice that echoed around the garage. He pointed at them in turn, going from oldest to youngest, and biggest to smallest. "Daddy Bear, Mummy Bear, and wee Baby Bear." He winked at the youngest man. "You're fucking adorable, by the way. Wi' your big spanner there, all slipping about in your wee paws. Put you in a bow tie and a wee bowler hat, and you'd be a viral fucking sensation, pal."

All three men looked at each other.

"You hearing this nunce mouthing, bruv?" asked Baby Bear.

"I'm hearing," confirmed Daddy Bear. The name suited him, his voice coming as a low, rumbling growl that made Hoon try harder to force the blood and the feeling back into his legs.

Chuck's MG was not the only car in the garage, but it was the only one that had the honour of still being fully intact. Two others—an Audi and a large, sporty-looking Mini —were both standing on blocks, and in the process of being reduced to their component parts.

"You lads are probably wondering why I'm here," Hoon said. And, if he were honest, he had some queries about that himself. This had seemed like a solid idea at the time, but his legs felt like two bin bags full of jelly, and if these guys went for him now he was done for. "It's a funny story, actually," he said, laughing. "See, I was in the boot this whole time."

"We know," said Mummy Bear, flatly. "We seen you get out."

"Aye, well, that's no' the funny part, son. Hold your horses. I'm trying to set a bit of fucking atmosphere here. Build up to the big moment, you know? That's foundation-level story telling."

He looked at the other two men and rolled his eyes, like they were all sharing a joke at Mummy Bear's expense. Neither man seemed particularly amused.

There was a scraping of metal on concrete as Mummy Bear bent and picked up an iron pole. It was about eighteen inches long, and thick enough that his fingers just barely met around the other side.

Hoon sized him up, then turned his attention to Baby Bear, who was slapping the spanner he was carrying into the palm of his hand. Hoon snorted. "The fuck you doing, son, auditioning for *West Side Story*?" he asked. "Put that down before you make even more of a dick of yourself."

Baby Bear side-eyed the largest of the three men. "You hearing this, bruv?" he asked again.

Daddy Bear confirmed, once again, that he was.

"You going to let him get away wiv' mouthing like that?"

"Ain't me he's mouthing at," Daddy Bear said. He had not taken his eyes off Hoon since he'd tumbled out of the car. It was like he was trying to beat him into submission with just his stare.

If so, he was going to have a long wait.

"Fuck him up, bruv," said Mummy Bear.

Baby Bear's grip tightened on the spanner. He did a sort of jig on the spot, his nerves interfering with the signals between his brain and his feet.

Hoon raised both hands to shoulder height, as if in

surrender. "Look. I don't want trouble," he said. "I just want your help."

"Our help?" Baby Bear sneered and shot another sideways look to the largest of the three men. "You hear him, bruv? Says he wants our help!"

Daddy Bear tutted. "I heard him fine."

"I just want to know about a car that got nicked a few months back. That's all," Hoon said. He reached slowly into his pocket, still keeping the other hand raised.

The three men tensed, then relaxed again when he produced his notebook.

"The fuck sort of bling shit is you carrying?" Baby Bear scoffed.

"This was a present, I'll have you know," Hoon said. He'd sensed some animosity from the others towards the youngest man, and decided to capitalise on it. "And unlike you, you bumfluff wee fudd, I'm man enough to be comfortable with it."

The young guy's eyes widened. He turned to Daddy Bear, who replied before the question could even be asked. "Yeah. I heard what he said."

"Here we go. Porsche Cayenne E-Hybrid. Blue. Nicked three months ago. Well, ninety-four days ago, to be exact." Hoon read out the registration number, then gave the MG a pat. "Same street you picked this one up on. I want to know what happened to it."

"You a Jake or somethin'?" asked Mummy Bear.

"A Jake?" Hoon asked. "You mean a jakey? Cheeky bastard. You try hiding in a boot that size for a few hours, and we'll see how fucking good you look."

"I mean you with the po-po. The 5-o," the carjacker continued. "You a Fed?"

"Oh. The polis? No. No' me," Hoon said. "Let's just call me a concerned citizen." He smiled at them all in turn, sweeping the room with his gaze. "So, you going to tell me what happened to that car, or do I have to beat the shite out of you all first? I'm easy, either way. If I was you pricks, though, I'd be leaning heavily in favour of that first option."

He stood, taking his weight off the car and testing his legs. They were working, for the most part. Still a bit sluggish, maybe, but not enough to stop him taking on these three no-marks.

"Who the fuck is this?" demanded a voice from the other end of the garage.

Hoon looked back over his shoulder to find three more men approaching from a door at the far end. The one in front was big. Serious looking.

Ah, shite.

"What was you saying, old man?" Baby Bear asked, the new arrivals doing wonders for his self-esteem. "You gone quiet all of a sudden."

"Just marvelling at your attempt at a fucking beard, son," Hoon told him. "Have you thought about doing a *Go Fund Me* or something, to see if you can pay some Taiwanese sweatshop to stitch you one on?"

Bolstered by the arrival of the other three men, or possibly just trying to earn their respect, Baby Bear made his move. He marched towards the MG, the heavy spanner clutched at a right angle to his body, his face set like a toddler about to refuse dinner.

Hoon folded his arms and smiled. This briefly interfered with Baby Bear's brain signals again, and his determined stride became markedly less so.

"Get him, bruv," encouraged Mummy Bear. "Waste this guy."

The youngest man's face was reddening now. Hoon was almost starting to feel sorry for him. The lad must've been expecting him to fall to his knees and beg for mercy, or to cover his head and curl up into a ball on the ground. Something, anyway.

Instead, he was just standing there, arms folded, smiling like he knew something that no other bugger did.

"I'm gonna kill you, mate. I'm gonna fucking kill you!" Baby Bear announced. He was maybe a dozen feet away now, his uncertainty washing ahead of him like a wave.

Hoon decided to put him out of his misery. He launched himself forwards, closing the gap, and drove his forehead into Baby Bear's nose, which promptly exploded in a spray of blood, snot, and gristle.

The other man gave Hoon a look of shock. Of betrayal, almost, like it was Hoon who was out of line here.

And then, he landed heavily on his arse. The spanner clattered to the ground, his hands covered his face, and he let out a muffled scream.

"That was self-defence," Hoon said. "Everyone saw that, right? Don't want the polis saying I started it. He was going to take a fucking swing at me." He clapped his hands and rubbed them together. "Now, then," he began, before a thought struck him. Or, less of a thought, and more of an urge. "Actually, give me a second."

In full view of the five men not currently burying their faces into their hands and crying, Hoon unzipped his fly, whipped his apparatus out, and began to piss on the floor. He groaned with relief, then met the eye of every guy in the place, holding each one long enough for them to become visibly uncomfortable.

"That's the stuff," he said. "I've been holding that in for Christ knows how long."

"The fuck...?" one of the new arrivals muttered, staring in disbelief at this fifty-something man proudly urinating on the floor of his garage.

None of the men looked happy about this turn of developments, but nor were they rushing to put themselves in the firing line.

"Won't be long now," Hoon said, rocking back on his heels. "Feel free to talk among yourselves. Or, you could tell me what happened to that car, and save us all a lot of hassle."

Keeping talking was important. It kept them distracted and off-guard. Although, to be fair, the public urination had already thrown them somewhat off-kilter.

He sized them up. Of the two originals, the big lad looked the handiest. Mummy Bear was all mouth, but Daddy had the fists and the flat nose of a fighter.

The newcomers were a lesser-known quantity. One of them—the one who seemed to be taking the lead—looked liked a biker, complete with leather jacket and handlebar moustache. He was probably the oldest man in the room, Hoon included. But age wasn't everything, and he held himself like he knew what he was doing.

The other two were less of a concern. Both young. Both gawky-looking. Barely out of school, Hoon reckoned, and currently shitting their pants. An inconvenience at worst, a couple of human shields at best. Nothing to waste too much time worrying about.

They all listened to the rattling of his urine stream as it

gradually faded into silence. He shook, bent at the knees, and tucked himself away again.

"Much better," he announced, before reaching into the boot of the MG and retrieved the baseball bat. He twirled it between the palms of his hands, making the nails spin like the blades of a helicopter, then he rested the bat on one shoulder and addressed the room at large.

"Now, then," he boomed, and his voice raced around the inside of the garage. "Which of you arse-eating spunk holes is going to talk first?"

CHAPTER THIRTY-THREE

IT WAS MUMMY BEAR, to his credit, who came running in first. He approached a little more cautiously than his younger colleague had done, partly because he'd seen what had happened to that poor bastard, and partly because he didn't want to traipse his shiny white trainers through a steaming puddle of piss.

He picked up the pace at the last few seconds, and swung with the bar in a wide horizontal arc that *whummed* above Hoon's head when he ducked.

"Fuck's sake, my granny could've seen that coming," Hoon told him. "And she's been dead for three decades."

He ducked a second swing, shook his head, then spat out another reprimand.

"Quit telegraphing it. You need to keep your movements shorter." He kicked the puddle of piss up over the guy's jeans, then beckoned him closer. "Try again. One more."

This time, Mummy Bear let out a cry of frustration as he swiped at Hoon's head with the metal bar. Hoon leaned back, waited for the wind to swish past his nose, then swung with the bat at knee-height.

There was a clunk. A *thack*.

"See? Like that," Hoon said, then he pulled the nail free with a *slurp*, and watched Mummy Bear fall screaming into the piss puddle.

The big biker hissed something to the two lads currently lurking behind him. They hesitated, then grabbed a couple of screwdrivers from a stained wooden worktop and approached the bat-twirling Hoon with trepidation.

"Two at a time. That's more like it," Hoon encouraged. "You're going to want to split up a bit, though. One there, one there. Not both in a row like you're in a fucking high school marching band."

He nodded approvingly when both lads moved to flank him. "That's better," he said. "Makes it harder for me to keep an eye on both of you at the same time, see? It's common fucking sense."

He feinted left, swung right, then enjoyed the sound of a nail puncturing the back of a hand, and the wail of pain that followed.

Hoon was moving before the screwdriver could even clatter to the floor, lunging with the narrow end of the bat and driving it into the other attacker's forehead with a comically hollow *thonk*.

He brought the main body of the bat down and his knee up, snapping the wrist of the hand still clutching the screwdriver.

Then, for good measure, he stepped back, drove an elbow into the throat of the first lad, turning him into a gagging, spluttering mess.

It was all going so well until a tyre iron caught him across the back of the legs, dropping him to his knees in a still-expanding ocean of piss.

"Looks like you didn't see that one coming," Daddy Bear intoned. He brought a foot up and drove the sole towards Hoon's face. Hoon twisted and raised his arms, deflecting the worst of it.

He heard footsteps splashing. Tried to turn, but too late. The biker's hands were on his face, fingers scrabbling to get a hold of a nostril and an eye socket. Hoon caught a glimpse of a mouth twisted in furious glee, then the sodden concrete floor came up to meet him, and something connected hard with his ribcage.

Once. Twice.

Again. Again.

Pain erupted like fireworks. He stamped it out, dampened it down. *Not now*, he told it. *Not yet.*

He tried to get up, hands sloshing around in the sea of urine, searching for purchase.

There was an impact. Jarring. Across his back. He splashed down, coughing and spluttering in his own acrid pee fumes.

The two men stood over him, saying something. Goading him, he thought, but the ringing in his ears was drowning them out, messing with his perception, making everything seem distant and far away.

He could still see, though. And right now, what he could see were feet. Four of them.

Handy, that.

He swung his arms up at his sides, brought them back behind his head, and reared up like a seal getting ready to perform its favourite trick.

Both the screwdrivers he'd managed to grab found their

targets, the long metal spears of each one neatly penetrating the top of a boot and a trainer, and driving down into the bone and flesh below.

He launched himself back, staggering upright on shaky legs, arms raised to protect himself from any stray punches or wild swings.

Neither one came. Both men were too heavily invested in the screwdrivers currently protruding from the tops of their shoes, and the blood oozing out through the soles. It mixed with the puddle, bringing swirls of amber to the otherwise uniform yellow.

He retrieved the bat, and leaned on it for support. The pain that he'd asked to hold off for a while now raised its ugly head again. It couldn't be reasoned with this time, so he flat out ignored it.

"Now then," he began, and when he spoke his breath wheezed in and out of his lungs. "One of you sloppy-boxed fucks is going to tell me what I want to know. The other is getting the jaggy end of this bastard right up the jacksy." He hefted the bat back up into swinging position, and twirled it in a circle a couple of times, like he was winding it up. "I'm going to let you decide amongst your-selves who's doing what. But, I'm no' the world's most patient man, so I suggest you hurry the fuck up and choose."

"Fuck you!" the biker hissed. He thrust a hand into his leather jacket, reaching for something. A knife. A gun. It didn't matter which.

A nail found his forearm, puncturing his sleeve and the flesh below. The bat drew back, then the wood hit his fore-head with enough force that he almost went horizontal in mid-air.

He fell hard. Fell silent. Lay there motionless in a rippling pool of pish.

Hoon made a show of checking his pulse, then gave a nod to indicate he was still alive.

"I'd move him into the recovery position," he said, "only there's a fairly good chance he'd drown." He smiled at Daddy Bear, who was leaning on a worktop, trying to work up the courage to pull the screwdriver out of his foot. "Still, good news for you, pal. You're the last man standing. Congratulations, big man! That means you get to be the one to tell me everything I need to know."

He tossed the bat aside, *cricked* his neck, flexed his fingers. The smile fell from his face. His voice, when it came, was like a symphony of doom.

"Might I suggest that you get a fucking move on?"

———

Chuck answered the phone within half a ring, before his brain had even fully registered the name on the screen. It was two in the morning, though. Who else would be calling?

"Hello? Boggle? That you?"

"Aye. It's me," Hoon confirmed, and Chuck sank back against the boat's semi-comfortable couch.

"Oh, thank God. Are you driving? You sound like you're driving. Is that my car?"

"Aye, it's your car."

"How is she holding up?" Chuck asked, then he bit down on a knuckle while he waited for an answer.

"Nothing too major," Hoon told him. "A few dents. Some light fire damage. Couple of new seats and a respray, and you'd never know the difference."

Chuck almost swallowed his fist. "What?!" he spluttered. "What the fuck happened?"

"Nothing. I'm winding you up. It's fine," Hoon said. "Maybe the faintest whiff of over ripe pish, but nothing that a couple of Magic Trees and a good airing won't sort out. I'm also alright, thanks for fucking asking."

"I was just going to," Chuck insisted. "I was worried about you."

"My arse you were," Hoon countered. "But I'm grand. Few bruises and a couple of broken ribs, just. Big red welt across the back of my thighs that'll be stinging for days, but otherwise dandy."

Chuck laughed, then realised that this time he wasn't joking. "Shit. Seriously? That doesn't sound good."

"Well, it's no' in my all-time top ten favourite fucking life moments to date, I'll give you, but it's nothing. The main thing is, I got something."

"What, besides a kicking?"

"An address," Hoon said.

There was silence while Chuck processed this. "An address?" he asked. "For what?"

"Jesus fuck. For where they delivered the car. The Porsche," Hoon spat.

"Right. Shit. Yeah."

"Turns out, one of the fellas I spoke to was a right fucking blabbermouth when he got going. Couldn't have been more helpful if he'd tried." Hoon shrugged. "Aye, might have been nice if he'd stopped crying, right enough, but he was full of useful information, all the same."

"Like what?" Chuck asked, reaching for a pen and a scrap of paper.

"They've got an arrangement with some other group of bastards. Monied, they think. They don't know much about them," Hoon continued. "They come in every so often, see what cars they've got in, then pay a few hundred quid to rent one for the night. They bring it back after a few hours, and it gets stripped for parts, or replated and sold on."

"Why?" Chuck wondered.

"My guess is Caroline's no' the only lassie these fuckers have taken," Hoon said. "I reckon we're dealing with some sort of ring."

"A ring of what? Like... serial killers?" Chuck asked. "I didn't know you got rings of them."

"No, no' fucking serial killers. People traffickers. Sex slave traders."

"Jesus, Boggle. You don't... Seriously? You don't seriously think that's what's happened to her?"

"Don't know, but I'm going to find out," Hoon said. He looked down at the notebook open on the passenger seat beside him. A smear of blood acted like an underscore to the address written there. "I'm headed to check it out now. See what's what."

Chuck coughed, almost choking on the thought. "What, on your own? You can't go on your own! You don't know what you're walking into."

"Well, I'm no' dragging your fat arse around with me," Hoon told him. "No' with the state my bastarding back's in."

"Me? Christ, no. No. My days of playing the hero are well and truly behind me," Chuck said.

"Don't you fucking flatter yourself, Bookish. We were many things, but heroes wasn't one of them."

"Aye. Fair point," Chuck conceded. "But I didn't mean

me. The police, I meant. Call the police. Tell them what you found out."

Hoon shook his head, tightened his grip on the wheel, and stole a glance at the satnav on his phone. "No. They'd take it off me."

"What?"

"They'd shut me out. I'm not having that. If Caroline's there... Or the bastards who took her..." He flexed his fingers and exhaled, cooling his swelling rage. "They're not shutting me out. No' when I've come this far."

"But there could be hundreds of guys there," Chuck warned. "With guns!"

"It's a warehouse on an industrial state, Bookish, no' the beaches of fucking Normandy," Hoon replied.

Still, Chuck had a point. He had no idea what he was walking into, and while he'd like to think of himself as the same unstoppable force he'd been in his twenties and thirties, the evening's activities so far had made him realise he was anything but.

Aye, there had been six of them, but they'd been nobodies. And they'd taken him down. Almost killed him.

Worse than that, he'd *nodded off* during the stakeout, like some sort of geriatric. They'd nicked the car, driven it a quarter of a mile through London, and he'd slept right through it.

And that was *before* his body and his ego had taken the battering. Now, he was driving with the top down so the cold night air would keep him awake and alert.

Storming the place on his own was not a sensible move.

Chuck seemed to read his mind. "What good are you going to be to Caroline if you get yourself killed in the first five seconds?" he asked. "We don't know what she's gone through, but I can't see that watching you bleeding out in front of her is going to do wonders for her mental health."

Hoon grunted. "Fine," he said, then he reached over to the notebook and flipped back a few pages. "I suppose there's no harm in bringing in some backup."

CHAPTER THIRTY-FOUR

IT WAS a full hour later when the headlights pulled up behind the MG, illuminating the inside of the car and briefly dazzling Hoon in the rearview mirror. He angled the mirror away, waited for the lights to go out, then readjusted it so he could see behind him without turning.

Turning, he had discovered, hurt. A lot.

The driver's door of the car behind opened, then closed. Hoon braced himself for the flash of the indicators and the cheerful *chi-chirp* of the alarm being activated, but thankfully the other man knew better than to draw that sort of attention.

Instead, he walked around the back of the MG and approached the passenger door. Hoon watched him getting closer in the wing mirror, and could just make out the sound of him muttering before his face appeared at the window, frozen in a red-eyed scowl.

Hoon had closed the roof shortly before reaching his destination, favouring stealth over the rolling chill that had been keeping him awake. There was no danger of him losing focus now. Not when he was so close. Not when the building he'd been looking for was just *right there*.

The door was opened, but DCI Balls made no move to get in.

"What the hell is this about?" he demanded.

"Get in," Hoon instructed. "I'll explain everything."

Balls tutted, glanced around, then clambered into the narrow confines of the car and gave a yelp as his lower leg bumped against one of the baseball bat's protruding nails. He looked between the weapon and the man sitting next to him a few times, then decided it was best not to ask.

He closed the door. Sniffed. Pulled a grimace. "Jesus. Do you smell piss?" he asked.

"I can smell nothing but," Hoon told him. "Cheers for coming. You came by yourself?"

"Yes, yes. Like you said." Balls sighed. "Although, I can't believe I came at all. I thought I was done with you."

"Aye, no' quite," Hoon told him. "I'll be honest, when I phoned I expected you to tell me to away and get fucked."

Balls groaned. "Should I have? What's 'the big finale,' you told me I had to be here for? What have you done, Mr Hoon?"

"Fuck all," Hoon said. "No' yet, anyway. But see that building?"

He pointed through a chain link fence and across a mostly empty carpark to where a single storey warehouse squatted in the darkness. The building had no windows in the walls, but light shone from a couple of glass panels in the roof, suggesting that someone was home.

"What about it?" Balls asked.

"There's a good chance the people in there know what happened to Caroline Gascoine."

Balls peered at the building. "What makes you say that? I don't see anything suspicious about it."

"Fuck me, what are you looking for?" Hoon asked. "A big sign saying, 'Baddies R Us'?"

Balls stopped staring so intently, and adjusted the collar of his jacket. "Suppose not," he admitted.

"I tracked the car she got into," Hoon explained. "Had a quiet word in the ear of the lads who stole it."

"What?! How the fu...?" Balls let the sentence tail off, then shook his head, accepting the situation for what it was. "Right. OK. What did they tell you?"

"The night Caroline was taken, the lads who nicked it hired the car out to some fucker they do regular business with. They got instructions to drop it off."

"And they dropped it off here?"

Hoon shook his head. "They dropped it off half a mile away. Same place they've dropped off dozens of other cars over the last few years."

Balls frowned, his brain working hard to keep up. It was late, and he'd barely been asleep for an hour before his phone had rung.

"So what are we doing here?"

"One night, they decided to hang back and see who made the pick-up. It was some white guy."

"A 'white guy'? And that's the only description again, is it?"

Hoon shrugged. "Guess we all must look alike," he said. He nodded to the building ahead. "They tailed him back here. Watched for a bit after he went inside, but didn't stick around to see him come back out."

"And so... what? You think he grabbed Caroline and took her here?"

"No' just Caroline, I'm thinking," Hoon said. "That's a big fucking building for one wee lassie. The lads I spoke to reckon they've had ten cars off them this year alone. You said yourself, people go missing all the time down here. Young women. What if they end up here?"

"For what?"

Hoon shrugged. "People trafficking. Prostitution, most likely. Tie them down, dope them up. Bad people will pay good fucking money for that sort of thing."

Balls ran a hand down his face, pausing when it got to his mouth. His fingers massaged his jaw as he considered the scenario Hoon had spelled out.

"That's... That would be massive," he said. "But we'd need evidence. We couldn't just barge in." He tore his eyes from the building and pointed them in Hoon's direction. "Could we?"

"Officially, no. But if you were to be in pursuit of a mad-looking Scottish bastard carrying a baseball bat with four dirty great nails through it, I'd say you'd be well within your rights to chase me inside. Wouldn't you, Detective Chief Inspector?"

A smirk tugged at the corner of Balls' mouth. "I'd say that would just be doing my duty."

"Aye. That it would," Hoon said. "And, if in the process of pursuing said mad-looking Scottish bastard, you happened to stumble upon a big room full of kidnapped lassies and sweaty-arsed perverts, that would just be the icing on the fucking cake. And you can't make a cake without breaking some eggs. So, if I happened to break some eggs before you could stop me, then... And by 'eggs' I mean..." Hoon tutted and shook his head. "I don't fucking know what I'm trying to say. My point is, are you in, or are you out?"

Balls groaned. "I don't know. This is crazy. Just me and you? This is..." He ran a hand through his hair, visibly stressing. "I've got a wife and daughter at home, you know?"

"You ask me," Hoon said. "All the more fucking reason to shut this down."

He reached for his bat, forcing Balls to scuttle his legs away before a stray nail could rip right up the side of his leg.

"So, Empty, are you in?" Hoon asked. "Or am I marching in there and killing all these bawbags myself?"

Hoon took point, leading them through the dark spots between street lights until they reached the fence. They jogged along it, keeping low, sticking to the shadows until they found a section where rust and time had eaten through the metal enough to let them slip through.

Hoon had been prepared for motion-activated lighting on the outside of the building, and was pleasantly surprised when no halogens kicked in. There were no wall-mounted cameras that he could see, either.

This was both good news and bad. Good because he didn't want anyone inside to know he was coming. Bad because if you were running a sex-slave ring from an industrial estate just outside central London, you'd probably have better security.

The lack of windows was a problem. Going in blind was never ideal, but it couldn't be helped in this case. Theoretically, he could've climbed onto the roof and looked in through the skylights. Realistically, though? With the bones in his side currently tenderising the meaty parts? Not a chance.

They did a lap of the building and found two doors—one massive slide-up garage door that had to be mechanically operated on the inside, and one person-sized entrance with a pane of frosted glass and a scattering of cigarette ends on the ground around it.

There was no light through the glass, the door presumably opening into some sort of side room away from the main floorspace.

Hoon considered waiting. Maybe someone would come outside to smoke. That would be a perfect chance to strike, giving them both entry to the building, and a hostage with which to negotiate.

But if Caroline was in there, then he had no idea what might be happening to her. He'd already waited long enough.

"Keep your eyes open," he instructed, dropping to one knee in front of the door.

While Balls kept watch, Hoon reached into his pocket and produced a small leather pouch. He flicked a few droplets of urine off it, before opening it to reveal a selection of lock-picking tools.

"This is me acting suspicious, by the way," Hoon pointed out, setting to work on the door's lock. "This is what first attracts your attention."

"Not the baseball bat with four big nails in it?" Balls whispered. He was shaking, his arms wrapped around himself to help stave off the cold.

"Maybe a combination of the two," Hoon said. He withdrew the tools and stood up again.

The DCI managed to look equal parts relieved and disappointed. "Couldn't do it?"

"On the fucking contrary," Hoon said. He pushed down the handle and the door swung a few inches inwards.

"Jesus. You did that quick," Balls remarked.

Hoon almost took the praise, but then shook his head. "It was already unlocked," he admitted. "Probably should've tried the handle first." He gave the other man a quick look up and down. "You ready for this?"

Balls swallowed. Nodded. "I'm ready."

"You're no' going to have a big fucking meltdown on me, or something?"

"No..."

"You're no' going to start crying, and then shite yourself?"

"Why the fu—? No! I'm going to be fine," the DCI insisted. "I mean, my career might be over, but otherwise I'll be fine."

"Over? No chance. This'll fucking make your career, son. This'll be a rocket jammed right up your career's hairy arsehole," Hoon promised. "They'll no' just give you a medal for this, they'll make one in the shape of your face, and then give that one to other, lesser bastards. The top brass'll be having frenzied fucking wank-fantasies about who gets to be the one to give you your promotion. That's what this is going to do for your career."

He patted the DCI on the shoulder.

"Unless you fuck it up, in which case we're both going to die. Either way, your career's the least of your worries."

Balls stared back at him for several seconds, then finally blinked. "Good pep talk."

Hoon placed the tip of the baseball bat against the door. "Ready?" he asked. Then, when Balls didn't object: "Right. Let's do this."

He pushed the door wider, revealing what looked like a staff canteen or kitchen area, with half a dozen mismatched wooden chairs clustered around a central table. Light spilled in beneath an internal door on the other side of the room—a thin line of orange light suggesting the main warehouse was blazing bright.

Hoon led the way, held the door for Balls, then let it close just enough so it was resting on the latch, but not quite shut all the way.

He adjusted his grip on the baseball bat and crept on into the darkness.

Halfway to the door, the light hit him. It burned from his left, a blinding circle of white that made his pupils contract and forced a hiss of shock through his teeth.

He turned with the bat, swung at the shape holding the torch, then felt his stomach flip as hands pulled at him from behind, wrenching him, twisting him, dragging him back.

There was an impact. Pain. His lungs cramped, ejecting all the air out of him in one short, sharp gasp.

He heard Balls cry out in panic. Felt the thump of the DCI hitting the floor.

There was a bag, thick and dark and heavy. It was pulled down over Hoon's head, saving him from the blinding torch-light, but bringing problems of its own.

A drawstring tightened across his throat, preventing his empty lungs from refilling. He twisted, turned, drove an elbow back but found nothing.

Something hit him across the cheek. A fist. A foot. A knee. He couldn't tell, but the result was much the same.

He felt himself losing balance, but he could no longer tell which way was up, so could do nothing to stop himself from falling.

His shoulder connected with something on the way down. A table, maybe. His chin, too.

The floor was hard. Cold. It did nothing to ease the pain or the shock.

He rolled onto his back, grabbed for the hood, kicked furiously at empty air.

A fist hit him in the centre of the face. *Bam*! Light exploded in the darkness. Blood washed back into his throat. The floor beneath him became melting tar, soft and sticky, pulling him down.

He heard DCI Balls wailing, pleading. "No! Don't! Don't! *Don't!*"

And then, the inky black void came to claim him, and the noise, and the shock, and the pain all retreated downwards into the dark.

CHAPTER THIRTY-FIVE

HELL WAS hotter than usual today. The mozzies were more insistent, too, trying to bite and pinch at him through his fatigues, drawn by the smell of his sweat.

Good luck to the little bastards. Given his current blood alcohol levels, he hoped they had a strong constitution.

It was almost noon, so the sun should theoretically be right overhead. The fucking thing was assaulting him from all angles, though, blinding his peripherals, even with his arm draped across his face. The heat of it was drying him out. Leeching the moisture from a body already ravaged by sunstroke, hangover, and quarter of a century of general abuse.

His head throbbed in time with the engine, a pulse of pain pushing his eyes forward until he thought they might pop right out of his skull.

Fuck it. If they did, they did. One less thing for him to worry about.

Two, he supposed.

Christ, he was suffering. Not just the headache, either. The nausea. The lethargy that weighed him down like a camel across his chest.

The regret, too. How much had he drunk? And how much of a tit had he made of himself?

He let his head roll all the way back. Let it be buffeted around by the movement of the Land Rover as it trundled across the sand.

"Boggle, you're up."

No. Fuck, no.

He peeled an eye open—a manual process that involved the use of a forefinger and thumb—and it did a couple of loops until it settled on the man in the passenger seat up front.

Bamber.

"Track's blocked. Your turn to..." Bamber studied him for a moment, then shook his head.

Something stirred in Hoon's gut. A snake uncoiling.

What was this?

What was happening here?

He knew what the words were going to be before they were spoken.

"Forget it. You're not worth shite," Bamber told him. "You can get the next one."

He opened the door, and where there should have been relief there was only panic. This wasn't right. This shouldn't be happening.

Not again.

Please, God. Not again.

Hoon tried to speak. To call after him. To tell him not to go.

But his mouth was full of sand now. His body made of lead.

He could only sit there. Frozen.

Could only watch as Bamber set off towards the blockade, AR held to his shoulder, head scanning for trouble.

Could only stare as Bamber reached the blockade.

Could only sit there watching, knowing full well what was about to happen, while utterly powerless to stop it.

His muscles screamed as he tried to force them to move, force them to obey, force them to do something—anything—to stop this from happening. To make this right.

"B..." he managed. "Bmb..."

There was a sound like the Earth itself cracking open. A sensation of movement. A wall of dust.

And the fires of Hell burned brighter and hotter than ever.

Balls' cries dragged Hoon back from the darkness, tearing him awake. They sounded different now. Shriller. More desperate.

Hoon tried to stand, but no part of him was where he'd expected it to be. He was slouched in a chair, bound to the arms of it by ropes across his wrists. An air conditioning system hummed overhead, and the cold air prickling across his skin told him he was naked.

Never good.

"No, no, stop, stop, ple—" Balls pleaded, and then the words gargled into a series of frantic muffled screams, like someone or something was filling his mouth, blocking it up.

There was a scream. A grunt of effort. A *clank* of something hitting metal somewhere close by on Hoon's left.

The bag was wrenched off his head. The light burned his eyes, forcing him first to close them, then to blink rapidly, and finally to squint. He was still in the same canteen area, but now sitting in one of the chairs.

Two men were in front of him. He recognised neither, and disliked the look of both.

On a table beside him, two bloodied teeth sat in a metal surgeon's bowl.

He listened to Balls' pained sobs, then studied the smaller of the two men in front of him while the other started screaming in his face.

He'd had plenty of people screaming in his face in the past, often in situations not unlike this one. Screaming in his face, this fucker would soon discover, was going to get him nowhere.

The smaller man wasn't shouting. He wasn't making a sound, in fact, and was instead giving Hoon an appraising sort of look, like a butcher might give to a particularly fine heifer.

He was shorter than the other man. Five-six, five-seven. He was aged somewhere in the mid-fifties, with wispy white hair that had receded to form a horseshoe shape around his pointed bald head.

He wore a heavy leather apron and delicate rubber gloves. Blood on the fingertips. His teeth were crooked. His mouth, too. It zigzagged asymmetrically below his hooked nose, like it didn't know how to smile or sneer without simultaneously doing the opposite.

The bloodied fingers on each hand danced with their opposite number, steepled together in front of his chest. Excitement radiated off him. He was positively buzzing about what was happening.

Or what was about to.

Aye, he was a concern, right enough.

Hoon had no choice but to retune his attention to the other man with the loud mouth when he forced himself into his field of view, blocking out the creepy bastard. He was heavily built. Bags under his eyes from lack of sleep. Face so ravaged by acne scars Hoon had an urge to sandpaper it smooth.

"...piece of shit! Don't you fucking ignore me! Are you fucking listening to me?"

"Sorry, pal, did you say something there?" Hoon asked. He felt the words backing up into his head, his nose blocked by plugs of blood. "I was miles away. Oh, and by the way..." He glanced up at the air conditioning vent above him, then down at his crotch. "It's cold in here, so no fucking wise-cracks, eh?"

The face in front of him puckered up with fury, then drew back. Hoon had nowhere to go, but the punch was telegraphed enough that he managed to twist his head and roll with it, saving his cheek and eye socket from the worst of the damage. He owed his neck an apology, though.

With his head turned, he tried to scope out the room behind him. His peripheral vision was still shot, though, and he couldn't see much of anything. Not the room. Not who else might be in it. And not DCI Balls.

That last one, though, he could hear loud and clear.

"Oh, thank God. Hoon. Thank God," the detective wept.

"Alright, alright, keep your fucking hair on," Hoon told him.

"They want to know what you know," the DCI babbled. "They want to know what—"

"*Shut the fuck up!*" the loudmouth roared, and Balls *yipped* and yelped into a sort of snuffling semi-silence.

Hoon tested his restraints and found them more than up

to the job of securing him to the chair. Someone knew what they were doing, then.

For the most part, anyway.

"Who are you? What the fuck are you doing here?" demanded the man still standing over Hoon, his fists clenched like he was getting ready to start swinging again. His accent was hard to place. English, but somewhere a bit further north. Yorkshire, maybe, but with the edges filed off.

Hoon answered his question with one of his own. "Who are you asking, me or him? Because he knows more than I do."

He heard a rustling as Balls twisted in his chair.

Damn. Sometimes, he hated being right.

"What? What are you talking about? You brought me here! You made me fucking come here! I don't know anything!"

"He does. He's the man you want," Hoon said. "Take another couple of teeth, see if that gets him talking."

"*What*?! No! No, don't!"

"Or a finger, maybe," Hoon suggested. "Thumbs are always a good call. Not a lot you can do without thumbs. The thought of losing their thumbs generally puts people in a pretty fucking chatty mood, I find. Not that I've ever threatened such a thing, of course. But, you know, I'd imagine."

The two men standing in front of him exchanged glances. There was uncertainty in the look from the loudmouth, but only impatience from the man with the bloodied gloves. None of this was of interest to him. This was foreplay, nothing more. And foreplay bored him immensely.

"Shut the fuck up, and talk!" the loudmouth seethed.

"Shut the fuck up *and* talk? That'd be quite a fucking trick," Hoon replied. He saw the fist draw back. The punch was inevitable. Might as well make it count. "I've got a right itch on my cheek there, any chance you could—?"

He rolled again, but his timing was less good. The room spun, and blood burst as a bubble on his lips. His comeback wasn't as snappy as he'd been hoping for, but he said it, anyway.

"That got it. Cheers."

Behind him, Balls went back to begging. "Please, Hoon, for God's sake, just tell them! Just tell them what you fucking know!"

"You tell them what you know," Hoon retorted. He looked up at the loudmouth. "He's polis, by the way. Your man behind me there. He's wi' the Met. A DCI, no less. None of your small fry." He spat a wad of blood onto the floor at his attacker's feet. "But then, I'm guessing you are, too. You've got that look about you. Like one o' them long balloons that instead of air's been filled with self-importance and then squeezed into a cheap suit two sizes too wee. That's what you are, son, you're a fucking balloon man. I want you to know that."

The news that he was 'a fucking balloon man' put the loudmouth onto the back foot. Either that, or it was the revelation that Hoon had clocked he was a copper that temporarily shocked him into silence.

"It was the car number plate," Hoon announced. "That's when I realised you were balls deep in all this. Pun totally intended."

The balloon man frowned. "What?" he asked, then the dying embers of his temper reignited again and he tried again, with more conviction. "What the fuck are you talking about?"

"I'm no' talking to you, ya fudd," Hoon told him. He

tilted his head back, indicating the man in the chair behind him. "I'm talking to this crooked fuck."

There was silence from DCI Balls. The loudmouth raised his eyes over Hoon's head. Said nothing.

"I told you that Bradleigh Combes had given me a car reg," Hoon continued. "You didn't ask what it was, which meant either you didn't give a fuck, or you already knew it. Neither one painted you in a particularly good light, I have to say, but I was still hoping you might just turn out to be a workshy skiving bastard." He shrugged. "But then, if that were the case, why would they strip me naked and no' you?"

He snorted up another wad of blood and mucus, then deposited it onto the floor. Behind him, wood creaked and fabric rustled. Hoon turned his head and watched Balls come pacing around on his right, not a mark to be seen anywhere on him, and all his teeth right where they were meant to be.

The loudmouth and the baldy both stepped back, like supporting players making room for the lead star to take his bow. There was no big moment of glory, though. No great reveal. Balls just looked weary, like he wanted, more than anything, to be back in bed.

"Fine. Good. I was getting tired of pissing about, anyway," he said. "I mean, I hoped you had a shred of human decency that would've made you talk to try to save my life, but I guess we'll never know, will we?"

"No, I wouldn't have," Hoon said. "Even if I hadn't worked out that you were an arsehole, I still *thought* you were an arsehole. Just a different sort of arsehole. Like, no' an *arsehole* arsehole. Just an arsehole. I'd have let them do whatever they liked."

"Yes. Well. I'll take your word for that."

Balls studied the man in the chair like they were meeting

each other for the first time. And they were, in a sense. The real them, anyway, fully exposed. Literally, in Hoon's case.

"So much for the 'cold north wind,'" Balls said, which drew a smirk from the other copper. "That's what you said, wasn't it? To the sex pest in the restaurant." Balls puffed out his chest and adopted a Scottish brogue so broad it was probably a hate crime. "I'm the fucking cold-fucking-north-fucking-wind, pal! I'll fucking huff, and puff, and blaw your fucking hoose doon, so's ah wull!"

From a pocket, he produced the silver pen he'd given to Hoon back in the office, and waggled it like it was a magic wand.

"This is the big city, Mr Hoon, not downtown Jocksville. We've got technology here. Gadgets. Proper spy shit. I've had people listening to every word you've said."

He chuckled and dropped the pen on the table alongside the metal bowl. "I must say, you've got quite a way with words. You've certainly broadened my vocabulary. I'm thinking of putting some of them in a book." He swiped a hand through the air like the arc of a rainbow. "I think I'll call it, '*Hoonerisms.*' Of course, it'll have to be published posthumously, but I smell a bestseller."

Hoon blinked, then made a little circle of surprise with his mouth. "Oh. Sorry, were you talking to me there? Didn't hear a word. I've been sitting here wondering whose fucking teeth they are."

"Aha! Yes. I thought that was a nice touch. The Prof here collects them. Or... 'collects' isn't quite the right word. 'Harvests,' maybe," Balls explained.

Behind him, the man in the apron and gloves smiled bashfully. Balls pointed to the side of his own head, twirled a finger, and crossed his eyes.

"Useful man to have around, though. You'd be amazed at the things he can find out. He can get blood out of a stone, this one. They call him 'The Professor,' like he's a man of science, but personally?" He leaned in closer to Hoon and let his voice become a whisper. "I think he's more of an artist."

The DCI winked, then straightened and stepped back, folding his arms in front of him. "He's going to get you to tell us what you know about the Loop, Mr Hoon. *Everything* you know."

"The fuck's the Loop?" Hoon asked.

Balls laughed and wagged a finger. "Nice try. But playing dumb doesn't suit you." He walked around behind Hoon and patted him on the shoulder. "I get it. You're a big man with a reputation to think about. You don't want the likes of me watching you crying your eyes out and begging for mercy. Straight face, stiff upper lip, show no emotions! That's the military way, isn't it?"

Hoon craned his neck, following the DCI as he paced all the way around him and back to the front again. "Let me out of this chair and I'll show you my fucking emotions alright, you dog-cocked pair of tits."

Balls licked the point of an imaginary pencil and mimed writing that one down. "Dog-cocked pair of tits. Lovely. That's a keeper," he said, then he gestured to the man he'd called the Professor. "We're going to leave you in his capable hands. Just the two of you, so you can be free to really share how you feel without fear of being judged. I appreciate that it might take time, but rest assured that you will talk. Eventually, you'll tell us everything you know. It'd be easier for all of us if you still had a tongue when that happened."

"Aye, well, joke's on you, pal," Hoon spat. "Because I know fuck all."

There was a moment of silence, then Balls raised his eyebrows and clicked his tongue against the back of his teeth. "Well, we'll see, I suppose."

He stepped aside and gave the bald man a nod. The Professor's face lit up, revealing all the gaps and overlaps of his uneven teeth. He reached below the table. Hoon watched as a battered old red leather doctor's bag was placed next to the stainless steel bowl with a *thunk* and a rattle of metal.

"What did you do with her?" Hoon demanded. "Where is she? Where's Caroline?"

Balls laughed again. "I'm not some Bond villain here, Mr Hoon. I'm not going to go on at length about who we are and what we do." He shrugged. "And, to be honest, I can't actually remember which one she was. Their faces all become a bit interchangeable after a while. You know? They sort of blend together into one."

He caught the impatient look from the Professor, and held his hands up, backing away. "But, I've said my part. Time for me and *balloon man* here—I like that, by the way. Funny stuff. Time for us to go and let you two get on with things."

He turned as if to leave, then did a full spin to face Hoon again. "Oh! By the way, we can't risk that you might have shared anything with anyone." He put his arm around the other copper's shoulder. "So this guy right here's going to go and have a word with... Gabriella, was it? Your mate's wife. Who, by the way, you *totally* should've shagged. I was rooting for you there."

The restraints groaned as Hoon's arms tensed. "Don't you fucking dare," he warned.

"He can be quite... not persuasive. Persuasive's not the word. *Forceful*," Balls said. "Although, by the sounds of things, she's crying out for the touch of a real man, so she'll probably enjoy it. Not sure how your bedridden friend will enjoy watching, of course, but I suppose that's the least of his worries."

"Touch her, and I'll kill you," Hoon said, and there was no rage behind it. No bluster. Just a cold statement of fact.

"I think you should be more concerned for your own wellbeing, Mr Hoon," Balls told him. He smiled, then turned to the Professor. "Call once you're done. We'll have someone get rid of him."

The Professor's voice was a breathless sort of giggle, like a nervous teenage boy having his first conversation about sex with a real live girl. "No rush, though?" he asked.

Balls looked Hoon up and down, then shook his head. "No," he said. "You go ahead and take as much time as you like."

CHAPTER THIRTY-SIX

CLACK.

It wasn't quite true that the Professor didn't enjoy foreplay. In fact, he took great pleasure in it, although only this one particular kind.

Click.

He hummed quietly to himself—an upbeat tune that Hoon found familiar, but couldn't quite place.

Mind you, he wasn't giving it his full attention.

Clunk.

A pair of needle-nose pliers were placed on the table beside a scalpel and a set of tweezers. The Professor took a moment to adjust their positioning, spacing them evenly and lining them up against some imagined marking on the wood.

Then, he reached back into the bag, took out a small, hand-operated drill, and set it down with the rest of his tools.

"Quite a fucking collection you've got there," Hoon told him.

A plastic cylinder full of wooden cocktail sticks came out next. The Professor rattled them next to his ear and listened, like he was checking they were still good, then placed them on the table.

A nutcracker was brought out next, and Hoon was suddenly very aware of his nudity.

"I've told you, I don't know anything," Hoon said.

The Professor shrugged. "I don't care," he said, then he went back to humming.

Something stirred at the back of Hoon's mind. Recognition flickered.

"What is that fucking tune, by the way?" he asked. "Is that the theme to *Casualty*?"

"I don't know," the Professor admitted, then he put one of his gloved fingers to his lips and called for silence.

Hoon spent a few moments wondering where the blood on the torturer's hands had come from, since it hadn't been from Balls, then decided it was probably best not to dwell on it.

"Tell you what, pal, I'm going to cut you a deal," Hoon said. "It's a juicy fucking offer, too, so I suggest you pin back your ears and listen."

A small block of wood was brought out of the bag, followed by another. The Professor knocked them together, smiled at the sound they made, then put them down on the increasingly cluttered table.

"Here's the deal," Hoon said, persevering. "Let me go, and I won't kill you." He replayed that in his head, then quickly offered a correction. "Sorry, I mean I *might not* kill you. Depends how quickly you get me out of these ropes."

The other man smirked, his crooked mouth twisting up at one end and down at the other. He said nothing, just kept on humming and producing items from his bag. A hacksaw. A toffee hammer. A guitar string.

"I don't have a lot of fucking time here, pal, so last chance. Yes or no. Are you going to let me go?"

The Professor shook his head, swishing his straggly horse-shoe of grey hair. "Why would I do that? We haven't even started."

He took a small dropper bottle from his bag, squeezed the rubbery bulb at the top, then removed the lid. A gloved hand was placed on Hoon's forehead. A bloody thumb forced back an eyelid. The dropper came closer.

"I'm fucking warning you, pal," Hoon hissed. "Last chance."

"Yes. You said that, already," the Professor whispered. "Now, hold still, please."

The shock of the liquid came first, but the pain overtook it almost at once. Burning him. Blinding him.

Hoon hissed through his teeth, threw himself back and forth in the chair, muscles bulging, ropes burrowing furrows into his flesh.

He tried to push back the pain. Bury it down, but it was like nothing he'd ever felt. Nothing he'd ever known. Every time he thought the burning had reached its peak, it doubled again. Tripled. His hiss became a roar, became a howl, became a scream. He spat blood and obscenities at the man with the dropper bottle, beams of concentrated hatred spewing from his one good eye.

"That deal is right out the fucking window now, by the way," he seethed between pulses of agony. "I'm no' just going to fucking kill you now, I'm going to cut you into pieces and post them to your maw in wee Jiffy bags. I'm going to make you into an advent calendar for the shrivelled old bastard. A finger or a toe behind every fucking door."

"That would only be twenty doors," the Professor

pointed out. He chuckled drily. "And my mother is quite, quite dead."

"Aye, and I bet you keep her mummified corpse in the attic," Hoon shot back. "And wank yourself off with her rotten cadaver of a hand, you grotty wee fuck."

The Professor studied him for a few moments, then returned the stopper to the bottle, and placed it on the table.

"On second thoughts," he said. "I think I want you to watch."

His hand hovered above the tools he'd set out on the tabletop. He began whispering under his breath. *"Eenie, meanie, minie, mo, catch a tiger by the toe, if it squeals, let it go, eenie, meanie, minie..."* The hand stopped above the pack of wooden cocktail sticks. *"...mo."* He clapped enthusiastically, his rubber gloves slapping together. "Yay. These are always fun. They fit in so many different places."

He made a show of unscrewing the lid. Plastic squeaking on plastic. Twist. Twist. Twist.

Pop.

He let them spill out into the metal bowl alongside the two teeth, then plucked one out and squinted as he studied the point.

"You fancy doing me a favour and cleaning my fingernails when you're down there?" Hoon asked. "They're mockit."

The Professor smiled, but there was irritation in it. This wasn't how it was supposed to go. He shouldn't be kidding around. This was a serious business, and the man in the chair just was not respecting the process.

But he would. Soon enough.

"Do you know how many nerve endings there are beneath each fingernail?" he asked, squatting in front of

Hoon. His fingers crept up Hoon's bare thigh like a spider, *incy-wincying* their way up his torso and onto his arm.

"Not off the top of my head, no," Hoon admitted.

"Nor me," the Professor said. He leaned in closer. Close enough that Hoon could smell him. He smelled of cleaning fluid, and of old milk, and of suffering. His voice became something soft. Sensual, almost. "Perhaps we could count them together?"

Hoon lunged. Twisted his head. Snapped his jaws tight shut.

He felt the sickeningly satisfying sensation of his teeth piercing flesh and tearing through cartilage. Tasted coppery warmth on his tongue.

With a growl of triumphant fury, he tore his grisly prize free, then leaned back his head and spat it up towards the ceiling tiles overhead.

The Professor fell back, hands clutched to his face, blood fountaining from the fleshy stump that had, until recently, been his nose. He squealed like a piglet being dragged off for slaughter, his feet kicking frantically as he tried to backpedal away from the man who had caused him this pain.

Hoon clenched his fists. Steeled himself. Whoever had tied him knew plenty about knots. Fortunately, they knew fuck all about common sense, and even less about chairs.

He struggled onto his feet, bent double like an inverted uppercase L. He picked a wall behind him. Ran at it, roaring to prepare himself for the impact and the pain.

They came in quick succession, the force of the collision slamming the chair into his back, slapping it against his arse cheeks, and jolting his arms up into his shoulders. Wood cracked, but the chair held firm, not ready to give up without a fight.

Through the shock, and the snot, and the tears, the Professor saw what Hoon was up to, and dragged himself to his feet. His apron, which was no stranger to blood, now shone with streaks of his own. He clattered around on the table, hands grasping like claws until they found the scalpel.

He ran as Hoon drove the chair back against the wall for a second time. A third. His body screamed at him, begging him to stop, demanding he let it rest.

The Professor's hand drew back. The scalpel blade glinted in the glow of the overhead lights.

And then, with a *shuck*, a six-inch sliver of wood was buried in the side of his neck, and burst out through the tunnel of his windpipe.

Hoon held it there, keeping the Professor upright, but at arm's length. The scalpel slipped from the Prof's blood-slicked fingers and landed, point down, in the lino.

He gargled. Wheezed. Mouth moving, eyes rolling back.

The piece of wood that was sticking through his throat was the armrest support of the chair, the arm itself still tied securely to Hoon's wrist.

Hoon waited until the other man's legs started to buckle, then yanked the wood free. Blood came in a heavy gush, then a finer spray. Hoon let it wash over him, speckling his bare skin. He watched as the Professor's legs gave way and he folded to his knees. There was a gurgling like a drain backing up, then the torturer flopped backwards until the top of his head touched the floor behind him.

He balanced there, motionless but for the flapping of his lips and the spraying of his blood, then gravity pulled him sideways, and he thumped down onto the floor.

Hoon breathed. That was important. That was the first thing. Breathe. Wait. Hold, don't act. Don't panic. Let the thoughts settle first. He'd killed a man, yes, but it was the most clear-cut case of self-defence he'd ever come across. Manslaughter charge at worst. A medal and a congratulatory handshake at best. Neither one something he'd care to face, but manageable.

He breathed. Let his pulse slow. His thoughts settle.

They settled on Gabriella and Welshy, and he knew he'd wasted all the time he could spare.

He hunted the room for his clothes, but they were nowhere to be seen. There was still light spilling under the door from the adjoining room, so he headed for that, safe in the knowledge that if anyone was through there, they'd likely have come running when the Professor had started screaming.

Still, better safe than sorry. He took a detour, grabbed the scalpel from the floor where it had fallen, and nudged the door open.

The main warehouse made him think of a makeshift military field hospital, with a dozen cubicles formed from grubby white sheets draped from a crisscrossing network of washing lines.

The place was eerily silent, but for the slow, monotonous humming of the overhead air conditioning. The chill pushed down, and the movement of the air made the bottoms of the hanging sheets drift back and forth above the floor like ghosts.

He found his clothes in a pile just inside the door. No phone, of course. That would be too simple.

The fire in his eye had dulled now, an ongoing stream of water from it working to cleanse whatever had been sprayed there. The vision in it was still mostly shot, though, and he missed a trouser leg twice before finally managing to step into it.

Once dressed, he forced his feet down into his boots, picked up the scalpel again, and wasted a few more seconds looking in the closest cubicles.

There was an attempt at a bed on the floor. A few dirty blankets on a thin plastic mattress, all twisted and knotted together. They smelled of sweat, and sex, and other bodily fluids. Two iron rungs had been cemented into the floor on either side, their dull grey surfaces scratched and scraped by something metal pulling against them.

"Jesus Christ," Hoon whispered.

He pulled aside the next sheet and found another cubicle almost identical to this one. Same excuse for a bed. Same fixing points for the restraints that must've been used to keep women here.

There were a couple of used needles on the floor, and an open wrap of something that might have been speed, or cocaine.

He stepped out of the cubicle, anger bubbling like lava deep down in his gut.

"Hello?" he called, and his voice rumbled like an oncoming storm. "Is there anyone here? I'm here to help."

He listened to the melancholy tune of the air conditioning, as all the raggedy ghosts swayed back and forth above the floor.

———

Gabriella opened her eyes, stared blankly at her husband lying in his bed, then woke fully with a snort and a start.

She looked around, taking a moment to fully get her bearings. She'd fallen asleep in the room with him. Again. It was becoming a habit. He liked her being here with him while he fell asleep. Even without words, he'd made that clear. She didn't even have to say or do anything, he just liked having her presence there with him in the room. Felt better knowing that she was there.

It helped with the nightmares, too.

She put a hand on the back of her neck, supporting it as she sat fully upright. She'd learned that lesson the hard way more than once before.

There was a string of drool on her chin. She wiped it away on a sleeve, muttered a quiet, "Classy," to herself, then squinted at the curtains.

Dark. Still late, then. She checked her watch, and after some whispered calculations, she was able to work out that the time was a little after three.

Odd.

Usually, when she nodded off in here, she'd sleep right through until morning, then wake up feeling like she'd been in some sort of industrial accident. That was what being a full-time carer did to you—left you so exhausted at the end of the day that you could fall fast asleep on a washing line with less than twenty seconds notice.

Waking up before the sun was up was rare. Something must've woken her.

She got up, crept to the bed, and listened to Gwynn's breathing. Slow, but steady. Not snoring, either, which was a refreshing change.

Not that, then.

She caught sight of her phone resting on the arm of the chair, just as the screen went dark.

Bingo.

Yawning, she plodded back to the chair, picked up the phone, and checked the screen. She experienced a brief spell of emotional turmoil—shame, guilt, annoyance, and a touch of excitement—when she saw Hoon's name there.

A message icon blinked. She tapped it, and stretched while she read the text.

'Coming over. Need your help with something. Sorry so late. Emergency.'

Gabriella read the text again, then once more to be absolutely certain that her half-asleep brain had understood everything correctly.

She tapped out a short response—'Fine. But keep noise down. Gwynn sleeping'—then, she slipped the phone into the pocket of her pyjamas, headed for the kitchen, and began brewing up a pot of coffee.

She was halfway through another yawn when the response came.

'Great,' it said. 'I'll be with you very soon.'

CHAPTER THIRTY-SEVEN

THE CAR WAS GONE. Of course it was. Not that he had the keys, anyway.

Hoon stumbled through the mostly dark industrial estate, his lungs on fire, his nostrils choked up with blood once more.

The night air was cold. It cut into him, sharpening his senses. Or most of them, anyway. The liquid that had been squirted into his eye was still hampering his sight, turning the occasional working streetlight into a flickering candle with a brilliant aura that smeared across the darkness when he moved his head.

His peripheral vision on that side was completely shot, so he wasn't aware of the car until he staggered out onto the road and heard the screech of tyres and the blasting of a horn. He turned then, hand raised to shield both eyes from the glowering glow of the headlights.

He let out a sharp cry of surprise when he saw the car. Big. Black. A glowing sign on top announcing it as a taxi. A lucky break. High bloody time.

The driver was mouthing something when Hoon limped around to the side door. He found it locked, and when he saw his reflection in the glass, he couldn't exactly blame the driver for not being in a rush to let him inside.

His wallet was still in his trousers. He produced his fake warrant card and pressed it against the driver's window. Held up a bundle of notes, too, to sweeten the deal.

The driver's jaw clenched. He was an older guy. Overweight and balding. Tired, too, by the looks of it. Too tired to argue, it turned out.

The door unlocked. Hoon practically fell inside, spitting out the address as he manhandled the sliding door shut.

"You alright, mate?" the driver asked, turning in the chair.

"Oh aye, I'm all fucking candy drops and unicorn cocks," Hoon spat back.

"You look like you need a hospital."

Hoon flopped onto the back seats. "I need you to shut the fuck up and drive, is what I need."

The driver gave him a quick once over, then shrugged, faced front, and pulled away.

Slouching on the seats, Hoon took a moment to assess the damage.

His ribs were fucked. Nothing he could do about them. His eye was getting better, but it was a slow process. The pain was manageable, though, so that was something.

His nose? Probably broken. His back, shoulders, and both arse cheeks had taken a right skelping from the chair when he'd smashed it against the wall. The pain there was just getting warmed up, he thought.

His wrists were two red welts of rope burns, one side of

his face was swollen and in the process of turning some exciting new colours, and his shoes were on the wrong feet.

That last one, he could fix, at least, although it took far more effort than he'd have liked.

He sat back and shut his eyes again. The inside of the cab was spinning in big dizzying circles around him, and he had to fight to bring it under control.

"How long until we get there?" he asked, eyes still shut.

"Ten minutes. It ain't far," the driver said. "You sure I can't take you to the hospital first?"

"I'm sure. Just drive," Hoon told him. "And give me a shot of your phone, will you?"

"You what? My phone?"

"Aye, your phone," Hoon said, forcing his eyes open. The floor of the taxi was rolling like the deck of a ship in a storm. An improvement, but only just.

"Who are you going to call?" the driver asked.

Hoon opened his mouth to reply, then closed it again. Who *was* he going to call? Whose number did he know? Not Gabriella's. Not Chuck's. Not even Logan's, up the road. He couldn't call the polis, because he didn't know who was involved, or who he could trust.

There was no one he could call in. No one he could turn to.

It was just him, then. Just him and anyone stupid enough to get in his way.

That suited him just fine.

"Forget it," he told the man up front. "Just drive. And don't spare the horses."

———

He tossed a sweaty fistful of notes in the driver's direction, half-fell out of the taxi, and went racing up the path towards the house. There was a car parked out on the street. The lights in the house were on. The front door was ajar.

He was too slow. Too late.

Too old.

"Gabriella! Welshy!" He flew through the door like it wasn't there, drawing the scalpel from the pocket where he'd stashed it.

There was a sound from the kitchen. A sob. A whimper. A groan. He barrelled along the hallway, all his own pain pushed from his mind by a growing panicky dread.

He found Gabriella in the corner, backed up against the kitchen worktops. She had a coffee pot in one hand—empty but for a half-inch of liquid and a few wisps of steam--and a cast-iron paella pan in the other.

Her head jerked up as Hoon skidded into the room, her face crumpling at the sight of him, her eyes welling up with tears.

"What happened? What happened?" he asked, hurrying to her.

He almost tripped over the man lying face down on the floor in a puddle of coffee and blood. Even from that angle, with only half the guy's face visible, and eyelids fluttering like the wings of an epileptic butterfly, Hoon recognised him as the loudmouth bastard who'd beaten him back at the warehouse.

"Fuck me, did you kill balloon man?" he asked.

The paella pan clanged and the coffee pot smashed as Gabriella lost her grip on both. Her legs seemed to give way and she fell into Hoon's arms, her body heaving with big, silent sobs.

"You're alright. You're alright," he told her, awkwardly patting her back and smoothing her hair.

"He came to the door. I thought he was you," she said, almost every word punctuated by a shaky breath. "He forced his way inside. So I ran. In here. And he came in. He came in, and I... I...."

"Fucking mangled the prick?" Hoon said. It perhaps wasn't the exact phrasing Gabriella herself would have used, but she nodded anyway. "You did good. You did really good," he assured her. "Is Welshy alright?"

"I... I think so. I... God. I'd better check." She wiped her tears on the heel of a hand.

Hoon rubbed her upper arms and arranged his face into something that might almost pass for a smile, provided you didn't look too closely.

"Maybe go in and shut the door. Pop some music on," he suggested. "But before you do that..." He glanced down at the semi-conscious figure on the floor. "I don't suppose you have such a thing as gaffer tape?"

————

Balloon Man woke up to find himself in quite the predicament.

He was still on the floor, roughly in the same spot he had landed after being scalded with hot coffee and then *whanged* across the temple with a cast-iron pan.

Since then, though, his situation had worsened considerably.

He was naked, for one thing. Half his face, one shoulder, one arm, and both knees were all in contact with the cool lino. His wrists had been tightly secured to his ankles, forcing him to thrust his bare arse aloft, presenting it like some sort of religious offering.

Terror compelled him to waste twenty seconds and a lot of energy trying to free himself, but the layers of silver tape refused to relent.

"Detective Sergeant Willoughby," said a voice from elsewhere in the room. The accent made his blood turn to ice in his veins. Scottish.

Oh God.

Oh God, no.

A pair of battered old military-style boots *clumped* into his line of sight. A pair of ageing knees creaked, and DS Willoughby's worst nightmare lowered himself into view.

"*Kevin*," Hoon continued, reading from the other man's ID. "Good to be properly introduced at last. I was really hoping that the two of us might get a chance to rekindle our relationship at some point. And look." He gestured between them both, grinning cheerfully. "Here we fucking are! Just like old times, too. Albeit, I'm no longer the one stripped naked and tied up."

He tilted his head so it was at a similar angle to Willoughby's. "By the way, I wouldn't make any sudden movements, if I were you. Trust me. It could cause you a whole fucking pile of problems."

Hoon leaned in closer and put the back of his hand next to his mouth like he was sharing a big secret. "There's a big kitchen funnel up your arsehole," he whispered.

Willoughby's eyes widened. He yelped, and then appeared to realise for the first time that his mouth had been taped shut.

Hoon gave him a friendly pat on the shoulder, then stood

up again. The Detective Sergeant's eye swivelled, desperately trying to follow him.

"Why have I put a plastic kitchen funnel up your jacksy, Kevin? That's a very good fucking question," Hoon said. "I actually asked myself the same thing while I was mid-insert. 'What the fuck are you doing this for?' I said to myself. 'This is fucking mental, even for you.'"

He chuckled, as if recalling some fond memory. Elsewhere in the house, music played, and jarringly cheerful it was, too.

"But why do we do anything, I suppose?" Hoon continued. "Why do we climb big fucking mountains, or wriggle around in underground potholes, or dive to the bottom of the sea? Because *we can*. Sometimes, that's all the reason we need, us lot. People, I mean. Why do we climb Mount Everest? Because it's fucking *there*. And so, for that matter, was your arse."

He paced around the kitchen. Willoughby couldn't see what he was doing, but he heard the clinking of glass containers being set, one by one, onto a worktop.

"Anyway, don't you waste a fucking moment worrying that a plastic funnel has been carefully inserted into your rectum, Kevin," Hoon suggested. "Maybe worry instead about what I'm going to pour into it. Because Gabriella— remember her? The woman you came here to rape and murder? Turns out she's got a very well-stocked pantry, and extremely exotic tastes."

There was a pause while he picked up a glass jar filled with a dark red jelly, and read the label.

"What's a Carolina Reaper, do you think?" he wondered. "It says it's two-point-two million SHU. Fuck knows what that means. Lot of exclamation marks after it, though. And that wee skull and crossbones can't be good."

Willoughby could only listen to the lid being unscrewed, and the subsequent gasp from the man holding the jar.

"Fuck me pink!" Hoon coughed. "That'll put hairs on your chest. And that's just the fucking smell. I can't imagine eating this. Or, for that matter, having an entire jar spooned up my arsehole."

There was a rumbling, then a click from elsewhere in the room. "And there's the kettle boiled," Hoon cheered. "That'll be the sort of palette cleanser between courses, I'm thinking. A wee half-pint of boiling water here and there, just to help things along."

Down on the floor, the DS whimpered behind his tape. The half of his face that was visible was red and blistered from where the steaming hot coffee had hit it. The pan had struck him on the opposite side, and blood smeared the lino as he squirmed.

"Honestly, Kev, I wouldn't move around too much, if I were you," Hoon warned. He pointed to the detective's raised back end. "If you fall and land on that thing, that's going right up you. It'll be like an open fucking manhole back there. You'll have guys from Thames Water climbing in and out of you at all hours of the day and night. So, maybe best you stay still, eh?"

He waited until Willoughby's squirming had abated, then gave him a big broad smile of encouragement. "Thatta boy," he said, then he squatted down again. "Here's what's going to happen, Kev."

He placed the open jar of red jelly on the floor by Willoughby's face. His eyes began to water immediately, and his breath got backed up somewhere in the scorched lining of his nose.

"I'm going to ask you a series of questions. If you answer one, I move on to the next, and everyone's happy. If you don't answer, or I think you're fucking lying to me, then I insert one or more unpleasant items into your lower intestines via your gaping rectal passage. I vaguely remember being told ginger is a good one for arses, so we'll probably start with that and work up to this Reaper stuff, but who knows? I might surprise us and go big early on." He shrugged. Smiled with the eyes of a maniac. "We'll just play it by ear, will we?"

He gave all that a moment to bed down, and watched Willoughby's face until he felt he'd had enough time to process it all.

"Right, first question," Hoon said. He placed a teaspoon into the jar of jelly with a *sploonk*. "What's the square root of eighty-one?"

What could be seen of Willoughby's brow creased. His eyes, which were streaming now, darted left and right in tiny twitches, like they didn't know which of Hoon's to settle on.

"No?" Hoon said.

Willoughby mumbled behind the tape, a series of frantic, muffled protests.

"I can't hear you, Kev. Speak up," Hoon said, touching a finger to his ear.

The detective's protests became louder and more desperate. A bare shoulder slapped against the lino as he went back to struggling with his bonds.

"Shite. The tape. Sorry," Hoon said. He caught one corner and pulled sharply. Willoughby's lips were stretched out, then snapped back into place again.

"Fuck! Don't! Don't!" he sobbed. "You can't do this!"

"Square root of eighty-one, Kevin. Clock's fucking ticking here, pal."

"I don't know! I don't know!"

Hoon made a clicking noise from the side of his mouth. "That's unfortunate," he sighed, snatching up the jar and getting to his feet.

"Wait! Wait! Don't! I'll tell you what you want to know!"

"I want to know the square fucking root of eighty-one, Kevin. And you're telling me you don't know!"

"Eight! It's eight. No, nine! Nine! It's nine, it's nine!

"Which one?"

"Nine!"

Hoon hesitated, spoon half out of the jar. "You sure? Final answer?"

"Yes! Yes! It's nine," Willoughby wheezed.

"Aye, well, I'll take your word for it," Hoon said. He squatted again. "Good, Now you understand the rules, let's start playing properly. You were keeping people in that warehouse. Where are they now?"

A battle erupted behind Willoughby's eyes, fear forming the ranks on either side.

"They'll kill me if I tell you," he whispered.

Hoon slapped his thighs. "Right, I actually think the boiling water first," he said. "Get things warmed up in there before the main course."

"N-no, no. Please, don't!" Willoughby begged.

"Then answer the fucking question, son," Hoon instructed.

"I mean it. They'll kill me. They'll kill my wife. My parents. They'll kill them all."

Hoon leaned in closer. He rested a hand on the other

man's scalded cheek. The levity that he'd been affecting fell away. The words that came out were a solemn lament.

"And what?" he asked. "Do you think I won't?"

He held eye contact. Stroked a thumb across the bridge of Willoughby's nose, wiping away a tear, and watched an expression of horror settle on the detective's face.

"Now, let's try that again," Hoon told him. "From the fucking top."

CHAPTER THIRTY-EIGHT

GABRIELLA JUMPED TO HER FEET, shielding her husband who lay awake in the bed behind her.

"Oh, thank God," she whispered, when Hoon entered the room and closed the door behind him. "You're OK. I mean, you look... But you're OK. Yes?"

"Well, I've been in better shape," Hoon admitted. "But aye, I'm dandy. What about you two?"

"Fine. He's... We're both fine," Gabriella said. She stepped aside, revealing Welshy lying at an angle so his shoulder was pressed against the metal bars of the bed guard. It looked uncomfortable. "He tried to get up. To help," Gabriella explained. "I couldn't get him propped up again on my own."

"Here. Let me," Hoon said. He crossed to the bed and caught his old pal under the arm. "Ready, Welshy?"

Gwynn's one good eye fixed on him. A low grunt fell from the pull at the side of his mouth. Hoon recognised it as a yes. Or took it as one, at least.

"Right, here we go," he said, then he grimaced as he

heaved Welshy back up onto his pillow, and tried to pretend that the movement hadn't dropped a napalm bomb on his ribcage. "There you are. Much better."

He leaned on the railing for support, lowered his head for a moment while he got his breath back, then half-turned so he could address both husband and wife at the same time.

"I'm really fucking sorry about this," he said. "I had no idea you two were going to end up getting involved."

He felt a hand slap down on his. Fingers tightened as far as they were able, squeezing his own. He looked at the man in the bed to find no blame or anger there.

"Did you get what you needed?" Gabriella asked.

Hoon nodded. "I think so, aye. I think I know where I need to go."

"To find Caroline?"

Hoon blew out his cheeks. "That, I don't know. But they've got other people, too. Women. Her age. Younger, even. I think I know where they are."

He hoped he'd find Caroline with them. At the same time, given what he'd seen back at the warehouse, a part of him desperately hoped he didn't.

"So, what now? Are you going to call the police?"

Hoon shook his head. "Can't trust them. That bastard in your kitchen? He's polis."

Gabriella's eyes went to the door, her face going pale. "What? But... I threw coffee in his face! I knocked him out! I can't go to jail. I can't!"

"And you won't," Hoon promised. "He's a dodgy bastard. Tied up in all sorts of shite. Only one going to jail here is him. But, that's going to have to wait until I get back."

"Back?"

"Aye. I need to go help those women."

"Yes, but... what? You're leaving him here? Just sitting there in the kitchen?"

"Well, he's no' sitting, exactly," Hoon said, scratching the back of his head. "But aye. For the moment. Maybe just don't go in until I get back?" he suggested. "Although, if you do, he might mention something about having a funnel sticking out his arse. Probably a side effect of the fucking brain damage you gave him with that frying pan. Just agree. Humour him. It'll keep him from trying anything."

"Jesus," Gabriella whispered, then she looked at her husband and nodded like he'd given confirmation. "Fine. I won't go in until you're back."

"Perfect."

"But what if you don't come back?"

"Thanks for the vote of confidence," Hoon said, scowling. "I'll be back, don't you worry about that. But, eh..."

"What?" Gabriella asked. "What is it?"

"Welshy. I remember he brought back a few... souvenirs over the years. Did he keep them, do you know?"

"Guns, you mean? And no. He handed them in. There was an amnesty."

Hoon tutted. "Damn."

"I made him. I didn't want them in the house," Gabriella explained.

In the bed beside them, Welshy made a sound like he was clearing his throat.

"Aye, fair enough," Hoon conceded.

"They were dangerous," Gabriella said.

"Says the woman who just scalded and brained a fucking policeman."

"*And* illegal."

"Would've been handy, though, considering I'm about to

go storm a building full of nasty bastards. No' sure a cafetière and some non-stick cookware'll do the job this time."

Welshy grunted. It was a two-syllable sound, and there was a sense of urgency to it that drew the attention of the others.

"You alright, Welshy?" Hoon asked.

Gwynn's good eye went to his wife, then raised to the ceiling. He grunted again. Twice.

"Upstairs? What's upstairs?" Gabriella asked.

Welshy was still staring at Hoon as his head twitched. Shook.

"Not upstairs? Further? The loft?"

The man in the bed's eye widened. He exhaled sharply, like some great effort had taken its toll.

"What? You'd better not have bloody kept any!" Gabriella warned him.

Welshy shot his wife the briefest of sideways looks, and even Hoon could read the apology there.

Gabriella rubbed her temples like she was nursing a headache. "God," she muttered. "Boys with their bloody toys."

Hoon grinned. "Aye, he's a sly bastard this one. You've got to fucking watch him," Hoon said, giving his old pal's hand a squeeze. He looked up at the ceiling, then back to the man in the bed. "One other thing, Welshy," he said. "Any chance I could raid your wardrobe?"

———

He'd found it in a hard plastic case at the bottom of a cardboard box, tucked away in the corner of the attic. It lay on Gabriella's unmade bed now, fastened in its case so she at least wouldn't have to look at it if she came in. No need to rub her face in her husband's betrayal, minor as Hoon considered it.

Taking souvenirs had been normal, back in the day. Expected, even. He had his own assortment of contraband weapons and ammunition stashed away up the road, where no bugger would ever find them. Foreign stuff, mostly. An AK-47, an old German Luger pistol, and half a dozen others that he couldn't remember off the top of his head.

Nothing to compare with what he'd found hidden in Welshy's loft, though. Nothing even close.

After leaving the forces, Welshy had gone freelance. There was always some organisation or foreign government looking for men with his sort of experience and skillset. He'd travelled the world—business class, no less—fighting other people's wars in return for far healthier paycheques than Her Majesty's Armed Forces had ever given him.

Hoon had no idea where Welshy had got his hands on the gun currently sitting on the bed, nor what the story was behind it. He could only assume that it was an absolute belter.

They were roughly the same size, Hoon and Welshy, and they shared a similar dress sense. The outfit Hoon had assembled from the other man's wardrobe was mostly made up of shades of black, from the combat trousers to the dyed NATO jacket bought from some army surplus store somewhere.

Plenty of pockets, too. That was never a bad thing.

He zipped up the jacket, finished transferring everything he needed from his own pockets to those of his borrowed clothes, then checked himself in the mirror.

The clothes looked decent, but his face was still a mess of bruising and dried blood. "It's like the *Milk Tray* man was in a fucking industrial accident," he mumbled, then a knock came and the bedroom door opened an inch or two.

"You decent?" Gabriella asked.

"Aye. In you come," Hoon replied, turning to face her.

She made it halfway into the room, then stopped when she saw him, a little jolt of shock momentarily staggering her.

"God. You look just like him," she said. "Welshy, I mean." She smiled, then held a hand up, blocking out Hoon's head. "If I do that."

"Oh aye, we're dead ringers if you do that," he agreed.

"You look good," she told him, then she blushed and directed her gaze at her feet. "And... listen. About what happened. What I... did."

"Forget it," Hoon told her. "It didn't happen."

She breathed out. Nodded. Only then did she look up, and Hoon could see that she was barely holding herself together.

"Don't die," she urged.

"Wouldn't fucking dream of it," Hoon told her.

She walked towards him, slowly at first, then picking up the pace until she flung her arms around him.

It hurt. A lot.

No way he was telling her that, though.

She crammed a full minute's worth of hugging into a few scant seconds, then turned and walked out the door without looking back.

Hoon waited for her to leave before crossing to the bed.

The plastic latches of the case *clacked* as he prised them free. The lid popped up until the case was open an inch or two. A faint golden glow spilled out onto the floral-patterned duvet cover, brightening as Hoon opened the case the rest of the way.

A Desert Eagle pistol lay nestled in the case, the ceiling light bouncing off its tiger-patterned gold plating. The grip was a tricolour of yellow, blue, and red jewels, forming the flag of Colombia. It was a ridiculous weapon—the sort of thing that could only have belonged to the head of a South American drug cartel or a comic book supervillain.

No wonder Welshy hadn't wanted to hand it in. Thankfully, he hadn't turned in the diamante-encrusted box of fifty cal rounds, either. Hoon filled the mag and the chamber, checked the safety, then tucked the pistol inside the jacket.

He gave himself a final check in the mirror. For the first time in a long time, the man beyond the glass didn't regard him with contempt.

"Right then, gorgeous," he told the other guy. "How's about you and me go fuck some shit up?"

CHAPTER THIRTY-NINE

HE TOOK DS Willoughby's car, and managed to plug the address into the in-built satnav system with only relatively minor difficulty. He'd never much liked driving in London, and being in a strange car wasn't making it any more pleasant. Nor was being partially blind, or having limited mobility due to the various physical traumas he'd had inflicted on him, for that matter.

The address Willoughby had given up was in Hackney, on the same side of the river as Welshy and Gabriella's place. With the thin night traffic, it took a little under fifteen minutes for him to make his way there.

It had been a residential three-storey tower block, part of an estate that had largely been demolished over the previous two years, until cash flow problems with the developers had seen the whole thing put on hold six months earlier.

The last remaining block now stood alone, the ground floor windows and doors boarded up, the frontage a magnet for local graffiti artists to show off their skills.

Or practice them, Hoon suspected, because a lot of the stuff that had been sprayed there was absolute shite.

A complete rip-out of the buildings had clearly started at some point, as there were stacks of baths, sinks, and toilets jammed up against the walls.

For a building surrounded by barbed wire fencing and supposedly empty, the car park was heaving. Three white transit vans stood huddled together against the darkness, their back ends facing the barricaded front door of the block.

There was activity on the second floor, too, where the windows were still glass and not big slabs of plywood. A faint light moved around, briefly darting across the ceiling and walls of one of the rooms up there. A torch.

Hoon took his notebook from his pocket, squinted at the number plates of the vans, and noted them down. Then, he got out of the car, locked it, checked he had everything he needed, and went scurrying through the shadows until he reached the fence.

The gate had been closed behind the vans, but not locked. Hoon opened it just enough to slip himself through, then shut it again.

He took a couple of steps along the fence, then returned to the gate and fastened the padlock, trapping himself.

And, more importantly, trapping everyone else in there with him.

The wooden board had been propped up over the front door so it wasn't currently attached to the frame. Hoon brushed his fingers across the grip of the Desert Eagle, checking it was easily accessible, then he shunted the board aside, backed through the door, and returned the plyboard to where he'd found it.

The hallway held nothing but a darkness so total and

complete that Hoon was unable to even get a sense of the scale of the place. It could stretch on forever, or it could end just beyond the reach of his arms, he had no way of knowing.

To his dismay, his other senses tried to compensate, and the thick, choking stench of rot and decay flooded his nostrils and coated the back of his throat. He buried his mouth and nose in the crook of his elbow, and listened while his eyes adjusted to the lack of light.

There were sounds somewhere ahead and above him. The next floor. Multiple people moving around. Male voices speaking. He couldn't identify the words, just the register. Harsh. Cruel. Taunting.

The black was becoming a murky swamp of charcoal greys, and Hoon could make out the bulk of what looked like the start of a staircase leading up. He made for it, moving as quietly as he could.

But detritus lay scattered across the floor—more by design than accident, he suspected—and there was a whipcrack of breaking glass beneath one of his feet.

He heard movement on his right. Footsteps. The clack of a handle being pushed down. The creak of a door.

A beam of torchlight cut across the hallway and painted the opposite wall in blinding shades of white. Hoon followed the light to its origin, his feet scuffing through the scattered rubbish.

The man with the torch swung it wildly, searching for the source of the sound, and Hoon became a shadow monster on the wall. A mouth opened to cry out. Hoon lunged, driving the tips of his fingers into the man's throat, turning the shout into a breathless gulp.

He was on the guy before he could recover, forehead

shattering his nose, hand clamping down over his mouth, forcing him to choke back his blood, snot, and squeals.

Once he was down, Hoon worked quickly to keep him there, taping his mouth shut, and tying his hands and ankles behind his back. He dragged him back into the flat he'd stepped out of, trailing his squirming body through a sea of plaster dust, and a few crops of mushrooms that had sprouted from the damp carpet.

Hoon abandoned him in what was left of a bathroom, then returned to the hallway and pulled the door closed behind him.

He picked up the torch from where it had fallen. It was a palm-sized black metal number, with a cluster of LED bulbs up front. He kept it turned off for now. Better to let his eyes adjust, and not to announce his presence.

The stairs were bare stone, flanked by rusted metal bannisters on either side. They zig-zagged up to the floor above, turning halfway at a small square landing rather than running straight from one floor to the next.

He stopped at the halfway point, listening to what was happening up above. There were lights up there. Dim ones, granted, but enough to cast shadows on the section of wall that Hoon could see.

He could hear women. Not their voices. Not exactly. But sounds they were making. Groans. Moans. None of it loud. None of it daring to be.

A male voice cut through it, making Hoon retreat to the back of the landing where the shadows were at their thickest.

"Will someone *please* get them to shut the fuck up?" it bellowed.

Balls. He was sure of it. The fucker was here.

Result.

Two other men started shouting, their voices pure London and harsh. Savage, almost.

"Quit your fackin' whining!" spat one.

"You fackin' heard him. Shut up, you dirty slags!"

There was a slap. A grunt. A sob. A whimper.

"L-leave her alone."

A woman's voice. A little slurred, a little shaky.

Silence followed. The men said nothing. Not at first. Even the weeping of the women abated, until the only sound Hoon could hear was the blood whooshing through his veins.

"What did you fackin' say?"

The voice was low. Controlled. Calm, even.

Disturbingly so.

"N nothing."

"Yes, you fackin' did. You got somethin' to say? Fackin' say it."

There was a *snink* of metal. A flick knife, Hoon guessed. It drew a series of desperate whispered pleas from the woman who'd dared to speak out of turn.

"No, no, please, d-don't, no."

Hoon's plan had been simple. Sneak in, get the lay of the land, then take out as many of the fuckers as possible without being spotted.

So much for that idea.

Taking the stairs in three big strides, he shone the torch in the direction the voices had come from, and locked his sights on a weedy-looking twenty-something in ripped jeans and a t-shirt with the word 'Fuck' spelled incorrectly on the front.

The high-powered torch beam was blinding, even in the half-light of the battery-operated lanterns standing in the corners of the upstairs hallway. The twenty-something blinked rapidly, turning Hoon's charge into a series of terrifying snapshots that ended when the circular butt of the torch handle hit him between the eyes, felling him like a tree.

"Jesus Christ!"

Balls' voice came from his right. Fifteen feet away, maybe more.

The more pressing problem was on his left. Sudden movements. Two men. Heavy. Hoon spun, and caught a glimpse of stocky bastards with extendable batons coming racing at him. A third and a fourth man were behind them, hurriedly shoving some bedraggled, dark-eyed women through a couple of open doors into the long-abandoned flats beyond.

Hoon had hoped the baton-wielders would swing wildly, but they knew what they were doing. The first went low, swiping at a knee. Hoon managed to raise a leg in time to block the worst of it, but it rattled across the side of his shin.

In a moment, it would be agony. All the more reason to finish this quickly.

He ducked the second guy's swing, and drove a punch up into his exposed armpit with enough force to dislocate the shoulder. The attacker's baton arm went limp. Hoon shoulder-barged him, and enjoyed the panicky scream and the diminuendo of thumps as he went tumbling down the stone steps.

The first guy was having another go. Hoon closed the gap between them, getting in close, making the baton useless. He swung with the end of the torch, but missed, and caught a glancing punch to his ruined ribs that made his lungs constrict and the floor turn to putty beneath his feet.

He heard another baton being extended. Saw one of the men who'd been shepherding the women through the doors stoop to pick up the fallen flick knife.

Balls was shouting something. Barking orders. But Hoon couldn't make out the words over the roaring in his ears.

Three of them. Tooled up. Younger than he was. Probably fitter, too.

Part of him wanted to fight them—to throw himself in there amongst the bastards, fists flying, teeth snapping at anything that came within biting reach.

Another part of him would've preferred to give up. To surrender to whatever came next. To rest. Just for a moment. Just for a while.

He compromised. The boom of the Desert Eagle filled the hallway, the fireball from its muzzle momentarily revealing the full decay of the hall.

Blood sprayed. The guy who'd punched Hoon went horizontal in the air, then landed on his front before he had quite worked out what the hell was happening.

And then, as the echo of the gunshot faded, he clutched his shin, opened his mouth, and screamed like his life depended on it.

The man who had picked up the knife dropped it again immediately, and thrust both hands up above his head. His friend was less compliant, though. He'd already started his attack run, and it was too late to back out now.

Instead, he doubled down, raising the baton above his head with both hands like it was the hammer of Thor, and roaring as he made his charge.

Hoon pivoted, avoiding the downwards swing of the baton. His leg swept out, knocking the attacker off-balance and sending him crashing to his knees.

Placing the gun right by the guy's ear, Hoon pulled the trigger. Shock and pain registered on the man's face, before

Hoon kicked him on the shoulder, smashing him so hard against the wall that he left an indent in the plasterboard.

Over his ringing ears and the sound of his own irregular breathing, Hoon heard the thumping of feet and realised the sneaky little bastard who'd pretended to surrender was on the move.

He spun, the Desert Eagle raised, and the man with the knife skidded to a stop just inches from the end of the gun's barrel. He dropped the knife and raised his hands for a second time.

"I'm sorry! I'm sorry!" he pleaded, eyes crossing and uncrossing as he tried to focus on both the gun and the man holding it at the same time.

Hoon lowered the weapon until it was pointing at the floor, and pulled the trigger. A foot exploded like an overripe watermelon. A second chorus of screaming filled the inside of the abandoned building.

Bringing the gun back up, Hoon turned in Balls' direction, only to find him gone.

"Fuck," he whispered, head snapping from side to side as he searched the gloom.

His eye, still damaged by the burning liquid drops, failed to pick up on the movement to his right. A baton cracked down on his forearm. The gun clattered to the floor.

He tried to turn, to block, to shield himself, but a well-placed kick found his knee, bending it inwards with a *krick*. He staggered, then fell when the tip of the baton caught him across the cheek out of nowhere.

The lights dimmed, then went out for a second. When they came back on, Balls was in mid-flow.

"...persistent bastard, aren't you? I can't even fucking imagine how you found this place, never mind actually got here. You should've been in little pieces by now. Your bollocks should've been in a jar. And yet, here you are."

Hoon struggled his arms into the press-up position, but pain flared along the arm that the baton had connected with, and he immediately collapsed back onto his front.

His eyes went to where the gun had landed on the floor. It was three feet away. An easy lunge and grab under normal circumstances, but in his current condition, it might as well have been on the moon.

Balls was pacing around him, ageing floorboards creaking under his feet, the baton *thwacking* against his palm like it was keeping time with his steps.

"You should've run, Mr Hoon. As soon as you managed to get away from the Professor, you should've run as fast and as far as you could." He stopped pacing for a moment. "Although, it wouldn't have done you any good. You're on their radar now. These people we deal with. They're aware of you, and believe me, that's the last thing you want."

Balls shook his head, tutted several times, then started circling again like a Great White Shark around a hapless swimmer. "You came blundering into all this, but you have no idea, Mr Hoon. Who they are. What they're capable of. And they're everywhere. All around us. The Loop, from the the lowest of the low, to the highest offices in the land. There's nowhere you can go to escape them. Nobody you can trust."

He crouched beside Hoon's head. The screams of the other men had become distant whimpers now, although Hoon couldn't tell if that was due to their pain subsiding or their blood loss. Either way, given how his own head was aching, he was grateful for the relative peace and quiet.

"I'm doing you a favour," Balls told him. "Ultimately, by

killing you now, I'm doing you a good deed. See, if you're dead, you won't have to watch them come for your family. Your friends. Your neighbours. Your fucking *pets*. Because they will. Now that you're on their radar, they will not stop until every trace of you is gone. Until they're sure that there's nobody out there you might have told about them. Because the Loop does not like attention, Mr Hoon. And it goes to extreme lengths to protect its privacy."

Hoon shuffled himself around so he was lying on his back, letting him look into the eyes of the DCI squatting above him.

"What is it?" he wheezed.

Balls raised an eyebrow. "The Loop? Now, there's a complicated question."

"I bet it's no' really," Hoon said. He coughed. "I bet it's a sex thing, innit? It's always a fucking sex thing."

Balls laughed. "I suppose it is, yes. Partly. It's a sex thing. It's a drugs thing. It's a political thing. It's a trafficking thing. It's all these things, and none of them. It's a network, really, that's all. A network of people, each powerful in their own way, but together, unstoppable." He shrugged. "I was investigating it for a while, but when I finally grasped the size of it. The scale. I knew there was nothing I could do. Not to stop it, anyway. And, like they say, if you can't beat 'em...'"

"Here, Empty, I nearly forgot," Hoon said, interrupting the other man's flow.

Balls frowned. "Forgot what?"

"I brought you your pen back," Hoon said.

Balls caught a glimpse of something silver flashing through the air, tucked into Hoon's clenched fist. The pen buried in his thigh, close to his groin. His legs propelled him upwards like a frog springing into the air, but the muscle was compromised by the metal ballpoint sticking out of it, and he fell backwards onto the floor.

Hoon rolled, grabbing for the gun. The heel of Balls' shoe caught him a glancing blow on the side of the head, and his fingers fell short of the target. He tried again, but Balls got there first.

He heard the click of the hammer being pulled back. The room stopped doing loops just in time for him to see the weapon being levelled at his head. Balls held the gun in one shaking hand, the other clutching his thigh just below where the pen was sticking out.

"Wait!" Hoon urged. "Don't. Don't shoot!"

Blood was pooling on the floor beneath the copper. It dribbled between gaps in the crumbling floorboards, and fell like rain into the room below.

"There's something you need to know," Hoon told him, but Balls wasn't listening. He squeezed the trigger. The gun, too heavy for his one trembling hand, let fly with a fifty calibre round that soared several feet above Hoon's head and punched a hole near where the ceiling met a wall.

Cursing, he levelled the gun again, but Hoon heaved himself over the edge of the stairwell and tumbled down into the sea of darkness lurking below.

"Kill you!" Balls hollered. "I'll fucking kill you!"

He dragged himself to his feet on the staircase railing. Blood trickled down the inside of his leg and left a trail behind him as he raised the gun and hobbled down the stairs in search of his prey.

CHAPTER FORTY

HOON WAS the first to admit that he was no doctor, but he had come to the conclusion that, in medical terms, his wrist was fucked. His knee wasn't in good shape, either. It was in the *wrong* shape, for one thing, the angle not conducive to bearing any weight.

The rest of him wasn't faring much better, from his bruised back to his swollen jaw. The blurriness in his right eye was easing, which was good. Unless it just afforded him a better view of the moments before his own death, in which case, he wasn't all that big a fan.

He had crawled into one of the downstairs flats, hoping to find something to defend himself with. Other than a foot-long section of soft foam pipe insulation, though, he'd found nothing in the flat but damp and mould.

He could hear Balls moving around elsewhere on this floor now. He'd thumped down the stairs a few moments ago, and then everything had gone quiet while he listened. So quiet, in fact, that Hoon had started to suspect he might have left, before Balls had shouted up to the whimpering men upstairs to, "Get it to-fucking-gether!"

After that, there had been the creaking of a door opening. Hoon was taking cover in a room that had presumably once been a kitchen, but was now an empty shell with only some rodent-nibbled lino serving as a reminder of its previous life. He had braced himself for Balls to come barging in, but then had heard the DCI moving around on the other side of the wall in the next flat over.

Good. The longer the fucker took to find him, the less blood he'd have in his body when he finally did.

Hoon shifted his weight from one leg to another, leaning on the windowsill for support. The decaying wood crumbled away beneath his hands, throwing his full weight onto his bad leg and drawing a yelp of pain from his lips.

He heard Balls react through the wall, and stumbled clear as two bullets tore through the plaster right where he'd been standing, punching holes in the door leading through to the living room.

The din of them rebounded around the small, empty room, so he didn't hear the front door of the flat opening until it was too late. Didn't hear Balls limping through the hall. Didn't hear a thing until the kitchen door opened and the gun raised, and there was nowhere left to go.

"You're a fucking dead man," Balls spat. "I'm going to fucking kill you."

He was shaking badly, now. The only colour on his face was his red-ringed eyes and a smear of blood from the hand he'd tried to stop the flow with.

The pen was still jammed in. Pity. If he'd pulled it out, he'd almost certainly be dead by now.

Hoon raised his hands for calm. "OK. I get that," he said. "But that gun holds seven bullets. Between us, we've shot six."

"One left," Balls seethed, hand tightening on the grip.

"Check out the fucking maths whizz," Hoon said. "Aye, one left. So, you probably don't want to waste it on me."

Balls' eyes, which had a vague, distracted look to them, narrowed until they found focus. "What?"

Hoon started to laugh, but it became a cough that lit fires up and down his body. "If that stuff you said is true. About the Loop, or whatever the fuck you called them, and how they value their privacy. If that's true, you'll want to keep that bullet."

"Keep it? For what?"

"For yourself," Hoon told him. "See, there's one thing about London that I do like. You can get anything. And no' just that, you can get anything *at any fucking time*. Day or night. You name it, somewhere'll have it. It's dead handy. I'll give it that."

The gun was thrust forward a few inches, the barrel swaying like it was tracking a moving target.

"What are you talking about?" Balls hissed.

Hoon flicked his gaze to the shiny silver ballpoint that was buried in the other man's leg. "That pen you've got stuck into your femoral artery there?" A grin spread across his face, showing the blood congealing in the gaps between his teeth. "That's no' yours. It's mine."

Balls blinked. His eyes flicked to the pen, but only for half a second.

"Bollocks."

"No joke, son. It's the same idea, of course. Wee microphone in it. SIM card so it can transmit everything it hears. The works," Hoon said. "And, I'm pretty sure it'll have picked up every fucking word you've said to me." He shrugged. "Maybe a bit muffled now, mind you, depending on which end the microphone's in, but it'll have got the main points. And you know what that means."

"You're lying!"

Hoon shook his head. "You're fucked, more like. You've no' just spilled the beans to me, you clumpin' fucking fuddhound, you've broadcast it to a very good friend of mine, who right now is relaying the whole kit and caboodle live onto the internet. These 'Loop' pricks are everywhere, you say? Then they know every fucking word you've said. They know you've told the whole world about them, and what they're up to."

Balls shook his head, shaking loose tears that had been building up behind his eyes. "N-no. No," he stammered. "No. You're lying. It's my pen."

"No, it's no'," Hoon insisted.

The gun shook in the DCI's hand. His eyes swam as his blood-starved brain tried to figure out the truth.

"It is. It's my pen. You're lying," he said, the words slurring together. He grabbed the end of the pen and tugged it free, then wiped it on his shirt, cleaning the worst of the blood off it. He forced his eyes to focus long enough to be able to see the name of the hotel stamped on the pen's barrel. "S-see," he mumbled. "T-told you it was..."

The pen and the gun both fell from his hand as his blood sprayed up his body and over the doorframe behind him. He fell straight forwards, like his legs had no knees in them. Hoon managed to limp back enough to avoid being hit by him, then stood by watching as what little life was left in the bastard leaked out onto the rotting kitchen floor.

"Aye, no, right enough," Hoon muttered. "Turns out that actually is your pen, after all."

CHAPTER FORTY-ONE

IT ALL TOOK SOME EXPLAINING. He was taken to the hospital first—him and everyone else in the building.

The men upstairs—the ones still alive, but injured—tried to paint him as the bad bastard, of course. It turned out all of them were polis, and their colleagues might well have believed them had it not been for the word of the twenty-three young women huddling together outside, camera flashes popping as three different press photographers documented the story.

Before the first responders had even shown up, Hoon had phoned the papers. It would be that much harder to make the women disappear again if the story was splashed all over the front pages.

He'd dragged himself up the stairs. They'd cowered at the sight of him, too wasted, conditioned, and afraid to do anything but turn their heads away and hope that whatever he was there to do to them was over quickly.

He had asked them about Caroline. Called out her name.

But he'd been met by hollow stares and silence.

She wasn't there. Whatever had happened to her, wherever she'd been taken, she wasn't there.

He'd slept fitfully in a private room at the hospital, the door flanked by two Uniforms. He'd insisted some seedy-looking bastard from *The Sun* be allowed to sit in the room with him. Chances were that what Balls' had said about the Loop were just the ramblings of a madman, but it was better to be safe than sorry. Even if that did involve breathing the same air as a tabloid journalist.

They patched him up while he rested, and pumped him full of painkillers, anti-inflammatories, and various other potions and brews to combat the side effects of both. When he woke, he hobbled on a crutch to the toilet, pissed more blood than he'd ideally have liked, then got dressed in the clothes he'd borrowed from Welshy, and told the Uniforms outside that he was ready for his interview.

He had one request, though—that he speak directly with Chief Superintendent Bagshaw. To his surprise, confirmation came through less than twenty minutes later, and a car was sent to pick him up and take him to Scotland Yard.

He snuck out before the car arrived, hailed a taxi, and travelled that way, instead.

That was when the explanations had happened. Bagshaw had sat, stoney-faced to begin with, then increasingly less-so, as Hoon had recited everything that had taken place.

A couple of trusted DI's were sent to collect DS Willoughby from Welshy and Gabriella's house, Hoon having completely neglected to mention him until that point.

Once he'd finished going over it all, Bagshaw sat back in her chair, drummed her fingers on the desktop, and gave a single nod. "There's been a question mark hanging over DCI

Balls for a few months now," she said. "DPS has been digging around ever since the death of Eduardo Gonzales, but he's been good at covering his tracks."

Hoon scratched at the brace on his wrist, like he could reach right through to the itch beneath it. "Is that why you sent me to talk to him?" he asked. "To see if I could draw him out?"

"No. I just wanted you to leave my office," Bagshaw admitted. "Everything else is a happy coincidence. Or an unhappy one, depending on your viewpoint."

"But you think he did in Eduardo, though?"

"Not personally. We think he might have been involved."

Hoon nodded. It made sense. If Eduardo had seen more than the other lads had on the night Caroline had been taken —a face, or a number plate, maybe—then Balls would have wanted to make sure he didn't talk.

"We checked the other address you mentioned," Bagshaw continued. "The warehouse."

"And?"

"It was on fire when we got there. Fire Brigade was battling it. Not much left when it was eventually put out. But this..." She flipped through a couple of pages of notes. "... Professor that you mentioned. Who you say tortured you?"

"What about him?"

"No sign. No bodies in the building. Could he have started the fire himself, do you think?"

"No' unless he opened a trapdoor from the pits of Hell," Hoon replied. "Trust me, that prick was going nowhere under his own steam."

"Yes. Well. Until such times as we have a real name or find a body, I don't really see there's much to prosecute on that front."

"Nice one," Hoon said.

"Don't get too excited, Mr Hoon," Bagshaw told him. "We still have two pages of charges we're considering." She sniffed. "Although, given the circumstances, and what you did for those women... I'm sure several of them will prove to be more trouble than they're worth. Still, much as I hate to say it, it would be best if you don't leave town."

Hoon shook his head. "Don't you shit your drawers about that, sweetheart. I'm going nowhere. I still haven't done what I'm here to do. I still haven't found Caroline."

Across the desk, Bagshaw clasped her hands as if in prayer. "Yes. Yes, I know," she said. "We took the liberty of showing a photograph of Caroline to some of the women you rescued. Most of them aren't making much sense yet—it's going to take months or years of professional care—but a couple of them recognised her."

Hoon sat forward. "What? Fuck. Who? What did they say?"

"They say different girls and women come and go. They're all moved around quite frequently. Sometimes they stay in the same groups for months. Other times, just a few days."

"Months. Jesus," Hoon whispered. "But they saw Caroline?"

"Yes. Two recognised her. One says she spoke to her two or three weeks back. They were in a van together. Being moved around. They got talking."

"And? What did she say?"

"You know I'm not at liberty to disclose those sorts of details, Mr Hoon."

"Fuck that!" Hoon spat. "I nearly fucking died getting those lassies out of there. Thanks to guys on your fucking payroll, might I add? If she said something about Caroline, I want to know what it was. You fucking owe me that much, at least."

Chief Superintendent Bagshaw pursed her lips, looked him over, then let out a little sigh of resignation. "There was something she said. Something Caroline told her."

"What?" Hoon demanded. "What did she say?"

"She claims the man who abducted Caroline knew her."

Hoon frowned. "Knew her?"

"Yes. Well... called her by her name, anyway," Bagshaw explained. "We're assuming that means she was targeted, and that the abduction wasn't simply random or opportunistic."

Hoon's chair creaked as he sat back, his gaze flitting left and right on the surface of Bagshaw's desk, like he was reading a map spread out across it.

"Christ," he mumbled.

"What is it?" Bagshaw asked.

Hoon threw himself forward and pointed to the phone on the Chief Superintendent's desk. "Find out where Bradleigh Combes is being held. I need to talk to the bastard, right fucking now!"

CHAPTER FORTY-TWO

THE YACHT ENGINE *PUT-PUT-PUTTED*, foaming the grey waters of the Thames. It had left the towers of the city in its wake, journeying through the Thames Barrier and onwards towards where the Estuary flowed out into the North Sea.

The river was wider here, the distant banks on either side a blend of light greenery and heavy industry. Up ahead, the Queen Elizabeth II Bridge rose above it all. Another obstacle to be navigated, but hopefully one of the last before the boat reached open water and hung a right towards France.

It was quieter this far east, too, the heavy river traffic through the city having gradually thinned to the point of virtual non-existence. There was some sort of barge far off on the port side, delivering or collecting what looked like an enormous pile of rubble. Ahead, beyond the bridge, a sleek white yacht was in full sail, a strong westerly gust helping it match the pace of Chuck's spluttering engine.

The sun was shining, dappling the water's surface with

droplets of gold. The smell of the river was far fresher here, and he allowed himself a well-earned deep breath. Navigating the Thames had been something of a nightmare, given his relative lack of experience.

Still, needs must.

He had a quick scope around to make sure nothing else was coming up behind him, then cut the engine. He'd been holding in what felt like a couple of gallons of piss for over an hour now. Given the wind, he hadn't dared risk peeing over the side in case it went everywhere.

He ducked down the narrow stairs, already working the buckle of his belt as he made his way to the bathroom tucked in at the back of the boat. His bladder, sensing relief was coming, began to swell in anticipation, forcing him to rush to the bathroom door and—

Thunk.

He blinked. Stared. Tried the handle again.

Thunk. Thu-thunk-thunk.

Locked.

"What the fuck?" he muttered, dancing on the spot.

From beyond the door, there came the sound of the pump-out toilet's electrically powered flush. Chuck stepped back as the snib on the other side of the door was unlocked, and the door was slid aside.

"I'd give that five minutes, if I was you," Hoon said, gesturing back over his shoulder with a thumb. "That hospital food played fucking havoc with my guts."

Chuck gawped. That was the only word for it. His mouth dropped open, his eyes went wide, and he just *gawped.*

"The fuck's wrong wi' your face?" Hoon asked him. "You look like you've seen a ghost."

"Boggle," Chuck wheezed, only partly because of the smell wafting from the tiny bathroom. "How did...? When...?" He smiled too wide. Too keenly. "Jesus Christ. I thought something must've happened to you. I couldn't get you on the phone. I went to scope out that warehouse you were going to, but there was no one there... Fuck!"

He threw his arms around Hoon and hugged him. Hoon patted him on the back a couple of times, before Chuck pulled away.

"I desperately need to piss," Chuck said, then he took a deep breath, ventured inside the bathroom, and slid the door most of the way closed. "Jesus Christ Almighty! That's not right," he said, his voice muffled by the neck of his jumper, then he sighed with relief as his bladder was finally allowed to empty.

He stepped out a minute or two later to find Hoon sitting on the couch, one arm draped across its back, one leg crossed over the other.

"We going somewhere nice?" Hoon asked.

"What? Eh... No. I don't know. Just getting out of the city for a bit."

"Why's that?"

Chuck shifted his weight on his feet. "Well, I mean... I thought, if something had happened to you. Maybe they'd come after me. Maybe I should lie low for a bit."

Hoon nodded slowly. "Aye. Makes sense," he agreed. "The good news is, they're not interested in you. Apparently."

Chuck swallowed. His fingers were knotting together like they didn't know what to do with themselves.

"Right. That's... that's good," he said, then a thought

struck him so hard he almost leaped into the air. "Oh! Drink?" he asked, scurrying over to the cabinet where he kept the booze.

"Aye, don't mind if I do," Hoon said.

He watched Chuck prepare a couple of whiskies, the liquid in the glasses sloshing around in trembling hands.

"They threatened Gabriella and Welshy," Hoon said, accepting the drink. "Sent a guy round to kill them."

Chuck looked shocked. Cartoonishly so. "What? No way. Jesus. Seriously?"

"Not you, though," Hoon said, bringing the glass to his lips. "Didn't say a word about you."

Chuck hovered by the drinks cabinet, nursing his own glass. "Well... that's a relief. Maybe they just didn't know about me."

Hoon shook his head. "Oh no, they knew. They knew everything," he said. "Fuckers were listening to us the whole time."

"God. That's... God," Chuck said, then he took a gulp of his drink.

"They'd have known that you knew way more than Welshy, but they didn't bother their arse with you," Hoon said. "Why's that, do you think?"

Chuck blew out his cheeks. "I don't... I don't know. Doesn't make sense. I mean, I've been the one helping you this whole time."

"Aye, but have you?" Hoon asked. "Really, I mean? When I think back, what have you *actually* done, Bookish?"

Chuck snorted out some nervous laughter. "Loads!"

Hoon shook his head. "No' really, though. Nothing that I couldn't have found out myself, or by asking Bamber."

Chuck clicked his fingers like he was warming up the neurons of his brain. "Um... no. The boyfriend. I found him."

"True," Hoon conceded. "But you didn't know he had anything to say that was worth knowing. And what he did have—the reg—was next to fucking useless. And there was always the chance that I'd decide he was the bastard I was looking for. That he'd killed Caroline. It could be argued you were throwing me off the scent."

"The constable who took the statement. Who changed it, I mean. Hid the car details. I found out who he was!" Chuck insisted.

"Aye, and then the fucker topped himself before I could speak to him. Convenient, that. And we know my thoughts on 'convenient.'"

Chuck frowned and attempted something like a laugh again. "What are you saying, Boggle?"

Hoon rolled his glass between finger and thumb, eyeing the other man over the top of it. "Ella Frewin. The lassie Bradleigh Combes was with in that restaurant. She never made it home that night."

Silence. Chuck's face went through a range of expressions, from confusion to surprise, like it was testing each of them out but finding none suitable.

"I don't... I don't understand," he said, once he'd run the full gamut. "What are you...? I don't..."

"The Met's opened..." He made quote marks in the air. "...'an inquiry' into her disappearance. But we know how effective those are, eh?"

"Yes. Well... God. If there's anything I can do."

Hoon laughed at that. It scraped at the back of his throat, then died as quickly as it had started.

"The man that took Caroline knew her name," he said.

Chuck blinked. Swallowed. "Oh. Did she... Did she tell you that? Did you find her?"

"No' yet," Hoon said. "But I will. I'll tear this fucking city apart, brick by bastard brick, until I do. And see everyone who was involved in her disappearance? See all they fuckers who contributed in some way? I'll be the last thing they fucking see. This face. These hands. Maybe one or two of their own internal organs. And then, boom. Darkness. Gone."

"Good. Yeah." Chuck cleared his throat. "Well deserved."

"Why did you do it, Bookish?"

In the silence, the dark waters of the Thames lapped solemnly against the hull.

"What do you mean?" Chuck eventually asked, forcing that laugh again. "What are you saying?"

Hoon took another sip of his whisky and waited.

"I don't know what you're talking about, Boggle," Chuck insisted. "I really don't know what—"

Hoon hurled the glass at the wall beside Chuck. It exploded, spraying sharp fragments and cheap Scotch in all directions. He rose to his feet, but his injuries slowed him, and by the time he was fully up off the couch he found himself on the wrong end of a Browning Hi-Power pistol.

The glasses had shaken in Chuck's hand. The gun, Hoon noted, did not.

"Don't," Bookish warned. "Boggle. Don't. I don't know what you're thinking, but whatever it is, it's wrong. Alright? You've got it wrong."

"No I haven't. I might no' be into books like you are, but I can fucking read you like one. You took her. Caroline. You waited for her, and you took her. Didn't you?"

Chuck shook his head. "No, Boggle, it wasn't... It's not like that."

"What's it like, then?" Hoon growled. "Because I'm all fucking ears, son."

He'd expected another indignant denial. Some protests. But the gun in Chuck's hand was changing the dynamic between them, and the truth—finally—began to flow.

"These people..." Chuck began. "You don't mess with them. They're serious bastards, Boggle. Way beyond anything we ever dealt with."

"I doubt that very much."

"Because you don't know them!" Chuck insisted. "Because you've got no idea who they are, or what they're capable of. Balls... the DCI? His wife and daughter are dead. Hit and run. Van ploughed into them this morning while they were walking to school."

"Bullshit," Hoon spat.

"No. It's not. It's true. They're dead. And that's just the fucking start, Boggle. These people, once you're involved with them, they don't stop. Once you're in the Loop, you're never out of it. You can't get out. You've got to keep doing what they tell you. Keep serving the greater fucking good. One big circle, one big Loop. Everyone watching everyone else."

The hand with the gun did start to shake now, and tears were blurring his eyes. He wiped them on his forearm, cleared his throat, then continued.

"I didn't want to. With Caroline. But I had to. I didn't have a choice. Same with the other girl. From the restaurant. It's like... like a quota. If I don't meet it, then..." He shuddered. "I have to meet it. It's the only way. I don't have a choice."

"There's always a fucking choice!" Hoon spat.

"No. No, not always. Not with them."

Hoon sighed. Shook his head. "Why her? Why Caroline?"

"I... I saw her seven or eight years back. Bamber's wedding anniversary. You weren't there. She was... God." His face took on a faraway sort of look, a smile tugging at the corners of his mouth. "She was fucking mesmerising. I couldn't take my eyes off her. I added her on Facebook next day. Using one of my other profiles, I mean. It was me who encouraged her to come to London. Told her how amazing it was. And then, a few months back, I saw she was going to be out that night, and, well... You know."

Hoon was still hung up somewhere back at the start of the speech.

"Seven or eight years back? Jesus Christ, what are you...? She'd have been a child, Bookish, she'd have been..."

It clicked. It all just clicked, right there and then.

"You're a fucking nonce," he realised. "That's why you're involved with these bastards. You're a dirty fucking child-molesting nonce. Jesus Christ. I should've seen it the way you were talking about her flatmate. I should've known. Jesus fucking Christ."

"It's not my fault!" Chuck protested.

Veins bulged in Hoon's forehead, the muscles in his neck standing out like ropes. "*No' your fucking fault?!*" he roared, only the gun keeping him from attacking.

"It's an illness! I can't help myself! It's not my fault! It's up here!" He jabbed angrily at his temple, his face puffed up with self-pity. "It's up here, it makes me. It's not my fault!"

"Did you hurt her?" Hoon asked, his voice levelling into something soft and quiet. The calm before the storm. "Before you handed her over to your wee fucking cronies. Did you hurt her?"

Chuck didn't reply. His jaw clenched, like he was fighting to keep something inside.

"Did. You. Hurt. Her?" Hoon asked again, each word punctuated by a pause.

"It was consensual," Chuck whispered. "She said she was up for it. I could... I could tell, from the way she was dressed. She was up for it."

Hoon clamped a hand over his mouth, as if holding back a torrent of spew. His eyes shone. Shimmered. "Jesus Christ," he whispered. "Jesus Christ. She's Bamber's daughter."

"I know! You think I don't fucking know that?" Chuck cried. "That's why I *was* helping you, even if you don't believe me. I thought... I thought, maybe you might find her. Maybe you could get her back. Maybe you could fix it. And I could see her again. I could explain."

"Explain?" Hoon hissed. "How the fuck would you explain? 'Sorry I gave you to an underground fucking sex ring, sweetheart. No hard feelings, eh?' Fucking *explain!*"

Chuck flinched, his cheeks burning with his humiliation. "No, not... That's not..." He groaned and shook his head, the gun now weighing heavy in his hand. "What happens now?" he asked.

Hoon shrugged. "Fucked if I know," he admitted. "Do you know where she is?"

"No. I wish I did, but I don't. I don't hear anything. I just do what I'm told."

"The other lassie? From the restaurant? What about her?"

"I don't have a clue," Chuck said. "I just... I make drops. We arrange it by text. I don't see who picks them up, or where they're taken, or any of that. I don't. I swear, Boggle. I don't know. All I have is a number in my phone. That's it."

Hoon regarded him for several long moments, then nodded. "I believe you," he said.

"Thank you. Thank you," Chuck said. "If I knew where she was, I'd tell you. I would. I don't like the idea of her being out there. Not like that." He shrugged. The beginnings of a wistful smile played across his lips. "Between you and me, I think... I think we had something. The two of us. I think we could've made it work."

"I highly fucking doubt that she'd have been interested in a sweaty, man-titted ball of donkey spunk like you," Hoon said. "But like I say, I believe that you don't know where she is. I believe that there's fuck all more you can tell me." He sniffed. Shrugged. Flexed the fingers of his good hand, then drew them into a fist. "Which means I'm left with two questions. One, can I get to you before you pull that trigger?"

Chuck's eyes became two circles of surprise. He yelped, his finger tightening on the trigger of the Browning before Hoon could so much as take a single step.

Click.

He stared down at the gun in his hand in slowly dawning horror.

"Like I say, *Charles.*" Hoon fished in his pocket and produced a handful of bullets. "I can read you like a fucking book."

He tossed all but one of the bullets aside. Closed the gap and prised the gun from Chuck's limp fingers. A jab to the solar plexus turned Bookish into a gasping, wheezing mess. He watched, struggling for breath, as Hoon inserted a single bullet into the Browning's magazine, and slid it into the grip.

"And that second question," he said, drawing back the

slide and shunting the bullet into the chamber. "If there's nothing else you can tell me..." He pressed the muzzle of the gun against Chuck's forehead. "Then what fucking good are you?"

Out on the Thames, with the boat bobbing alone on the murky grey waves, a gunshot boomed like thunder.

CHAPTER FORTY-THREE

HE'D LIED about not leaving London. He wasn't going to be gone for long, though, and some things you had to do in person.

The evening had tipped over into night, and the rain rattled down on him as he approached the front door. Rang the bell. Waited.

It was Lizzie who answered. Bamber's wife. Made sense, right enough, given his reduced mobility.

She took a moment to recognise him. Her face, when she did, seemed to melt and harden at the same time. She glanced anxiously into the darkness behind him, searching for something he would dearly have loved to have brought with him.

He watched the realisation settling on her like a lead weight across her shoulders, and felt a pain like a knife to the heart.

"I just... I wanted to tell you that I'm going to keep looking," he said. "However long it takes. Whatever I have to do. I'll keep looking. And I'll find her. I promise. I owe Bamber... I owe both of you that much."

He didn't bother waiting for a response. Instead, he just nodded, pulled up the hood of his jacket, then turned back to face the rain.

He was almost at the garden gate when she finally spoke.

"Do you want to come in?" she asked. "It's wild out there. That north wind'll cut you in two."

Hoon stopped and looked up, letting the rain wash over him, cleansing all the many sins he had committed.

And all those he was yet to.

"Another time, maybe," he told her.

Then, bracing himself for the storm ahead, he pushed onwards into the dark.

AFTERWORD

This book was always going to be a challenge.

When I first introduced the then Detective Superintendent Bob Hoon in my DCI Logan crime fiction series, he was so foul-mouthed and unpleasant as to feel almost irredeemable. A larger than life bully with a penchant for bad language, Hoon was a deliberately over the top caricature—a barely human monster who existed largely to make the lives of the other characters that bit more difficult.

Some readers hated him. Others, inexplicably, adored him. And, as the series progressed, I took a perverse delight in making Bob that bit worse in every book. He was a thug, a drunk, and an ever present pain in the arse.

In late 2020, I first had the idea of giving Hoon his own novel. It was ridiculous, I knew. Here was a character so thoroughly unpleasant that even if readers enjoyed his scenes, surely they couldn't cope with a full length novel in which he took centre stage? Surely they couldn't actually empathise with such a man and cheer him on?

I tried to push the idea from my mind, but Hoon—

because this is what he does—soon forced his way back in. The man is nothing if not persistent, and before long I had stopped thinking about whether it was possible for readers to root for him, and had started thinking about the *how*.

What would need to change about his character to make reading a full-length novel about him an enticing prospect? How could this snarling boggle-eyed bully become the hero of his own story?

If you've read the DCI Logan series, you'll have noticed Hoon becoming a little more sympathetic in the later books. He was still the same potty-mouthed monster, but he became other things in his brief appearances, too.

He has become a confidant. A mentor. A strong right arm offering words of wisdom. You might even say that he has become—reluctantly—a friend.

I wanted to keep all those elements of Hoon that divided readers so much, but add more layers to him, and give him that bit more depth. It's a tricky balance keeping a character the same while also making them different, but that's what I set out to do.

The Robert Hoon in this book is the same Robert Hoon as first appeared in Thicker Than Water, the second DCI Logan book. He's also not remotely the same. He has evolved since then. He's still a blunt instrument with a vocabulary full of creative obscenities, but he's no longer *just* that. And at least we now have some idea of why he is the way he is.

If you're discovering Bob Hoon for the first time, welcome. If you've enjoyed this book, then I think you'll also like the DCI Logan series, which starts with A Litter of Bones.

If you've followed Hoon through the Logan series, I hope you've had fun catching up with him again on his first solo adventure. I know I had fun writing it, and am happy to report that there are still two more books in the Hoon series to go.

Whether you're an existing reader or a new one, I'd love to hear your thoughts on this book, so I encourage you to drop me an email at jd@jdkirk.com.

Thanks for taking the time to read this first Robert Hoon thriller. I really do appreciate you taking a chance on the curmudgeonly old buggery, and I'm sure he'd appreciate it, too, though he'd never tell you.

Finally, if you want to find out Hoon's opinion on you, then you can check out the Bob Hoon Random Insult Generator on my website. You'll find it at link.jdkirk.com/insultme. Be warned, though, he doesn't hold back, so it's not for the faint of heart!

All the best,

JD

ACKNOWLEDGEMENTS

I'm not sure whether I should be thanking people for this book or blaming them for it, but out of politeness, I'll stick to the former.

This book would not have been possible without the love and support of my wife, Fiona, and my children, Kyle and Mia, who work hard every day to keep me grounded. Without their relentless piss-taking and put-downs, I'd almost certainly be some sort of raging egomaniac by this point in my career, rather than the jittery, anxiety-ridden shell of a man who stands before you now.

I suppose I should thank Alex Smith and David J. Gatward for all the virtual water cooler chat, the words of wisdom, and the photographs of delicious looking food, but they're both insufferable enough as it is, so I won't.

I'd like to thank my editor, Hanna Elizabeth, who knows where commas are supposed to go, and my eagle-eyed proof-readers, Penny Willow, Bob Brews, and Jacqueline Beard, all of whose names I'm tempted to spell wrong on purpose just to annoy them.

Thanks, too, must go to everyone at The Highland Bookshop in Fort William, who have been tireless supporters of mine since they first opened their doors, and who have sent literally hundreds of signed copies zooming off to readers all over the world. Check them out at highlandbookshop.com for all your book-related needs.

I'm continually amazed by the kind words and support I receive both from readers online and those living in and around the Highlands, that latter of whom regularly stop me in the street and warn me I'd better not even *think* about killing off any main characters. To those people I say, "No promises."

And also, "Please stop shouting at me."

I'd like to thank my Dad, who reads all my books, and my Mum, who is sadly no longer here to do so, but would if she could. I'm not sure she'd be keen on some of Hoon's language, but wish, more than anything, that she was here to tell me off for it.

And finally, dear reader, I'd like to thank you for sitting through this book all the way until this, the last page. That's some serious dedication, and while you can't see or hear it, just know that I'm applauding you. Albeit quietly. In my head.

So, yeah. Thanks, everyone. You're all bloody excellent.

Southpaw

HAVE YOU READ?

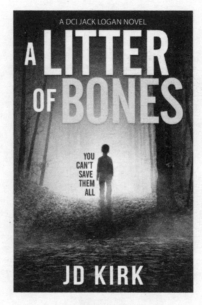

A Litter of Bones

The first book in the million-selling Scottish crime fiction series from bestselling author JD Kirk. Available now.

ABOUT THE AUTHOR

JD Kirk is the author of the million-selling DCI Jack Logan Scottish crime fiction series, set in and around the Highlands.

He also doesn't exist, and is in fact the pen name of award-winning former children's author and comic book writer, Barry Hutchison. Didn't see that coming, did you?

Both JD and Barry live in Fort William, where they share a house, wife, children, and two pets. This is JD's 13th novel. Barry, unfortunately, has long since lost count.